Married by Monday

ALSO BY CATHRYN BROWN

Wedding Town Romances

Runaway to Romance

Married by Monday

Alaska Dream Romances

Falling for Alaska

Loving Alaska

Crazy About Alaska

Merrying in Alaska

Alaska Matchmakers Romances

Accidentally Matched

Finally Matched

Hopefully Matched

Surprisingly Matched

Merrily Matched

Married by Monday

CATHRYN BROWN

For permission requests, write to the publisher, addressed "Attention: Permissions Coordinator," at the address below.

Sienna Bay Press

PO Box 158582

Nashville, Tennessee 37215

www.cathrynbrown.com

Cover designed by Najla Qamber Designs

(www.najlaqamberdesigns.com)

Publisher's Note: This is a work of fiction. Names, characters, places, and incidents are a product of the author's imagination. Locales and public names are sometimes used for atmospheric purposes. Any resemblance to actual people, living or dead, or to businesses, companies, events, or institutions is completely coincidental.

Married by Monday/Cathryn Brown. - 1st ed.

ISBN: 978-945527-51-7

Created with Vellum

DEAR READER

I had a lot of fun writing *Married by Monday.* The characters in Two Hearts are people I'd like to spend time with in person, so I'm glad I got to go there again.

It's time for you to have another visit to this sweet town. I hope you enjoy being there, maybe having a piece of pie at Dinah's Place or spending time in the park.

I also hope you enjoy Bella and Micah's story!

CHAPTER ONE

Bella Bennett eyed the red fire alarm on the wall. "When I was a kid, I always wanted to flip the switch on these when I saw them. One in my first school caught my attention every time I walked by."

Her friend Cassie laughed. "Troublemaker." She folded the flaps on a box and stood. "You're right, though. I wondered exactly what would happen if I pulled down."

"You see, that's why we're friends."

Cassie raised an eyebrow. "Because we're both troublemakers?"

"Because we have the same sense of adventure." Bella reached for the switch. "Besides, what better time to fulfill an old whim than to do it now with a disconnected fire alarm in an old building?"

"Bella, wait! What if it *is* connected?"

She waved around them with her left hand. "In this dump?"

"It's a charming brick building from the 1890s with original details."

"One overhead light—"

"But it's a gorgeous period fixture."

Bella continued. "We found a single wall plug that worked. The rest of them—of the few there were—didn't."

Cassie frowned. "I may have made the wrong decision when I chose to put our mini bridal event in one of the old storefronts on Main Street. I hoped the brides would see themselves getting married in the small town of Two Hearts if I immersed them in it."

"Cassie," Bella added gently, "Every store around this building closed years ago. There's no charm."

"You're probably right."

Bella shifted the mood back to playful. "But I can knock one childhood wish off my list." She pulled the handle down, breaking the glass rod, a spike of concern rushing through her in spite of her bravado.

A horn honking in the distance was the only sound they heard.

"I know you enjoy living in Nashville, but Two Hearts is my home now. I see only the potential in the old buildings, especially these historic storefronts on Main Street, but I guess you're right."

Bella shrugged. "See? I told you so. I know you love this town, Cassie, but—"

An ear-shattering ringing came from over her head. Shoving her hands over her ears, Bella raced out the front door. Cassie emerged right behind her.

"I may have made a mistake," Bella shouted over the alarm. "At least there isn't a real fire."

"Real or not . . ."

Bella's heart sank, and she groaned. "A fire truck is on its way. Cassie, the firefighters will be angry when they find out what I did." *Just when you thought your situation couldn't get worse, you do something stupid, and it does.*

"You're right." Cassie pulled her phone out of the purse she'd apparently thought to grab as she'd exited the building. After a few swipes across the screen, she shoved it back in the bag. "Greg isn't answering. I remember him saying something about helping his mother with a project, so maybe he can't hear his phone."

Bella hadn't thought about Cassie's fiancé, the town's sheriff, being annoyed too.

"I'll run over to his mother's house to see if he's there. Maybe he can contact the station before the volunteer fire department's men and women load up the truck and come over here."

Cassie raced across the street and through the walkway to what Bella knew was the residential area behind Main Street's empty stores. As Bella turned around, she saw people hurrying down the street. Toward her. Well, not her specifically, but toward what they assumed was a burning building.

Was there a hole big enough for her to escape into? At least she could hope that Cassie would find Greg and that his car would come down the street at any moment to save her.

A siren in the distance, much louder than one man's police car, told her Cassie hadn't. Would she need to pay a fine for a false alarm? She could barely afford gas money right now, so that could be a problem.

Sighing, she looked down and realized she still wore a wedding gown. Running inside, she ignored the sound that would probably be in her ears for a week and grabbed the blue dress she'd worn this morning.

Turning toward the mirror they'd placed against the wall for customers to use, Bella reached for the row of buttons that ran down the back of her dress. One, two, three buttons slipped out of their loops. As she stretched for the fourth button, a woman stopped in front of the window and pressed her face against it to see inside. More people joined her.

Facing them in a partially unbuttoned wedding dress while the alarm blared heralded a new low in her life.

Could the humiliation grow any worse?

Never ask a silly question.

Bella started for the back room, but had only taken a step when flashing red lights reflecting in the mirror said her time was up. She picked up her purse and turned toward the door. She squared her shoulders and waited for someone to enter. She'd explain her mistake to, hopefully, a kind firefighter and ask for forgiveness.

Someone—man or woman?—wearing firefighting gear, including a helmet with a shield, entered the building, clutching the end of a fire hose. The person stopped and stared at her. When they flipped up the face shield, the puzzled face of Greg's friend stared at her.

Micah. The man who had accidentally showered her with fruit punch at Cassie and Greg's engagement party. And ruined her dress.

"Isabella?" His green eyes stared at her as though she must be an apparition—and she had to admit that it would be rare to find no smoke or fire, and a woman in a wedding dress. He continued through to the back room. A minute later, the ringing blissfully stopped.

When he returned, he had his helmet under one arm and the fire hose under the other. "I don't see anything that looks like an emergency. Now, please tell me what happened?"

A voice from outside shouted, "Did you say 'now'?"

Micah shouted over his shoulder. "Yes, but I don't want—"

The fire hose shot water across the room. Micah struggled to stay upright as the hose he'd barely been holding onto went wild. The wet stream sprayed everywhere—including right into her wedding dress display.

"No!" Bella threw herself in front of the dresses. "Turn off the water!" she sputtered as it pummeled her. Shouting between Micah and the firefighters outside continued, but she could barely hear it over the rushing deluge.

When the barrage ended, a stunned Micah stood before her.

He blinked and stared at her. "That shouldn't have happened." He shook his head and seemed to be muttering to himself when he added, "Of course, it shouldn't. We must need more training."

Three dresses had blown off the rack and lay wadded up in a grimy pool on the floor. The others hung dripping on the rack. She leaned closer. Some of the embellishments looked damaged. When the crowd outside shifted, allowing more light in, the water on the floor glittered with either sequins or crystals, maybe both.

Her inventory. Every sample. Ruined.

Micah seemed to be talking to himself. He might have continued—if she hadn't screamed.

He hurried over. "I'm so sorry, Isabella! Are you hurt?"

Fighting tears, she shook her head.

A man and woman in firefighter gear rushed through the door. "Need help, Chief?" the woman asked.

Bella shook her head. More people would not be better.

"I think we're good here. I'll let you know when we need cleanup."

The man said, "I'm sorry about the water," before the two of them left.

Right. Water. Lifting a limp and soggy dress off the rack, with beading hanging off it by a thread, she knew nothing could save the former beauty. Bella held it up facing Micah.

"It's nothing that can't be fixed, right?" His shrug told her he knew nothing about silk and handmade lace.

Bella swallowed hard as she realized the implications of her stupid decision to pull that alarm.

Financial ruin.

What would she do?

"Isabella?" Micah's voice from beside her made her jump. "Are you okay?"

She shook her head. "No," a small voice she barely recognized croaked.

Micah stared at Bella. She looked like she might be on the verge of tears. "It's just water." When she didn't answer, he added, "We can throw them in a dryer."

Isabella's whimper told him the problem might be bigger than he realized.

"Silk and handmade lace. Beading. Sequins."

Those things meant something, maybe that she didn't want to put the dresses in the dryer. When she stared at the rack of clothing like she'd lost her best friend, Micah knew he had to do something.

His grandmother liked to hang clothes on the clothesline in the backyard. She said it gave them a "fresh" scent. "They could hang outside."

Turning to him with a glimmer of a smile, she said, "Okay."

Whew. Crisis averted. "Then let's pack them up and take them to my house." He started toward the rack.

"Wait!" She put her hand on his arm. "I'm staying at Cassie's. I can hang them up there."

Her hand slid away when he turned toward the back room. Even though he had barely felt her touch through his heavy coat, he missed it. "You can't." He plucked the box of large trash bags off the shelf where he'd seen them earlier.

"Of course I can," she continued as soon as she could see him again. Some of the fire had returned to her voice.

"No, you can't, Isabella."

The sun came out from behind a cloud, bringing a sunbeam onto the water and showing him a problem that loomed larger than he'd thought from his original position. They'd have to get someone with equipment to suck up the water and dry the place out as soon as possible. He hoped the ancient electric outlets could handle the fans they'd need to plug in.

"Micah—" Isabella pulled him from his thoughts.

That was the first time she'd used his name since they'd met, and he liked the sound of it from her.

"My grandmother helped when Cassie moved into the house and lamented a time or two about the lack of what she considered the all-important clothesline," he explained.

Isabella grabbed the box from him. He'd wanted to snap her out of her sadness, but it seemed to have been replaced with anger. "It would have been easy at Cassie's." Pulling out a bag, she huffed. "But we'll go to your house."

Why did that thought not bring him joy?

"I'll run up to the fire station to get my truck."

She nodded, but didn't say anything. From the little time they'd spent together at Cassie and Greg's engagement party, he suspected that silence wasn't normal for her.

After a jog up the street, he returned with the old pickup he liked to knock around in. There was something satisfying about a truck that was older than he was. He also didn't mind hauling fifty-pound bags of seed in it for a friend, as he'd had to earlier in the day.

Isabella waited outside for him, and she stepped up to the back of the vehicle when he stopped, peering over the tailgate. Her gaze went from his truck to the store. "Micah, I don't know if this is the best way to haul white dresses." She sounded nicer than before, but he had noticed her rubbing her eyes like she'd been crying when he drove up.

Guys could be clueless, and he certainly was more often than he should be. He surveyed the bed of the truck. "What if we put a layer of trash bags down and the dresses on top of that?"

She considered his suggestion. "That could work. We have to be careful, though. No rust. *Please*."

They carried the dresses out one by one and laid them on the trash bags. When they'd all been set there, Isabella touched them almost lovingly. With a sigh, she went to the passenger side, opened the door, and stared at the seat with a frown. "Micah, I'm wet."

He pulled open his door. "Don't worry about it. I haul all sorts of things in here. We get in wet and dirty after fishing."

She grimaced but climbed in, slamming the door. Or did it take that much energy for someone her size to swing it shut?

Every few seconds, he glanced in the rearview mirror to make sure the precious cargo hadn't picked up birds or anything else. When they arrived at his house, he slowly rolled into the driveway.

Isabella stared at the house. "You live *here*?" The incredulous tone of her voice grated on him.

"Why wouldn't I?"

She turned to him and shook her head. "It doesn't seem guy-friendly. It's so . . . small-town."

He laughed and popped open his door. "Isabella, I live in a small town." At the back of the truck, he let down the tailgate and reached for a dress. "It's probably easiest if we carry these through the house to the backyard."

She picked one up and followed him. When the tapping of her heels stopped, Micah turned toward her. Her gaze went up and around the house, pausing for a moment on the planter filled with petunias before coming back to him.

"Problem?"

"It's charming." She shrugged.

Her "charming" didn't sound the same as when someone like Cassie said it.

He charged back toward the door with the dress. The sooner they finished this task, the better.

CHAPTER TWO

She knew Micah wore a leather jacket and rode a motorcycle. That had translated in her mind to a minimally decorated, very masculine home. Basically, the opposite of Cassie's beloved house. There would be dishes in the sink, and dirty socks lying on the floor. Furniture might be passed down from relatives or friends. Or it could be modern metal and wood if he'd shopped for himself.

Instead, his truck had stopped in front of a house that might have even more country charm than Cassie's yellow cottage. But was that possible? A wide front porch with brick steps leading up to it held white wooden rocking chairs waiting for her to try. Not that she was a rocking-chair kind of girl.

Painted a soft blue-green with white trim, the older house—maybe Victorian—had yellow curtains billowing out of open windows.

Bella shook her head. She wasn't sure if it was to show disapproval or clear it from the jarring image in front of her. "This is a surprise."

"Did you expect to see the loft apartment I had in

Charleston?" He opened the front door and seemed to be waiting for her to follow him.

She silently scolded herself. "I'm sorry, Micah. It's a pretty house. I clearly love pretty, or I wouldn't make wedding dresses."

When his shoulders relaxed, she realized she had been rude. Something about Micah put her on edge.

When they stepped inside, she almost stopped but followed him through without a pause. What crazy world had she stepped into where hot guys lived in houses with sunshine-yellow curtains and floral-print furniture?

Each dress Bella hung on the clothesline added to the gravity of her situation. None of them could be sold. Not one. At least not by her. Sure, she could find a buyer for a low price, but selling these with her name attached to them could ruin her business's reputation. And she still wouldn't be able to pay all her bills.

With them hanging side by side, moving in a gentle breeze, the moment felt almost peaceful. She sat on a porch swing on his screened-in back porch and closed her eyes, that same warm breeze lifting some of her stress up and carrying it away. Birds sang and crickets chirped.

For a second—barely a whole second—she knew why Cassie liked living in a small town.

Then she returned to her senses, opened her eyes, and plotted a way to save her business.

When she stood, her clothes felt stiff and somewhere between wet and dry. Looking down, she realized something she should have an hour ago: She hadn't just been wearing a wedding dress, she had the dress for the Michelson wedding on. The bride's family had cancelled the order after it was completed, but Bella had planned to, *needed to,* sell it. The water had ruined Honoré Michelson's dress. *She* had ruined it.

That, along with the loss of the sample dresses, meant she only had the inventory of fabric, notions, and embellishments in her shop to save herself. Financial issues had prevented her from buying anything beyond the necessities weeks ago. Her inventory was much under what it would normally be.

Micah stepped out of the house with a glass in each hand. "Iced tea?"

"Does a rabbit have floppy ears?"

He stopped in mid-stride. She felt heat climb her face.

"That's a yes?"

"It is."

"I know a lot of country sayings. I spent most of my time here when I was growing up. That's a new one."

"I made it up. But I know what you mean. 'Fruit basket turnover' is the one that surprised me the most when I moved to Nashville."

He grinned. "Chaos. I can see it if I picture it. An upside-down basket with fruit rolling everywhere. Some sayings made a lot more sense to our ancestors. I hear that one more from my grandmother's generation."

She tugged at the bodice of her dress, which seemed to be shrinking slightly as it dried.

"Uh, Isabella, why are you wearing a wedding dress? I didn't want to ask earlier because you were so focused on the other dresses being ruined."

"It's all lost." She fought the whimper that tried to follow those words. Standing, she knew she had to do something, but she wasn't sure what.

~

Micah gently eased her back into the rocking chair and knelt in front of her. "Isabella, you aren't making any sense."

He was probably right. The stress of keeping this secret must have gotten to her. She should have shared it with someone. Cassie would have cared about her situation. Of course she would. Bella felt like such a failure that she hadn't gotten up the nerve to tell her yet.

Micah was still gazing at her with those steady green eyes. His intense focus must stand him well as a lawyer in a courtroom.

"I'm broke. Bankrupt." She made a *pfft* sound. "Zip. Nada."

He cocked his head to the side. "I know Cassie does well with her business. And I have seen a bride in a dress you made, haven't I?"

"Yes. But I made a huge mistake with my business. There doesn't seem to be a way out of it, either. Well, my only possible way out was to sell all my sample dresses. I'd made sure they were in tip-top condition. *This* was the big mistake." She stabbed at her chest with her finger. "It was for the Michelson wedding."

"Honoré Michelson?"

"You know her?" Honoré's parents were one of the wealthiest power couples in Nashville. How would a small-town boy like Micah be familiar with the family?

He hesitated and seemed to be flustered at her question. It was a simple one.

"My grandfather was friends with her grandfather and father." He leaned forward. "I still don't understand, Isabella. Why are you wearing Honoré's wedding dress? And how did that drive you into despair?"

She may as well confess everything. She hadn't gotten to tell anybody else so far. Maybe talking about it would help her find a solution. "I always take a deposit of half down on a wedding dress. Always."

"That makes good business sense. Go on."

"I did with this one. But it was on the projected project. It was a fairly simple dress when we started. So simple that it actually surprised me. But I do whatever the bride asks for whether or not it makes sense to me."

She remembered that day when the bride, her mother, and aunt had come in for the first fitting. "I had made my sample as I always do. It basically looked like the lining of a dress. It's only for style and fit. Nothing more than that. Honoré's aunt saw that and went into a . . ." How could she explain this to someone who knew Honoré without casting too bad of a light on the woman? "She wasn't pleased with the simplicity of it. No matter how many times I assured them this was not the final dress, the family would not be consoled."

"That sounds like her mother and aunt."

"Once we'd made the finished dress, which the family was too busy to see and have Honoré try on, we added a sprinkle of sequins on the skirt to make it sparkle when she moved. It was still the simple dress design she had asked for.

"The next fitting was when the wheels came off the bus. Honoré put on the dress and stepped out of the dressing room. Her mother and aunt were both there again. The aunt shrieked. I thought she was in trouble and needed first aid. Then she said, 'My niece will not get married in a dress like that.' When I picked my jaw up from the floor, I said, 'This is the dress Honoré chose.' The woman shook her head so vigorously from side to side that I worried about her.

"'It needs *more*. Honoré, this is the wedding of the year. You're going to be featured online and in magazines. I will not have my niece being humiliated by the simplicity of this dress. It does not suit her stature in the community.'"

"Was that Sandy?" When Micah spoke, she realized she might have gone too far. She'd gotten so caught up in the story that she'd forgotten to filter it for a family friend.

Bella gave a slow nod.

"That sounds exactly like her. Continue."

Relieved that he didn't sound offended, she continued. "I added more sequins. It really was beautiful. Well, it had been beautiful at every phase, but at that point, it was a gorgeous dress a princess could wear." She paused to calm herself. "But it wasn't enough for her aunt, and her mother had gotten on board. Honoré herself even seemed to adopt their opinion as her own and forget that she was the one who'd started off with a simple dress."

He chuckled. "I'm sorry. I know this isn't funny. But this is so them."

"I added crystals. It was still gorgeous." She closed her eyes as she remembered the next meeting. "Her aunt came alone to see that version of the dress."

"Is it normal to have that many fittings of the dress before they take it home for the wedding?"

"Never. Even when there's a major shift in weight or a pregnancy." She pictured that day, and her stomach tightened at the memory. "The dress still wasn't enough for them. At this point, it was so embellished that it looked like a costume a country music performer would love for the stage. The woman needed more. Pearls were the embellishment of choice this time. Genuine pearls. I thought tiny pearls added an elegant touch to the bodice of the dress." At his confused expression, she added, "The bodice is the upper part to about the waist. Anyway, I knew those wouldn't be enough, so I added larger pearls, too."

"And that still didn't make them happy?"

A mix of anger and depression washed over her. "Worse than that. At some point between these fittings, the ladies had decided that this dress wasn't going to work out. They didn't tell me that, of course. Sandy came in, took one look at it, and said they had another dress. From a New York designer, no less." She put her nose in the air as she said the final words the way that her client had.

Micah stared at her for a moment, and then his eyes widened. "You didn't get any more money from them for that gloriously hideous dress, did you?"

"No. I added lace, sequins, pearls, and crystals. But more than that is the amount of labor that went into it. I don't stitch everything on myself. I have a team who does. Many, many hours with rushed timelines were needed to make the changes." She looked down at her fingernails, pretending to see something important there. "It's my fault, Micah. I thought this dress was going to put me on the map for social events. Her family doesn't just play in Nashville's high society; they're in it on a national and even an international scale."

"Isabella, I think you're selling yourself short. Haven't you done dresses for music stars? Carly Daniels wore one you'd made for her wedding, right?"

She all but whispered, "Yes." Still in a low voice, she added, "I've done well. At least up until now. But this was a different group. I got greedy, I guess. My business had been extremely successful. Up until now."

"You could start over."

"You need money to do that."

"It can't be that bad, can it?"

"It *can* be that bad. It is. I have salaries to pay, rent on my business property, vendors who want to be paid for supplies. And don't get me started on my personal life. I have apartment rent and a car payment."

He winced.

"There's another little problem. I've started getting feedback that word has gotten out that I'm difficult to work with, and my designs are outdated."

He shook his head. "That sounds like Sandy's doing. You're smart. You'll figure something out."

He thought she was smart? She was usually the flashy one in high heels that nobody thought much about as far as intelligence went. "I *had* a plan. I planned to sell all my sample dresses."

"What are those?"

"A custom designer often has dresses in different styles. The potential customer can try those on and get an idea of the cut that flatters her. Which style she prefers over another. The dresses get tried on a lot and can get rather shopworn. But I fixed up the best of them, a total of six, to make sure they were in perfect condition. I brought them and Honoré's dress here for Cassie's small bridal event with her newest clients. I hoped that one of her brides would be happy to buy one off the rack. Sadly, none of them did. I did get a commission for a new dress."

"That's great!"

"This bride also wants a simple gown, but she wants it in a fabric that I don't currently have in stock and will need to order from a supplier that I haven't paid yet because of this." She smacked her hand on her lap. "It's a circle." She rotated her finger in the air. "You need the money for supplies to make the dress. And now—"

"What about the sample dresses?"

Bella made a sweeping motion at the clothesline, now overloaded with heavy, soggy garments.

"Oh, no! Now your samples are wet."

"Not just wet. *Damaged*."

She'd lose everything. Maybe have to move home to Texas to live with her less-than-warm mother. Or New York to be with her father and his new wife and family. Neither option held much appeal.

If she asked her parents for a loan, she'd get a lecture on her career choice, and probably their usual suggestion that she go to medical school. That would be all.

If she moved in with one of them and got a job at a bridal dress shop, she could start saving her money again and start over. It might take a few years to pay her debts and put away cash for a new business, but it wouldn't be bad.

It would be horrible.

She watched Micah's Adam's apple as he gulped, the full impact of what had happened hitting him. "I'm so sorry, Isabella! If the water hadn't come on . . ."

In the end, this was her fault. She had to confess. "I pulled the alarm."

"You what?"

"I didn't think it would work." She gave what came out as a brittle laugh. "I was wrong." Definitely wrong. Unbelievably, unbearably wrong.

"Why?" His one word said it all.

"Didn't you ever look at one of those when you were a kid and wonder what would happen if you pulled it?"

He grinned. "All the time."

A pitter-patter sound made her look up and around.

"Rain." Micah answered her unspoken question.

The gentle rhythm increased to a steady beat with a lot of bass. "My dresses!" She watched them being doused by Mother Nature. "At least I don't have to figure out how to wash all of them in the bathtub."

Micah laughed from beside her. "I thought they couldn't get wet."

"Not usually. But they were dirty, so I thought the first step to trying to salvage parts of them would be to get them clean." She gestured to the clothesline now in a downpour. "That's being taken care of."

"Do you want that one washed too?" He pointed to what she was wearing.

"Micah, this is all I have to wear." The damp dress had begun to cling to her skin as it dried. "I tried this one on to show a bride not long before, well, you know."

He stood. "Let's get you something to put on. And I'll hang that one on the line too."

The dress crunched as she stood. She followed Micah into the house and down a hall to a bedroom—also decorated for someone fifty years older than him with a penchant for country decor. But the room charmed her against her will. A quilt, probably handmade, in pinks and blues covered the bed, and lace curtains hung at the window. An attached bathroom told her updates had been made to the old house at some point.

"You can take a shower. I'll leave clothes for you on the bed." He surveyed her up and down as though deciding her size. When she slipped off her shoes and dropped inches in height, he added, "I will need to be creative."

He went toward the door, and she remembered her earlier dilemma. "Um, Micah, I need a favor." She turned her back to him. "Please help unbutton me."

When she didn't hear him move, she glanced over her shoulder. "Don't get any ideas. I'm stuck in this dress."

He did as she asked, fighting with the damp button loops over the covered buttons. His fingers skimmed her neck at the top of the dress, then met her undergarments as he went lower.

"I'll take it off and set it outside the door."

He made a gruff sound in his throat. When the door closed behind him, she released a breath. She removed the dress and hefted the garment into her arms before depositing it where she'd said she would. With it off, she felt better than she had in a while.

What more would this day bring?

A shower washed away the grime. Now, she needed to free her heart and spirit from the tangled knot they were in. Was it okay to use someone else's comb? With no other option available, she did that and left her chin-length, wavy brown hair to dry and do whatever it wanted. Once she was done, she rinsed out her undergarments and dried them with a hairdryer the best she could.

Clothes lay on the bed, as promised. On top was a navy-blue T-shirt that boldly proclaimed *Two Hearts Fire Department* in white block letters on the back. The man must have more shirts than this, so he'd been making a point about the day. A clothespin lay on top of a pair of his running shorts that would never stay up without help. Chuckling, she slipped them on and clipped the waist to shrink it. She did better with the pink flip flops, which must have belonged to a woman in his family.

With that taken care of, one main thought loomed in front of her: She needed to figure out how to ask her best friend for a loan.

CHAPTER THREE

Bella settled into Micah's car. As she did, she considered her words to Cassie. Asking her for a short-term loan should be easy. They'd been friends since their freshman year of college. They could talk about anything and had often discussed their businesses and financial matters.

Do you have money to spare?

That was a weird question to ask someone.

I've gotten myself in a spot of trouble. It's nothing for you to worry about, but could I get a loan?

The second she said "nothing to worry about," her friend would start worrying. Then Cassie would be sucked into the mess of Bella's life and want to do more than she should.

Would you be able to do a short-term loan? I promise to repay you in full—with interest—within six months.

Succinct. Businesslike. Bella hated to ask Cassie for money because she had recently had the expense of moving herself and her business. Still, this wasn't the worst timing in the world. Her friend had another wedding she'd planned taking place this afternoon, which would bring in more income, so that was good news. And Cassie had declared her new-to-her house nothing short of perfect.

"We're here."

Bella blinked and looked at him.

"Cassie's house." He pointed to the yellow building that Cassie claimed was charming beyond words. Bella saw "old and in need of modernization." Micah stepped out and came around to open her car door. First time ever for that. As much as the modern woman inside wanted to say she could do it herself, a part of her enjoyed the chivalry.

As she stepped out, she noticed Greg further up the driveway untying a tall extension ladder from his car's roof. Micah hurried over to help him with it.

Bella heard Micah ask, "What's going on?" as she neared them.

Greg frowned. "I need to check for storm damage."

Micah shielded his eyes with his hand and looked up and around them. "Tree fall?"

"Fortunately, no. We were eating lunch when the storm came, and something hit the roof." He extended the ladder and rested it against the side of the house.

"I'll go up with you." Turning toward her, Micah said, "Could you steady the ladder?"

"Sure." Bella would make certain she did one thing right today.

The men scaled the ladder.

Cassie came out right after they went up. "I hope they're okay."

Bella caught glimpses of them as they walked around the roof. "I haven't seen a falling object or heard a thud, so I think they're alive."

Cassie's eyes widened. "Don't do that to me!"

Bella chuckled. "I'm sure they're fine."

Minutes later, they came back down, with Micah taking the lead as she steadied the ladder again.

Greg stopped in front of Cassie. "A branch fell on the roof but didn't damage anything."

Cassie's face lit up. "That's great news!"

Her fiancé rubbed his hand over his face before continuing. "Sweetheart—"

Bella held back a sigh at his word of endearment.

"We thought the roof was fine because it looked good from here and there weren't any signs of water damage inside."

"Yes." Cassie said the word slowly, then her gaze went up to the roof.

"Parts of it are in rough shape." He winced. "I think you're going to need a new roof. Sooner rather than later."

Cassie groaned. "First, the heating and air conditioning system needed to be replaced, and now this. I still love this house, but these big-ticket items will clear out my savings."

"I wish you'd let me help."

Cassie shook her head vigorously from side to side. "Not until we're married."

Greg frowned.

"When is the big day?" A change of subject seemed to be in order, and Bella knew they'd planned to decide that today.

Greg's frown deepened. "September 15."

"That's great. Just a couple of months." It wasn't long for the grand affairs Cassie usually managed, but Bella knew that could work.

"Of next year," he added. His glance toward his fiancée told Bella he might have preferred sooner.

Then Greg's words sank in. "What?"

Cassie smiled up at her groom-to-be as she said, "Bella, you of all people know how long it takes to plan a wedding."

Bella didn't respond. Did her friend not want to get married? Then again, Cassie would want to create the best wedding possible for herself. The delay might give Cassie extra funds now for the loan. If Bella was willing to pry it out of someone who was stressed out because of her house.

"Besides, the wedding is irrelevant right now. I need to call a roofer." Cassie's voice sounded glum.

Micah jumped in. He hadn't said anything for a while, but Bella had sensed him standing beside her. "I have a buddy who's a roofer. I think he'll give you a good price."

"Bring him on. I'm saving every penny for my wedding. I'm not even going to get lunch from Dinah's for a while."

There went the last hope of a loan.

The men took down the ladder and reattached it to Greg's car roof.

Cassie turned to Bella and leaned back. "What are you wearing?"

Bella fingered the neckline of her oversized T-shirt. "Everything got wet."

"You were out in the storm?"

"Fire hose."

Cassie's raised eyebrow made her barrel forward and explain. "You left. The fire truck came. Micah—completely covered with firefighting gear, so I didn't know who he was—entered the building. You know, to put out the fire." Bella pursed her lips, then blew out a breath. "So, he said not to turn it on, someone misunderstood, and here I am in Micah's clothes." She blinked to avoid crying.

"Bella, where are your wedding dresses?" Concern was in every syllable.

"Hanging on Micah's clothesline."

Cassie gasped. Micah might be clueless, but Cassie knew what that meant. "Are they . . ."

"I don't know about a couple of them. They all sustained damage. I may be able to save pieces of them, though." Bella blinked furiously. She would not cry. Again.

Cassie leaned forward and hugged her. "I'm so sorry. I hope it doesn't take too long to get them fixed up. There goes your extra cash, at least for a while."

Bella felt tears leaking out of her eyes and trickling down her cheeks. More than extra. *Essential.* But Cassie didn't need to know that.

Her friend stepped back but kept her hands on her shoulders. "Are you okay?"

Bella swiped at her cheeks. "You know me. I'm a survivor."

"That's one of the things I love about you. You get back up when you're kicked down. Remember the time a bride's little sister used a permanent marker on the wedding dress two days before the ceremony? You covered it up with lace, making it so pretty and saving the day."

She had done that, hadn't she? Maybe there was a way to save her business. She simply hadn't thought of it yet.

"I have lunch leftovers."

"What you mean is your future mother-in-law sent over more than you could eat."

"Hey, now, I could have made it myself."

Bella stared at her.

"You're right. But I can now cook six meals that don't kill people or set buildings on fire. Greg's mother is a patient teacher."

"I'd love to try one of those meals and judge for myself."

"Greg survived all of them. I'll let you know when I'm willing to have new guinea pigs taste my food. Let's go inside."

They passed the men, who were chatting beside Greg's police cruiser.

"Bella," Greg said, "I understand that you had an unexpected shower. Twice."

"Thank you for sharing that, Micah." She knew she'd scowled as she walked past. "And Greg, since you seem to be making fun of me, you can help me take the dresses off the clothesline later and transport them back to Cassie's."

"Uh, okay."

Both men were silent as the women continued on to the back entrance of the house. Once inside, Cassie turned to her. "Okay, give it to me." She gestured forward with her hands.

Bella shrugged. "What?"

She pointed to Bella and then outside. "You. Micah. What's going on? And please tell me it's something good."

Bella rolled her eyes. "Only you would try to find romance in my day. I was wet. The dresses were wet. He took me and the dresses to his house to dry out."

"Why not here?" Cassie had a knowing expression.

"Wipe that smirk off your face. You don't have a clothesline."

She leaned over to check out the kitchen window. "You're right. I've never had a need for one, so I didn't check for it."

"Micah's grandmother commented on it, so he knew."

Cassie crossed her arms. Her stance didn't fit her next words. "He's nice, though, isn't he?"

Thinking back to the time alone with him, she almost sighed. He'd been beyond nice. There had been moments—

"You have a happy expression."

Matchmaking for the two of them made no sense. "I'll admit that he was nice, but I'm not interested." The leather jacket and flowery couch did not go together. "He's the guy I'd call if I got a flat tire on my car. Not the one I want to knock on my door to pick me up for a date."

CHAPTER FOUR

Micah pulled out his phone. His grandfather. *Again*. He could choose to ignore it or answer it. Whatever he wanted—and he had been persistent the last few days—the odds weren't good for it being anything Micah wanted to hear.

He answered using his most jovial voice. "Hi, Grandfather! How is everything in the big city today?"

"They'd be better if you were sitting in the empty office down the hall."

And so it began. *Again*.

"You know I'm happy in Two Hearts."

"I paid for a Yale law degree, and you took it to that town."

Micah didn't have anything new to add after five years of the same argument. "You know that I love living here. It's my home."

"Nashville is just as much your home."

There was no point in arguing that he'd grown up in Two Hearts and only visited his grandparents and other family in Nashville. Edmund Brooks wanted what he wanted, and he almost always got it.

When his grandson didn't reply, he cleared his throat before continuing. "I need your expertise on a new case."

This had also been happening more often during the past year. "You have an excellent team." Micah's grandfather's grandfather had founded one of the most powerful legal firms in the city. They were known in Nashville and far beyond for work on certain law specialties, one of them corporate, the type of law Micah had studied most intently in law school.

"We do at that. I'd like to take you to lunch."

Why couldn't he have the grandfather of films and books? One who greeted you with a hug and couldn't wait to take you fishing? His wanted to make him a partner, and he'd been talking about it since Micah had decided to be a lawyer when he was fifteen. Probably even before that.

Maybe he could find a plausible excuse to not go.

"I'm getting older."

Micah knew he'd been beaten when this vibrant and strong man talked about his age.

With a sigh, Micah asked, "What time?"

They set up a lunch date for the next day, with them meeting first at the law firm.

Micah waved to the receptionist as he passed her and walked down the hall to his grandfather's office. He stopped in his tracks when he reached the door to the office always pointed out as his, the one he used every time he worked on a case here. A sign bearing the name *Micah Walker* with the title *Partner* under it now hung there.

Partner. During college, he'd toyed with the idea of working at a major law firm, dreaming of the day he would become a partner. Happiness surged through him. Becoming a partner in a law firm took years, if it happened at all, and he could accept that title today.

This was why he'd been asked to meet here today instead of in a restaurant as they often did. A trickle of annoyance seeped in, tainting the joy. More than a small amount of manipulation was going on. This must have been planned long enough for a sign to be made.

His grandfather's deep, controlled voice sounded almost jovial. "Micah, my boy!" He strode over and tapped the wooden door. "Looks good, doesn't it?"

"It does. But I like the people I work for in Two Hearts and the surrounding county."

"You might like the people here too."

Micah doubted that. When you practiced corporate law, you worked for a mix of people who did and did not commit crimes. You often weren't sure which category the client fit into.

"No matter." His grandfather changed subjects. "Let's get lunch. You didn't come here to see a door sign."

Herded out of the office with his grandfather's arm a steady pressure on his back, Micah wondered what might happen over lunch. This man had clear patterns to his life, and nothing that had happened today fit those.

They went to a restaurant they'd come to before, one in downtown Nashville that he knew because his friend Nick was head chef. They weren't too far from tourist destinations such as the Country Music Hall of Fame and Ryman Auditorium. And his friend usually had time to visit for a minute when he was there.

Micah had absolutely no question that this lunch was going to be one more pitch to get him to come to the law firm to work. One more that would fail. The requests had become more and more focused and intense in the last year or two. Every time he had turned his grandfather down, he'd hoped it would be the last time he'd have to, but here they were again.

"So, son, do you have a special lady in your life?"

Micah slumped back in his chair. Where had that come from? They never discussed personal subjects like his dating life. "No, sir. I'm not seeing anyone special right now." *And I hope you never ask that question again.*

"It's just that you're approaching thirty."

"My thirtieth birthday is Monday. But I'm sure you know that."

"And Maisie and Margo, how are they doing?"

Now he was completely thrown off. Now his grandfather had moved on to idle family chitchat. This man didn't do *any* chitchat. He was a good person and had been a good grandfather in his own way, but warm and fuzzy family moments weren't his thing.

"My sisters are well, thank you. Maisie got accepted to her college of choice for engineering. And Margo got accepted to three colleges and now has to pick the one she wants."

"She still plans to be a doctor?"

"She does. She's currently leaning toward dermatology."

His grandfather gave a firm nod. "Good to hear." The older man leaned back in his chair. With a steady gaze, he said, "I'd like for you to join the firm, Micah. As you know, I'm not getting any younger. Your mother would have made a brilliant lawyer, but she chose to go a different direction."

Yes. She took a left when she was leaving Nashville and ended up with my father in Two Hearts. Definitely not what this man would have expected from his only child. "Everyone is wonderful, Grandfather. And you know that I have no intentions of coming to work for you. I'm building my own career."

His grandfather smashed his fist on the table, making silverware jump. Diners at tables around them turn to stare, but Micah just shrugged. "I know that isn't what you want."

"I can offer you so many more opportunities here. Things you can't even dream of in that small town of yours."

"Two Hearts. But you know that well. It's a good place to be, Grandfather. I like it there, and I plan to stay there. I gave the big city two years of my life after law school, but it wasn't for me."

His grandfather's gaze turned shrewd. "As I mentioned, I'm not getting any younger. There are things that I need to have happen in my lifetime. You at the firm tops the list. Who else am I going to pass this place on to?"

Micah was certain that some of the top partners would jump at the chance—leap, even—to be first in line for this firm when his grandfather retired.

"The best I can do is a day a week every once in a while. If you have a special case that I might be interested in, I'm game."

"That isn't what I was hoping for. But I do have a proposal for you." The older man's voice had changed to one that Micah recognized from the courtroom. The one that put fear into the hearts of the opposing lawyers and the witnesses on the stand. This couldn't be good.

Not that he would fall in line with whatever this man wanted. But he was his grandfather, so he would treat him with respect.

"Instead of waiting until I'm gone for you to know the terms of my will, I've decided to put those terms into action now."

Micah had always been told that he and his twin sisters would receive everything. They'd been told that for years. He didn't need the money, but it was nice to know it was coming.

"Give it to me straight." Micah crossed his arms and gave a stare worthy of his grandfather.

The older man chuckled. "You are a chip off the old block, aren't you?"

Micah shrugged.

"If you join the firm—and notice how I said *if*—then you receive your full inheritance when I'm gone."

Micah should have seen this one coming. His heart twisted a

little over the cruelty of the situation. His grandfather knew that this was not what he wanted for his life. Micah pushed back his chair. "Then I guess our conversation is over."

His grandfather motioned him to stay seated. "I knew you'd say no to that. I do have another option. Get married."

Micah laughed. "I always expected to get married. If that's all I need to do—"

"By Monday."

Micah felt his eyes widen. "Excuse me?" And then it dawned on him. "By my thirtieth birthday. Is that what you're saying?"

"Do we have an understanding, then? You'll join the firm next week." He didn't have a question at the end of that sentence. It was a statement. He thought Micah would fall right in line.

"So I only get the inheritance if by Monday I either join the firm or I get married? Why those two choices, Grandfather?"

"One brings you here to the family business. The other one would give you stability. My hope is that the little lady would also think that joining the firm was a good idea. Small-town life versus the successful lawyer's life in Nashville?" He wavered his hand back and forth. "Which one might she choose?"

"Any woman I'd marry would choose the one that made me the happiest." He leaned back in his chair. "But neither of these are going to happen in less than a week. It's what today? Thursday? Friday?"

His grandfather sighed deeply. "See, this is what I'm talking about. You live such a lackadaisical life that you don't even know what day of the week it is. It's Wednesday, Micah." His grandfather's expression changed to one of concern, but Micah also recognized it from the courtroom. "How do you think your sisters will feel about this news?"

Micah froze. "My sisters? How do my decisions impact them?" A chill ran down his spine as he watched the determined expression on his grandfather's face.

"The money in trust for the three of you is to be divided equally upon my passing. If one of you doesn't meet the terms . . ." He stretched out his words, and Micah realized where this conversation was going.

Micah said what he knew to be true. "They're smart. They'll do well in life. Not that they'll be thrilled about not getting an inheritance, but—"

"Son, *your* college education was paid for out of that trust fund."

Micah jumped to his feet. "Are you telling me you aren't going to pay for Maisie and Margo's college? You know that my parents can't afford it. These are bright girls with a great future ahead of them—*if* they go to college and get the degrees they have been dreaming of for years."

His grandfather leaned forward in his chair. "You know my terms. Find someone to marry you by Monday." His eyes narrowed. "Convince me it's real. Don't go marrying somebody you just met on the corner. And the marriage has to last at least a year." He shrugged. "Or I'll see you in your office at the firm Monday morning." His grandfather pushed back his chair and stood. "I'll pay the check on the way out. Think about this, Micah. You can have a great future."

Micah gulped as he watched his imposing figure of a grandfather cross the room. He'd never expected him to stoop so low. Now he knew why his parents had eloped.

CHAPTER FIVE

As her employees filtered in one by one, Bella realized that her responsibilities went far beyond her own life. A squeal went up from across the room, and she hurried over to see what was going on. "Everyone okay?"

Bonnie pointed at April. "Give her the news!"

"I'm pregnant." She shyly put her hand over her mouth. "I'm due in January." Her expression changed from glee to one of concern. "I can work right up until the baby's born, though. We're buying a house."

Bella pushed her troubles to the side for right now. The last thing she needed was a stressed-out mother-to-be. "Of course, I will let you work as long as you're able. Are you coming back after the baby's born?"

"Yes. I love working for you."

April was one of the best employees she'd ever had. She was amazing and did detailed work on the dresses without complaining. Some things would have driven Bella out the door screaming. April simply did the jobs and seemed to enjoy them. Once, she'd had her embroider the front of a wedding dress, a task that had taken over two weeks. It had come out stunning and had been in a magazine article in a well-known publication. A lot of Bella's dresses had over the years, but that one was special.

April clapped her hands together. "Everyone, let's get to work before the boss gets cranky." She gave a sideways grin to Bella, and Bella couldn't help but smile back in spite of everything.

She had to save the business. She paid her employees more than the going wage because she wanted to retain them and because they deserved it. What they didn't deserve was being told they'd lost their position overnight.

Her answer was to get a second job. Somehow, appointments would be made around the job's hours. She'd downsized to a studio apartment from her one bedroom a month ago, but she might have to move to something on the outskirts of town in an area with more affordable rent.

Bella went back to her office and sat at her desk. Her phone rang, and she picked it up, expecting to silence the call, but it was Cassie.

"How's everything in the small town?" Bella forced happiness she didn't feel into her voice.

"Everything's okay with me, but I keep thinking there was something you wanted to tell me before we had that disaster with the fire alarm."

Bella laughed. Or she thought she was laughing until she heard the hysterical edge in her own voice.

"What's going on, Bella?" Cassie's insistent tone did not allow for backing away from the conversation, but Bella didn't want to burden her friend who'd recently fallen in love and moved to her dream home. Not until things became too serious to handle, and right now, she still had hopes of this working out.

"You know the wet dresses from Saturday?"

She could almost hear Cassie shrug through the phone. "Of course."

"They may be a bit ruined."

After a few seconds' pause, her friend shouted, "They're ruined, and you didn't say anything? You lost thousands of dollars."

Bella held the phone away from her ear and put it on speaker so she wouldn't get her eardrums damaged. "Yes." One word, but packed with so much meaning.

"This is causing you financial problems? I can help you out." A second later, she added, "Some."

"Cassie, you just bought a house, and you're getting married. You uprooted your entire business and moved it to the middle of nowhere, where you're starting fresh. You can't give me your money. I won't let you."

"I can scale back on something."

"I can't let you do that. You're my friend. I will figure this out."

"But—"

"I *will*." She emphasized the last word with enough force that Cassie grew quiet.

"Remember that I'm here. Greg and I don't need a fancy wedding. And I think my business is going to do very well. I just haven't had enough time to be certain."

"I will remember your offer." And she would. She wouldn't take her up on it, though. Friends helped friends. But she couldn't let a friend who worked so hard at her own business suffer because of Bella's actions.

"On a happier note." She told Cassie about April's pregnancy. Cassie exclaimed in delight at the news. They got sidetracked talking about a baby shower, as well as wedding details for a client they shared, thankfully never returning to the earlier topic.

When she hung up, Bella stared at her phone, wanting to pick it back up and say she'd changed her mind. She couldn't do that, though. She'd dug a hole, stepped into it, and started to shovel the dirt around herself. She had to figure a way out of this problem on her own.

CHAPTER SIX

Micah caught himself grinding his teeth as he drove away from lunch with his grandfather. Forcing himself to relax, he took deep breaths and considered his options.

The old man was wily. He'd asked his grandson about joining the firm enough times that he knew the odds were against Micah willingly doing that. As his grandfather would have in a courtroom, he had played his hand perfectly. The name on the door with "partner" had eased Micah toward that option ever so slightly. Would he dislike it, or was he just being stubborn?

He felt tension rising again.

Working in the city or getting married in the next—he counted the days on his hand—five days. Both were impossible to imagine.

It was time to drown his sorrows. He'd soon be in a familiar location where he could numb his senses. Ten minutes later, he pulled up to Dinah's Place, stomped up the steps, and went inside, choosing a stool at the bar.

Michelle came over and stood with her pencil over her order pad. "Don't you look handsome!"

When he glanced down, he remembered the suit and tie he'd put on for the meeting. "Thanks." Tugging at the tie to loosen it, he added, "I can't wait to put on jeans."

"Lunch?"

"No. Coffee. And keep it coming." She started to walk away. "Wait! And pie."

"We have pecan, blueberry, and coconut cream today."

She'd pulled her dark brown hair up in one of those messy buns. Smiling, she really was pretty. No one in Two Hearts had a bad thing to say about her.

Could he ask Michelle to marry him? Picturing the ceremony, he got to the kiss at the end and stifled a shudder. She was more like his sister. Randi from the motel was the same way. In fact, every woman of a marriageable age within twenty miles either felt like a sister or had a significant other in her life.

"Micah?"

He realized he'd been staring. "Sorry. I'm trying to sort something out. Bring me whatever flavor you think I'll like. Dinah doesn't make a bad pie."

Michelle grinned. "That's the truth." She leaned forward and whispered. "But she did try a spicy chocolate jalapeño pie once that I wondered about. I tasted it, and it was okay, but a slow burn after a bite of pie was odd. She decided against selling it."

Spice. That was what he needed in his life. A non-sisterly woman who would be willing to join him in the bonds of matrimony for a short time. Someone who would benefit from it as much as he would. Not to be a true wife in every sense of the word, but someone he could pretend with for a year. A woman he enjoyed being around.

He went through everyone he knew again.

Then Isabella came to mind.

The idea was nothing short of crazy. And that was what he'd

be if he had to spend every hour of every day with her. Her high energy would push him over the edge. And he was teetering on the rim of a cliff as it was.

But she'd been nice too. Pleasant once he'd gotten to know her.

No, the best option had to be moving closer to the city and taking the position there.

Michelle set his coffee and a slice of pecan pie in front of him. A moment later, she added another slice of pie with peaches on top. "Dinah tested this recipe today. I volunteered you as a taste tester."

He put his fork into it and found a creamy base under the peaches. Sliding it into his mouth, he sighed. "Please tell Dinah to put this on the menu. She won't be able to keep it in stock." After another couple of bites, he felt as though his world was righting on its axis. Life would go on.

Nothing like soothing your troubles with a piece of pie. Or two.

He went to his Two Hearts office for an appointment about a will, wrapped that up, then went home to put on jeans and a T-shirt. Looking in the mirror as he brushed his hair, the man there appeared much more relaxed than the man in the suit had. Just one more reason to stay here.

If only he could get his sisters money for college—but that would probably be hundreds of thousands of dollars when it included medical school and the engineering graduate school Maisie needed to meet her career goals. He didn't want either of them to start life after school with massive student loan debt. That wouldn't be fair when he'd been offered two solutions to the problem.

What he needed was a friend to help him talk through this. Greg had mentioned that he was on duty today, but maybe they could meet after work and talk it over. He hoped. Because he needed someone else's input.

Micah called Greg as he left Dinah's. His friend usually had good advice.

A siren sounded from nearby. Greg's clipped voice said, "I'll call you back."

The phone went silent. Micah sat in his truck and tried to decide what to do next. A few minutes later, his phone rang.

"Sorry about that. That Thompson kid decided to race down the highway again. This time I caught him." Micah heard satisfaction in his friend's voice. The town was blessed to have someone like Greg who cared about his job.

Their usual night out in a nearby town might be a good place to talk without anyone from Two Hearts listening in. "Pizza?"

"Sure. I'm done about five. Cassie and I don't have any plans for tonight."

Did he mean he could come alone because they didn't have plans or that he wanted to bring his fiancée? "Just a guy night?"

"Okay," he said slowly. "What's going on?"

"I had lunch with my grandfather—"

"Say no more. I'll pick you up at your house when I'm off duty."

Micah should have been used to it by now. His friend always wanted to drive, apparently in case he needed to transport a felon or join a high-speed chase. Thankfully, neither had ever happened while they'd been eating.

A phone reminder sounded right after the call ended, and it was a good thing he'd set it. With all that had happened, he had completely forgotten about a late appointment today. He headed back to his office, grateful for the distraction of working with a client to set up a trust for her grandchildren. *She* wasn't making her family jump through hoops. It would be nice to have a grandparent like that.

When Greg picked him up in his sheriff's car, Micah had gone through his limited options a dozen times. He needed a friend's input. Unfortunately, this friend spent the whole drive to the pizza parlor on his phone dealing with a police situation, only hanging up when they were minutes from their destination.

Micah had rarely seen anyone else from Two Hearts at this restaurant, but the moment they walked in, it was clear today's streak of not-so-great things happening wasn't over yet. Just inside the door, Randi and her brother sat enjoying a large meat lovers' supreme. Personal conversation would be out.

Without missing a beat, Greg said, "Let's get it to go." Nothing beat having a buddy who knew you well enough to know to do that.

They each had a soda while they waited for their pizza to bake, neither saying much, but Greg studied him with a focused gaze every once in a while, much as Micah imagined he would a possible criminal. There was something unnerving about a man with a gun at his hips who kept giving you suspicious glances.

As soon as they got into the car, Greg asked, "What's going on?"

Micah ran his hands over his face. "I think I need to eat. Then I'll tell you my woes."

"It can't be that bad?"

Micah didn't reply because it actually could be. When they neared Two Hearts, he said, "Can we go to your place? I don't want to be distracted by Grandma's flowers and girly colors right now." He couldn't help picturing Isabella's face when she'd first seen his house.

"Sure." Greg made the turns to his home, which was an apartment over his mother's garage that would be his until he married Cassie.

They climbed the stairs to Greg's home and went inside, crowding around the small dining room table with the pizza box taking up most of it. By the time he'd finished his third slice of their usual pepperoni, Micah felt strong enough to tell his story.

"If you're ready to listen, I'll get started."

Greg kept chewing and waved him on.

"Grandfather has offered me two options."

He repeated their conversation.

When he finished, Greg shook his head. "You're moving to Nashville next week? I'll be sorry to see you go."

"Did you hear my words? I have *two* options."

Greg laughed. "Since you aren't even dating anyone, I saw it as one option." He took a sip of soda as he reached for the final slice of pizza. Micah would have normally argued with him over it, but tonight he didn't care.

"I don't want to move. I tried city life, and it wasn't for me." Charleston wasn't even as large as Nashville, but he'd learned his lesson.

"Then you need to find a woman to marry you by Monday."

"When you say that, it seems all the more ridiculous. I should pack up my life here and take the job."

Greg got up and carried his drink over to his small couch, gesturing for Micah to take the chair across from him. "Sit. Relax."

Micah did with a grimace. "I don't have time to relax. My life implodes on Monday."

"That's a little dramatic, isn't it?"

Micah focused on his hands, realizing he had been rubbing them back and forth on the chair's arms. "I'm not sure what to do next."

"You're a grown man, Micah. Your grandfather can't choose your major life directions." Only his best friend could say that. "But, if you don't want to move, and you want your sisters to get their college money—because you do, right?"

Micah nodded.

"Then your one option is to marry. Do you have anyone in mind?"

Isabella was his first thought, but he dismissed it. "I've considered Michelle and Randi."

His friend scowled.

"Then I realized that I couldn't marry either of them."

"That's my thought. I know they do best-friends-to-lovers romances in movies and books, but I can't see you with either of them. Anyone else?"

He took a deep breath before answering. "Isabella."

"Who's—wait! Do you mean Cassie's friend? The same one you doused with punch, then soaked with a fire hose? That Isabella?"

When he said it that way, Micah realized he'd made a mistake even considering it. "Bad idea. Forget I mentioned her."

Greg studied Micah again before speaking. "Cassie said she thought something was up with her. That she wasn't acting like herself."

Isabella had only revealed her situation to him after a crisis and a lot of crying. He probably shouldn't share her secrets. "Let's say that I think she could use some extra money right now."

"I see a massive problem with your plan. You're in Two Hearts, and she hates small towns."

"Isabella made that abundantly clear on more than one occasion."

"Bella."

"What?"

"She goes by Bella."

Micah laughed. "Great. So I've been calling her by the wrong name too."

Greg tapped his fingers on the couch. "I've been looking into what we need to do to get married—you know, because I've been engaged for a while." He stared at Micah and shook his head. "You'll need a marriage license, so she'll have to agree to this and be available in town during the county clerk's regular business hours this week—or else you'll have to wait until early Monday morning."

Micah winced. "You're right. And I don't know how to make that happen." He narrowed his gaze at Greg. "Wait. Did you agree that this could work?"

His friend frowned. "This is the only plan you have. Let's see if we can get her here and to agree to it."

Micah's sense of desperation ramped up about fifty notches, though he wouldn't have thought that was possible. In the end, they devised a simple yet detailed plan to bring Isabella—no, Bella—to Two Hearts to have dinner with him.

After a second's pause, Greg said, "Wait. I think Cassie mentioned that Bella would be here later this week for a wedding." He made a quick call to his fiancée and kept glancing at Micah as he spoke. That might have concerned him if he didn't know Greg as well as he did. When his friend smiled widely once he'd ended the call, Micah worried anyway.

CHAPTER SEVEN

With both eyes still on the paperwork in front of her, Bella reached for her phone. How had she gotten so far into debt so quickly? Her caller's name surprised her.

"Greg?"

"Yes. I have a favor to ask. I know you're coming out tonight for tomorrow's wedding, but I'd like to take Cassie out for a nice dinner."

That left her with nowhere to go while they were gone. She supposed she could ask Cassie for a key to her house and knew she'd give it to her.

"Micah said he would have dinner with you at his house. If that's okay with you. I know Cassie would feel guilty if she abandoned you."

"That sounds like a date." Two people alone for dinner? *Date.*

"It definitely isn't one."

"I don't know, Greg. Why would he do that?"

"He said you got along well after the fire alarm incident." Greg paused. "Oh, right, we didn't discuss the use of town resources for that."

She quickly agreed to the plan to get him off the phone. "I'll be at Micah's house by seven o'clock."

When she set down the phone, she wished she'd had the guts to tell him no. But she certainly didn't have the funds to pay for the alarm incident.

After the ridiculously long drive from Nashville, she was ready to have a quick dinner—long enough to avoid being rude —and get out of there as soon as she thought Cassie might be back. The weather was so nice that she could wait for her in her backyard.

Micah answered the door wearing a suit and tie. The man may have dressed this formally for work, but she doubted he sat around at home in that. She felt like she'd been set up. Had Greg worked alone, or was Cassie in on it too? One step into the house confirmed it.

This looks like a date.

A bouquet of fresh flowers took center stage on the table, with a candle flickering on either side. Lights were low enough that she barely noticed the grandma decor.

Micah adjusted the tie at his throat, which seemed to be strangling him, if his gulp as he did so was any indication. She'd apparently underdressed for what seemed to be a formal occasion in her businesslike daytime dress and heels. When he dropped his hand and didn't seem to know what to do with it next, she realized he appeared . . . nervous.

Nothing about this made sense. They'd sat in this very room before with zero tension.

He gestured toward the dining room table, which had been set with plates, silverware, napkins and had two candles in glass candlesticks glowing in the center. "Isabella, I'm glad you made it. Please, sit here." Micah hurried over to a chair and pulled it out.

She did as he'd asked, too confused to argue that she could seat herself.

He asked, "How was your day?" as he sat across the table from her.

"Fine. Thank you. And yours?" Could their conversation get any more stilted?

Micah pushed back his chair and stood. "I forgot. I bought dinner from Dinah's, but I made iced tea for us."

He placed a filled glass in front of her and set down one for himself. Then he placed a long iced tea spoon beside each of those.

Staring at him, she shook her head. "What's going on?"

He gulped again. "Going on?"

"Yes." Bella slapped her hands on the table. "*This* isn't you." She tapped a nail on the glass.

When he became indignant, she felt like the man she knew had reappeared. "I can be nice."

None of this made sense. "Yes, but you made tea? Why not get it from Dinah?"

"It's the South, so iced tea goes with everything. I wanted to add a personal touch by making it myself."

"Why?" Not only was this a date, it felt like more than a casual one.

He put his hands over his face and slowly rubbed them down. "Isabella, I'm in trouble."

"As in a crime?" A chill went down her spine. Could someone be after him? "Wait! You're a lawyer. Don't they stay on the right side of the law?"

"Shh. I don't want words connecting me with a crime mentioned here. Besides, my problem isn't criminal. It's my grandfather."

A wide grin spread across her face. "My grandfather's a sweet man. For my birthday, he sends me a card with a $10 bill tucked inside."

Micah rolled his eyes. "This grandfather is far from *sweet*. I may as well tell you everything. He's wealthy. My mother's side of the family is."

"The fancy motorcycle?"

"I bought that when I lived and worked in Charleston. But he has given me many expensive gifts over the years."

"So you're wealthy?" Did that make him more appealing? That would mean she was shallow.

"No. He's a successful lawyer in Nashville. *He's* wealthy. And my family tree on his side is, well, loaded."

Now it all made sense. He gave off a vibe that didn't match with the place he lived. "What's he done?"

Micah gave a weak smile, even though it seemed far from humorous. "After asking me for most of my life to join the family legal firm, he's found a way to push me away from here and to there. I have to go to work for him on Monday. His plan seems foolproof."

For a second, she pictured Micah living in Nashville and the two of them able to date. She found that idea . . . appealing. One glance at his face said he didn't like the idea. "You don't want to do that?"

"Not in this lifetime. I'm needed in Two Hearts, in Dogwood County. People are friendly here. My friends are here. I tried city life in Charleston, and it wasn't me."

"So tell him no." She brushed her hands together. "Done."

"He paid for my college education. My twin sisters are going to college in a year. He says he won't pay if I don't do what he asks, and I can't let them go into massive debt. My parents earn a decent middle-class income, but they can't afford this."

The older man knew how to play his grandson. "Then I don't see a choice." She took a sip of her tea. "This is great." When he stared at her without speaking, she set the glass down. "Am I here to help in some way?"

He cleared his throat. "He offered me a Plan B on the same timeline."

She couldn't think of a single connection between them that explained why she was here. "What is Plan B? He wants a wedding dress?"

Micah sighed. "In a way. He wants a wedding. For me."

Her brow furrowed. "Had you planned to get married at some point?"

"Sure. When I met the right woman."

Bella shrugged. "Then you're fine, right?" His previous words came to mind. *Monday*. "You have to be married by Monday?"

He blew out a deep breath. "Yes. Isabella, I wondered—"

He couldn't be asking what she thought he was. Leaning away, she said, "I barely know you."

"Please don't look at me like I'm crazy. This could be a win for both of us."

Chills came over her. There was no wondering if he'd lost his mind. He had. Completely. She pushed back her chair as she stood, the wooden legs grating across the floor. "One word. No."

She ran toward the door as fast as her high heels would carry her.

"Isabella, wait! I can pay your debts. Save your business."

She stopped and slowly turned. "Because?"

"He's giving me access to my inheritance early. At least part of it."

So she could run from this crazy situation. Or she could consider his crazy offer. Either way, she saw *crazy* as part of it.

"Please. Sit back down and talk to me."

She brushed her bangs off her face, then slowly returned. "I'm only here because of my business."

He raised his hands as he spoke. "I'm only here because of my sisters."

She took her seat again. "Are we talking forever? Because I was hoping to find the man of my dreams, get married, and have little bambinos with him."

"He said one year. I'm sure there will be an agreement that he has us sign."

She considered it. To save her business, she could do that. He seemed kind—he was doing this for his sisters, after all—and he was so handsome he made her heart flutter whenever he walked into a room. His dark-brown hair, green eyes that tended to have a mischievous sparkle, and fit body called to her more than they should.

"Would you pay my apartment rent?"

He shook his head. "You aren't seeing this right. We will be married."

She shrugged. "Sure. Ring. Ceremony. Married. Weddings are my business."

"Sharing the same home, Isabella. *Married*."

"Wait! You want me to live *here*." She gestured to the room around her. "In Two Hearts?" Not a plan she wanted to be part of. "Sorry, but no."

She started toward the door again.

He hated to do this, but he didn't see a choice. "Before you go, what's your plan to save your business?"

She turned to face him, and her angry expression told him she didn't have an answer. "Get a job and work at my business part time."

"Do you have employees?"

"Of course I do."

"You need to pay rent and utilities for your business?"

"Yes." Her lip quivered. "It won't work, will it? I want it to."

He went over to her, needing to pull her into a hug but knowing he couldn't. "Not unless it's an amazing job."

She gave a single shake of her head. "That isn't likely." She paused. "Micah, one of my employees is pregnant and buying a house. Losing her job now might stress her out so much—"

"Don't think like that."

She rubbed her eyes. "Are you sure I couldn't live in Nashville?"

His heart leapt at the possibility that she'd marry him. To satisfy the terms, of course. "Saving your business will likely take most of the money I'm getting. We can't support two households."

Her defeated sigh made him want to take it all back.

"I could put an air mattress in my office," she said.

One thing he knew for sure: Isabella didn't want to live in Two Hearts. That brought him full circle to needing a bride in the next few days. He didn't have any other options. They had to make this work. "We can try that. You'd need to be here every weekend, though."

Happiness lit up her face, and her glowing beauty stunned him. Sure, he'd thought she was attractive, but this took his breath away. "Every weekend when I'm not needed at a wedding, and that's most weekends. Only a few brides pay extra to have the dress designer on site in case there's a last-minute problem."

"Let's hope that's enough."

"In one year we would have the marriage annulled?"

She was detail-oriented. He liked that. "I checked, and it looks like we'd have to get divorced. We won't fit the reasons in this state for an annulment."

"Divorce. I'd hoped to avoid that one after my parents managed it multiple times, twice to each other." After a pause, she said, "I have to live in this dinky, nowhere town, and get a divorce."

She would never agree to that. "Isabella—"

"I'll do it."

"You'll what?"

"I'll marry you, Micah."

"That's . . . great." At least, he hoped it would be.

"We need your grandfather to buy that we're in love, right?"

"Yes. We have to have instantly fallen madly and deeply in love." The more he spoke, the less plausible this sounded.

She cocked her head to the side. "You don't seem like an instant love kind of guy."

Bella saw more than most women did.

"You're right. But I am today." That got him a glimmer of a smile.

"Maybe we should tell him we've known each other for a while. That adds a realistic note. There has to be a sense of romance about the whole thing, though."

"Hmm. We need to make this look real."

She tapped her chin with her finger, then she grinned. "A romantic proposal should help. One I can put on social media."

"Everyone will know." He laughed self-consciously. "That was a ridiculous comment. Everyone needs to know for this to work."

He dropped to one knee.

"Wait!" She put her hand out. "Don't you need a ring for this?"

He stood. "You're right. But this was a whirlwind romance. Would I have a ring?"

She frowned. "I think you would have run to the store early this morning and bought one. You know, your love would have made you do everything you could to make this special for me. You'd be that kind of guy, wouldn't you?" There was a hopeful note in her voice.

She was right. "But jewelry doesn't appear from thin air. Or does it?"

As he raced down the hall to his grandmother's room, he said, "I have an idea."

Sorting through his grandmother's jewelry box, he found a

ring that might work—the simple band of diamonds his grandmother had worn for decades. When he returned, he showed it to her. As soon as she slid it on her finger, he knew this was a bad idea. Bella would have chosen a modern design. "No, I can get something you'd like instead."

She held up her hand, turning it from side to side. "This ring is beautiful."

"It is?" He heard the incredulous tone of his voice. "But it's old-fashioned, and belonged to my grandmother."

"That makes me like it even more. Is your grandmother . . . gone?"

He nodded. "Yes. Since January."

"Oh, I'm so sorry." Her sympathetic expression seemed out of place.

"She enjoys living in her condo in Florida," he said, puzzled.

Bella laughed. "I thought she'd died."

"Sorry! She moved to the beach. She worked for years saving every penny so she could do that when she retired."

"Micah, I make wedding dresses, so I like pretty things. Other than a necklace my grandmother gave me, I don't have any family heirlooms. The family connection is special. Sure, I personally prefer modern, clean lines—"

He put his hand out for the ring.

"But this has those. I love it." She certainly sounded sincere.

His grandmother had always said he could use that ring "if and when" he married. She'd tended to emphasize the "if."

Bella slid the ring off and dropped it into his outstretched hand.

Kneeling, he said, "Isabella Bennett, will you marry me?"

She pulled out her phone and snapped some photos of the ring. "Now I'll get video. Ask me again." She propped the phone up against a vase sitting on a side table, then hit Record. As soon as he asked her, she squealed, "Yes!" and threw her arms around him, almost knocking him over. Then she hit Stop and stood. "That should do it."

For a second, he'd thought she meant it, and he'd felt weirdly . . . happy. He must be more of a romantic than he'd realized. That emotion certainly had nothing to do with the cantankerous woman standing in front of him who was now focused on her phone.

"Did you upload it yet?"

She stopped with her finger above her phone. "Almost."

"Don't. Let's figure out our plan first."

Bella dropped the device in her purse. "Good idea."

"What do we do now?"

Micah stood in front of her and took out his own phone. "Today is Thursday. When do you want to get married?" The craziness of his question was not lost on him. "Unless we're going to wait until Monday, we need to get to the county office tomorrow for our license. We could get married over the weekend that way."

"The sooner the better."

Did she *want* to marry him?

"Waiting will only make it worse."

She did not.

CHAPTER EIGHT

"Let's get married Saturday." Her words made her pause. "It just got real, didn't it?"

Micah laughed. "Yes, it did. We probably need witnesses. Don't we? They do in movies."

"Witnesses aren't required in Tennessee." A trickle of nervousness raced down her spine.

She had gotten engaged. What had she been thinking?

Oh, yeah. She was trying to save her business and her home. She didn't want to end up back on her mother's or father's doorsteps.

That was why she'd just done what might be the stupidest thing of her life.

He nodded slowly. "Right. Weddings expert."

"Pretty much." She shrugged. Maybe she wouldn't panic if she saw it as another wedding on her schedule.

Looking down at his feet, he said, "Isabella, Greg already knows about this. I talked to him, and he suggested tonight."

"He told you to lie to me?"

"I've never lied to you. He took his fiancée out for a

romantic meal. And you must know the long hours she's been working. All of that is true."

"She wants her business here to succeed."

"And it is doing well. There's one other thing."

Only one? "That sounds easy."

"I don't want to lie to anyone. If word leaks out, Isabella, this whole thing could fall apart. We'd be married for nothing. We need to tell the truth, but in a way that doesn't give away our secret."

Right. Because he wouldn't want to marry her otherwise.

"I don't want to lie either. But I have to tell Cassie the whole truth." Or could she? Cassie would try to give her money if she knew that part of the equation.

"No one else, though."

She tapped the side of her face as she considered the solution. "Maybe we could say we knew we should be together."

He smiled slowly. "I like that. It's true and simple."

"That's settled, then. By the way, Micah, it's Bella."

"Sorry! Greg told me too. I'll get used to it once we're married." He gave her a long look. "That's too bad. Isabella suits you."

She'd never thought of her adult self as anything but Bella. But it was a sweet thought that her husband would call her by a different name. "My parents called me Isabella, but if you prefer—"

"I'd like to have a special name for you." He winced after he said those words. "That sounded . . ."

"Perfect. Keep talking like that and everyone will buy into this marriage." When had she gotten so into the plan?

He checked the time on his phone again. "We'd better hurry, Isabella."

That sounded wrong. "On second thought, I think I need to be Bella. A pet name would still be cute, though." She turned toward the door, and her heel caught on the edge of a throw rug.

Micah grabbed her arm to steady her, then slid his hand down to hold hers. As his fingers intertwined with hers, tingles shot up her arm.

"We have to get used to looking like a couple," he said.

It was her turn to gulp. She would be married soon. On their way to Cassie's house, she realized that all her employees could keep their jobs. Her Monday-to-Friday life could look the same.

Micah's phone sounded. "That's Greg. I asked him to text when he and Cassie were at her house."

"It may be best if I call Cassie first and let her know I'm on my way." When she did, Cassie told her what they already knew —that she was home now.

Driving over, she tried to picture her friend's reaction. How could she explain this to her without her trying again to give her money?

She felt her footsteps slow as they stepped out of the car and approached Cassie's back door. When Micah reached up to knock, she put a hand on his arm. "Wait a second."

He turned. "Isa—Bella, I understand if—"

"I'm not backing out."

"Whew. That's a relief. I don't think I'll rest until everything's taken care of."

She rolled her eyes. "What, you mean 'everything' as in our wedding?"

"Your *what?*" shouted a voice she'd know anywhere as Cassie's.

She turned slowly and wanted to run the second she saw the expression on her friend's face.

"We're here to talk to you and Greg."

"He's inside." She glared at Micah. "Or did you already know that?"

He shrugged.

Cassie asked, “I guess you’ve planned getting married for a while?”

Bella laughed. “You must be joking. No, this is fairly new.” As in this afternoon, but she wouldn’t add that now. Maybe later.

“You decided to get married on a whim?” The rising voice and frown that accompanied those words confirmed Bella’s thoughts.

~

Greg came to the door. “Everything okay?” He looked directly at Micah when he spoke.

“As good as it can be.”

With Cassie to one side and Greg on the other, he felt a glimmer of doubt about their plan.

A gray and white kitten darted out the still-open door. “No, you don’t, Romeo. We’re all going inside.” Cassie scooped up her kitten. “Let’s talk about this somewhere more comfortable.” She leaned closer and dropped her voice. “And more private. I’ve noticed that Mr. Gilmore next door seems to sit outside more when I have guests, and he’s pulled his chair closer to the fence between us over time.”

“He’s probably bored,” Bella replied as they went through Cassie’s kitchen, where they usually sat to talk.

Cassie set Romeo on the living room floor, and he pounced on a nearby kitten-sized toy ball. Then Cassie sat on a chair, and Greg chose the one beside her, leaving the couch for Bella and Micah. Bella sat on one end, Micah on the other. When he realized they must look like the virtual strangers they were, he scooted closer to her.

Cassie spoke up, surprising him with her bluntness. “Is this a practical joke? I know for a fact that it’s nowhere near April Fools’ Day.”

Micah took Bella's hand in his. Maybe that would convince Cassie. He was surprised to find Bella shaking.

"This isn't a joke. We're getting married." He swallowed hard. "This weekend."

Cassie jumped to her feet. "That's insane! Bella, why are you doing this? Are you being coerced somehow?" The dark, possibly even threatening, gaze she directed toward him made him squirm in his seat.

Bella stiffened at her friend's words, but the meaning was clear. "What's not to like? He's gorgeous."

Bella thought he was gorgeous? He figured she hadn't found him unattractive, but this surprised him.

"I'll give you that. He is attractive."

Micah sat up straighter. This was going well.

"But he doesn't have much of a future. I know that last week, he took a workday off to go fishing." Cassie shrugged. "Small-town lawyer without much ambition." He could picture her putting the phrase on social media with that hashtag.

He turned toward Bella. Surely, she'd stand up for him.

Instead, his fiancée sighed. "I know."

Before he could say anything, Greg—his *good* friend—chimed in. "His grandmother gave him that house, and he hasn't touched it."

"Hello? I'm sitting right here." He tapped his chest. "And I left the house that way because I wanted her to feel comfortable when she visits. Besides, I'm a bachelor. What do I care about decor?"

The three people who'd stomped all over him turned in his direction. Greg chuckled, and Cassie's eyes sparkled.

Bella laughed. "Cassie winked at me when you turned away from her. I knew she was messing with you."

He leaned back in his seat. "Wow. I'd hate to see what happened when you didn't actually like someone."

Cassie said, "I'd never really say something like that."

"Me either, buddy. You care about home decorating as much as I do."

"But the apartment over your mother's garage is nice." Cassie stared at Greg, who flushed red.

"That's nicely done because she decorated when they remodeled. The place is exactly as it was the day my mother gave me the key. With occasional dusting and vacuuming."

The knot in Micah's stomach loosened.

Cassie crossed her arms and gave him a long stare. "Why should I let you marry Bella?"

Bella spoke up. "This is mutually beneficial."

Cassie asked her fiancé, "Marriage should always be that. Right, Greg?"

Greg said, "Absolutely."

"It's a business arrangement." Not able to sit still another minute, Bella jumped to her feet, knocking her tea to the floor, which startled Romeo, who let out a yowl of surprise.

Cassie ran into the kitchen and returned with paper towels to wipe up the tea, which had thankfully missed the rug and landed on easy-to-clean hardwood floors. With that done, she tucked the roll under her arm and said, "What are you talking about? Did he make you sign a prenuptial agreement?"

Micah muttered, "That's a good idea." When Bella smacked his arm, he added, "For both of us. Then we're both guaranteed to get what we expect."

"What are the two of you talking about?" Cassie raised her hands in frustration, the paper towels dropping to the floor. "Wait! You don't *need* to get married?" Her gaze settled on Bella's abdomen for a long, uncomfortable moment, then she changed her focus and glanced from one of them to the other.

Bella laughed in a deep throaty way that made him chuckle. "So not the case."

"Then start talking."

"My grandfather—"

Greg stepped in and helped the situation. "His grandfather is a little controlling."

Micah scoffed. "That's an understatement." He began. "He gave me two options: join the firm or get married."

Cassie turned toward her fiancé. "You know the law better than I do, Greg. He can't do that, can he?"

Greg sighed. "He's using the terms of his will to make things happen now. He's holding back college money from Micah's sisters unless he complies. It's time that I admitted that Micah came to see me yesterday."

Cassie glared at him, and Micah expected Greg to get the full force of her anger about leaving her out later.

Micah rubbed his hand over his face. "That's it in a nutshell."

Cassie jumped in. "You don't want to live in Nashville."

"Right."

"So you need to get married," Greg added.

"That makes sense for you, Micah, but Bella's been quiet. An unnatural state for her, I might add." Cassie sat down and faced Bella. "Why marriage to Micah, Bella?"

"If I tell you, you have to promise not to try to sacrifice to help me. Deal?"

Cassie said, "No deal. I won't promise that."

"Then I can't say anything beyond the fact that we're getting married. Soon."

Cassie turned toward Micah. "Why don't you explain Bella's involvement in your situation? I understand choosing marriage over leaving your home, no matter how crazy the whole thing sounds, but what I don't see is why you've picked her. You've met once or twice and never spent time together."

"I helped her after the fire alarm fiasco."

She nodded. "That's right. Those were his clothes."

"His *clothes*?" Greg glared at Micah.

Micah held up his hands in a stop position. "Not what you're thinking."

Bella clapped her hands. "Everyone. Micah helped me after I got hit with water from the fire hose. We sat and talked while my clothes were drying on the line. I shared something about my current business situation. I'm okay with getting married. *We're* okay with it." She glanced around the room at everyone else. "We need to feel supported."

Cassie blew out her breath. "Okay. I'm in."

Bella added, "Can you keep it quiet? Both of you? Because Micah's grandfather has to believe this is a love match."

Cassie softly asked, "Why are you lying to everyone?"

"I'm not lying. Ever." Bella squeezed Micah's hand.

"What about the 'love, honor, and cherish' part of the wedding vows?"

Micah groaned. "I think we'll use something a little less conventional."

"I agree," Bella said. "Besides, when you've seen as many weddings as Cassie and I have, being different is highly desirable."

"Where are you having the ceremony? Who's invited?" The planner in Cassie had apparently kicked in. "Have you chosen a dress? What about the reception?"

As panic surged through her, Bella experienced a sample of what a real bride felt. She held up her fingers, folding them down as she ticked off the answers. "One, we don't know. Two, you two are. Three, I have no idea, but I'll figure something out. Four, no reception."

"I agree with almost all of that," Micah answered. "But the town may not let us get away without a reception." He shrugged. "And I have no idea about the dress."

"I had hoped to have a simple ceremony with the two of us, Cassie, and Greg. And we could go out to dinner afterward. It's one thing to tell friends and family we're getting married. It's completely different to announce it to a whole town."

"But everyone will know. You will be wearing a wedding ring."

The blood rushed in her ears. "I know that." She closed her eyes. When she opened them again, she found Micah focused on her. "But I didn't know that. If that makes sense?"

Micah squeezed her hand. "It's all going to be okay."

When he looked into her eyes as he spoke, she believed him.

"I'll have to leave you to figure this out. I have an early morning tomorrow," Greg said. After much back slapping with Micah and a one-sided man hug, he left.

Then Cassie turned toward them. Bella had seen this expression before. Her mild-mannered friend had changed from sweet and laid-back to in-charge with excitement in her eyes. "Let's get going on this wedding. What do you have planned so far?" She raised an eyebrow in expectation.

Micah had apparently never seen this side of Cassie, because he made the mistake of saying, "Nothing." One word that would never make a wedding planner happy.

"When are you getting married?"

Bella didn't immediately reply to her question. "I do have an idea for the dress. But I have to make a call."

"Okay. Now we're getting somewhere. Bella, you think about your dress while I jot down some ideas about the rest of it."

What would she do without a wedding planner friend?

Bella considered her dress choices. She needed one she could wear immediately. The only one that fit well was the dress she'd worn a week ago. The one Micah had doused with water. That dress was too sparkly. Too poofy. Too *everything*.

She could pull an everyday dress out of her closet and use that, but her business was making special wedding dresses. She couldn't walk down the aisle in anything less.

An idea came to mind. She stepped away and phoned April, quickly making arrangements. Her best seamstress would contact two others, and they would strip away the sparkly layer, de-poof the skirt, and turn it into something she would like to wear. Maybe not the dream dress she would have created if she'd had time, but a dress she hoped wouldn't be embarrassing.

"I'll have someone pick it up early Saturday morning."

"Is the bride one I've met? Oh, and we'll need her measurements."

"We have this bride's information on file from previous special occasion dresses we've made." Bella tripped over the next words. "It's me."

As had happened often recently, silence greeted her. "Did you say you're getting married? *Saturday*?"

"I am."

"Okaaay. The team will make something beautiful for you."

They hung up with Bella feeling like she'd done something wrong by not waiting to get married to a mysterious someone in the future. And she probably had, but she'd come too far to give up now and this was still the best option.

One day was pushing it—even for her best seamstresses—but she thought it would be possible.

When she came back into the room, Cassie pounced. "There's the venue, the officiant, flowers, cake—"

Micah spoke up, his voice rising on every word. "But this isn't a real wedding."

Cassie gave him a steady gaze. "Doesn't it have to appear that way to your grandfather?"

"I'd planned to show him the marriage license."

She shrugged. "Okay. If you believe that will satisfy him."

Bella said, "Micah, I've never met the man, but from what you've told me—"

He sighed. "You're right. The more convincing we can make this, the better. Do your best work on it."

Cassie beamed as she grabbed a pad of paper and a pen off her coffee table and started scribbling notes. Her glee at being given carte blanche scared Bella. *What happens when you let a wedding planner do whatever she wants?*

She stopped with her pen on the paper. "You didn't answer about the date."

Bella and Micah looked at each other, then he gestured with his head toward her. He'd chickened out. "Saturday."

The pen clattered to the floor. "It's late Thursday. Please tell me you don't mean in two days."

"I do." She and Micah said the words at the same time. Bella felt heat rise in her face, and she noticed him turning pink as they both realized what they'd said.

Cassie grinned. "That's good practice." She picked up the pen and tapped it from side to side. "I have done a few elopements. I'd better get to work. You need to decide who will perform the ceremony."

He immediately answered. "The minister from the church, of course."

"That would be fine for me normally, but Micah, this isn't a real wedding."

"It doesn't matter anyway," Cassie said, jumping in to what might have turned into an argument. "I have it on good authority that he's at a theme park in Florida with his family."

Micah frowned. He looked handsome even when he did that. "Then who *can* m-a-r-r-y us?" She heard what almost sounded like a stutter every time he said "marry." He'd have to fix that before he told his grandfather about it.

Cassie leaned back in her chair. "In Tennessee, there are a lot of options. Judges, the county clerk, the mayor. And lots more."

A smile started on Micah's face and grew. "The mayor? Let's get him to do it."

"Why him?" Cassie's voice rang with hesitation.

Bella glanced from Cassie to Micah. "Why not him? Have I met him?"

Cassie frowned. "Probably not."

"Wait! Isn't he that old guy who nods off at the restaurant? You told me about him."

Micah crossed his arms. "He stays awake when he needs to."

"Isn't there someone else?" This may not be real, but she didn't want it to be a farce either.

"He's like family to me." Micah's expression told her to give in on this one and hope it all turned out well.

"Fine. The mayor does the ceremony. Now, for the cake, we need to see if Simone can pull a rabbit out of a hat—a beautifully frosted and decorated bunny. Should I call her?"

"I'll take care of it." Cassie made a note on her pad. "If I didn't love you like a sister, a rush wedding would be pricey."

"I will call the mayor in the morning." Micah's expression still held overwhelm even though he'd won that one.

"Wait!" Cassie cried. When they turned toward her, she said, "Where are you going to have the ceremony?"

They must have had similar blank expressions, because she added, "Your backyard, Micah? Or mine? The weather's supposed to be great this weekend."

"I think mine is a little larger. And the neighbor's dog probably won't be watching our every move at that time of day." Everyone must have had similar confused expressions because he added, "Finn is an Irish Setter who stands on his back legs and peers over the fence."

Bella wondered how embarrassing this event would be. An officiant falling asleep. A backyard with a neighbor whose dog could be watching the proceedings. And a bride wearing whatever dress they could cobble together.

She hoped Cassie forgot to schedule a photographer.

As she pictured the big day, she realized they had a problem. Whirling around, she asked, "Cassie, where will everyone sit?"

"Good point." Her friend frowned. "There isn't enough time for one of my vendors to supply chairs. Or is there?" She tapped her foot on the floor, then made another note on her pad. "I'll see what I can do."

Bella walked Micah out to his car.

"You can trust Cassie," she said. "She's good at what she does."

He didn't look any more confident, but that was probably because of the occasion and not her friend.

Micah put his hand over his mouth as he yawned. "I've had some very long days. I'll go now, then I'll pick you up—" He checked the calendar in his phone. "Tomorrow morning at about ten."

"For?"

"The marriage license."

It felt more and more real.

CHAPTER NINE

When Bella returned to Cassie's living room, her friend gave her a steady glare and sat beside her. "What's really going on?"

"I can't tell you."

"Because I'd try to help."

Bella nodded. She hated not being able to talk to her best friend.

"I'll leave it this way. For now. But I'm going to demand the information if I think you're in trouble. Okay?"

"I can agree to those terms."

The next morning, Bella tried to sneak out of the house before Cassie was up, to avoid awkward one-on-one time, but her friend was already dressed and at her kitchen table with a mug of coffee in her hand.

"Have a seat." Cassie pointed at the chair across from her own.

"I thought I'd take an invigorating morning walk."

Cassie chuckled. "You have never in your life taken a morning walk, invigorating or otherwise."

Reluctantly pulling out the chair and sitting, Bella realized a mug of something that smelled wonderful sat in front of her. Leaning forward, she took a sniff. "Chai?"

"I'm trying to be more welcoming to tea drinkers."

Wearing what she knew was her first genuine smile in days, Bella took a sip. "Thank you. I feel seen."

"As hard as it is for me to picture, I've come to realize that there are those who don't want coffee."

A moment of uncomfortable silence later—something they hadn't experienced since the day they'd met in college—Bella set down her mug and shrugged. "Do you want me to tell you everything right now? Or do you want me to wait until after we're married?"

"I want to know everything, but it's selfish of me to try to make you do something you don't want to do."

"If you're sure . . ."

"I'm sure." Cassie picked up a mug that Bella knew would be filled with coffee. "So you're going to marry him?" Her friend stared at her over her mug, then took a sip. "That's so good. How can you not love this?"

Bella grinned. Their usual relationship was back. "Yes to Micah. And because it tastes like battery acid. Or what I imagine battery acid tastes like."

"On a completely different subject: Bella, are you just coming to the wedding itself today or also helping with the bride and her dress?"

Her friend's words took a while to sink in. "Wedding! I forgot that was why I'd driven to Two Hearts in the first place. Amelia was such a fun client that when she invited me to her wedding, I said yes. I'm a guest. Of course, I thought it would be in the city. And I hadn't paid enough attention to notice that it was on a Friday." That meant taking a whole day off work. But she wasn't going to make the rent, anyway.

"Her parents and grandparents married on Fridays. It seems to be a family tradition. And she always wanted to hold it in a barn. I had expected to find one closer to Nashville."

"But now that you're in Two Hearts . . ."

"Exactly. She loved Cherry and Levi's barn when she saw it and immediately wanted to book it." Cassie got up and refilled her mug. "The country-chic dress you made is perfect." She started for the doorway to the living room. "I'd better get to work on a wedding someone dropped in my lap last night. I'll see you here at three. We can ride together."

"I'd better go alone. I probably won't stay until the end of the reception."

"Right. Because you may need to discuss something with your *groom*. I'll see you here tonight. The key will be under the cushion on the lawn chair."

"I thought you didn't need to lock the door in a small town."

"Too much of the city in me to do that quite yet."

Bella made a fresh cup of tea. She sipped it, trying and failing to picture her life two days from now. She barely knew the man she'd be married to. Would she keep her name or take his? Laughing, she realized she didn't remember what his surname was.

She'd told Cassie she was going to take a walk, and she might as well. For better or worse, she'd be spending more time in Two Hearts, so she may as well learn where things were.

A couple of blocks away, a woman called to her from her front porch. "Bella? Is that you?"

Bella stopped and stared. She knew her. That's right—she was Greg's mother and Cassie's future mother-in-law. "Yes, ma'am."

"Come on inside. I just pulled brownies out of the oven." She waved her forward.

The older woman was doing the small-town thing and being welcoming. Bella really didn't know her, but it would be rude to say no. Then she realized what the woman had said. "Brownies still warm from the oven?"

Mrs. Brantley nodded.

"I'm on my way." As she drew closer, she asked, "Do you have tea?"

"I'm happy to make a pot. It would go well with the brownies. But then, everything goes well with brownies."

That was true. When Bella got closer to the door, a small black-and-white puppy peered around his or her owner. "Is that the dog—?"

"From the engagement party? Yes." She patted the puppy's head. "We couldn't find her owners, so I took her home that day, and . . ." Mrs. Brantley shrugged. "Cookie stayed."

A dog named Cookie? That seemed about right for Mrs. Brantley, who Cassie claimed was always baking something. Bella stepped inside the welcoming home. Cassie had been fortunate with her future mother-in-law.

She was directed to sit at the kitchen table—that seemed to be a Two Hearts thing to do—and a square of brownie on a plate was soon followed by a cup of tea in a delicate china cup.

Mrs. Brantley set what looked like a homemade treat on the floor for Cookie. What brings you here on a weekday?" Mrs. Brantley paused for only a beat before adding, "That's right, there's a wedding today."

"Yes, ma'am." Should she tell her about her own wedding? There was no doubt that she'd find out about it tomorrow. "I'm also here for another reason." She took a fortifying sip of her tea before continuing. "I'm also"—she struggled to say the words —"getting married to Micah tomorrow."

Mrs. Brantley choked on her tea. Sputtering, she said, "What?"

"I'm marrying Micah tomorrow." It was a little easier the second time she said it.

"I didn't even know you two were dating." She leveled her gaze at her, and Bella fought the urge to squirm in her seat.

"Um, it happened fairly quickly."

"Let me get this straight. Micah Walker?"

That's his last name! "Yes."

"You aren't—"

"No!" Why did everyone think she was expecting?

"I'm surprised you aren't madly planning the details."

"Cassie's working on it. The ceremony will be in Micah's backyard tomorrow afternoon." At least, she assumed it would be in the afternoon. "The mayor is officiating."

At her last words, Mrs. Brantley's eyebrows shot so high they disappeared behind her wispy bangs. "Will your parents be driving in for the ceremony?"

Bella laughed. "Definitely not. I haven't seen them in a couple of years." More like five, but who was counting?

"I'm sure he's told you his parents likely can't come. They moved to Houston, Texas, years ago, so his father could find work. His sisters are out there with them, of course, so I guess he won't have family here."

Bella knew she should have the answer to this, but they hadn't talked about his parents, only his sisters.

When she didn't reply, Mrs. Brantley continued. "Then who is walking you down the aisle?"

She hadn't thought about that, and she should have. Many times, she'd asked herself that same question when a father and daughter went arm-in-arm down the aisle at a wedding. She'd assumed someone would be obvious for the role when the time came.

"You're Cassie's best friend," Mrs. Brantley said. "Maybe Greg could do it."

When she pictured that, it seemed right. "Perfect! Micah can ask him today." Bella popped the last bite of brownie in her mouth and washed it down with tea. "That was delicious."

"Well, you're welcome here anytime. Remember that. You'll be almost like family and living a few blocks away."

Bella didn't have the heart to correct her and say that she'd be spending most of her time in the city.

They said their goodbyes, and Bella went back toward Cassie's house. Her phone rang when she was almost there, and Micah's name appeared on the screen.

"I didn't call earlier because I don't know when you wake up. That's one of the many things I need to learn about you in case the subject arises."

"I've been up for hours. In fact, I had a brownie and tea with Mrs. Brantley."

Silence greeted her.

"I told her about the wedding. It seemed better to have it arise naturally than to have it come as a complete surprise after it happened."

"You're probably right." She heard a sound that she guessed was him rubbing his hand over his rough beard. He did that a lot. "But it does make it seem real, doesn't it?"

She couldn't argue that point. At Cassie's, she lifted the cushion, finding the key where she'd said. Bella explained about Greg's possible role tomorrow, and Micah said he'd call him when he got off the phone.

"I can think of only one more thing that's vital. We have to get to the city office today if we want to get married before Monday."

Unlocking the door, Bella said, "Let me change into something nicer. You can pick me up here in a half hour."

"I'm sure you're beautiful, as you always are, but I'll wait before driving there."

Micah thought she looked good all the time? Her heart warmed a little at his words.

Once she'd put on a dress and heels, she felt like she could conquer the world. Heels had a way of doing that for her, and probably for other women hovering just over five feet tall. Micah's appreciative expression confirmed her choices.

Bella got into his car. "Let's do this." She'd managed to ignore almost everything about her business today, but a text from her commercial landlord brought it back into focus. She considered opening the full text, but Micah pulled up to a large, old building and stopped. She'd deal with it later.

The stately building greeted them with signs pointing to the county clerk's office. A woman Bella's grandmother's age greeted the groom-to-be.

"Micah, what brings you here today?"

It made sense that a lawyer would be known at the courthouse.

"And is this one of your sisters? It's been so long since I've seen them."

Or maybe it was simply another small-town thing.

"Hazel, this is my fiancée, Bella."

The woman's gaze went from him to her. "Bella, it's a pleasure to meet you." Then she glanced at the phone, and Bella knew she would be burning up the line as soon as they walked out. She'd have thought the county clerk would have privacy regulations, but maybe those were overlooked in small towns.

"There will be a lot of broken hearts when one of our last single and handsome men ties the knot. Besides, I always expected you and Michelle—"

He shook his head. "We were never more than friends."

That must be the Michelle she'd met, the waitress at the diner.

Micah spoke quickly, probably wanting a subject change. "Bella, Hazel keeps track of almost everything in this county."

The older woman chuckled. "I threaten to retire every once in a while just to keep them on their toes." She produced a form for them to fill out, which they did, and she handed them the license. "You have thirty days to use this before it expires."

Bella knew the wedding would happen long before that. In a month, she might be regretting this decision.

Be positive. Her business and her employees' jobs would be saved.

They said goodbye to Hazel and walked out, Micah staring at the license in his hand. "Crazy. This must be the craziest thing I've ever done." He looked up at her. "And I did some crazy things in college. Maybe a few after college. Not to mention the time Greg and I and a few of our friends took a raft out on the creek and sank it in the deepest part."

Bella felt her heart sink like that raft. He'd changed his mind. "Micah, you don't have to go through with this." Cassie would let her stay in her spare room while she figured out her life. Everything would . . . not be okay. But she could pretend it was for a while.

CHAPTER TEN

Saturday morning arrived faster than any day had in Micah's life. The days since he'd asked Bella to marry him were a blurry memory of activity.

All morning, people had hurried along the path beside his house to the backyard, their arms loaded with everything from flowers and ribbon to the runner that now went down the lawn. He'd turned away for a short time, and chairs had appeared.

What had he gotten himself into?

This wasn't a simple "I do" at the courthouse as he'd first pictured. This was a full-on wedding.

Cassie stepped inside and surveyed the area. "Micah, it's time for you to get ready."

He looked down at himself. The suit and tie *were* his idea of ready. "This is it." He pointed at his chest.

She made *tsk tsk* sounds. "That won't do at all. Bella's wearing a white dress. You're wearing cream." She tapped the collar of his dress shirt, which had, he realized as he looked down, narrow navy and cream stripes. "Please change into a shirt with white. A solid white if you have it." The smile she gave after her words softened them. But he knew he needed to obey.

He was witnessing firsthand why she was a great wedding planner. Issues were firmly, but kindly, resolved.

Ten minutes later, she gave a single nod when he reappeared in his dark-gray suit, white shirt, and gray and white striped tie. "Perfect. Bella's getting dressed in one of your spare bedrooms. Why don't you go outside now so you don't see the bride in her dress before the ceremony." There was no question mark at the end. This wasn't a request.

"But"—he leaned closer and looked around to make sure no one would overhear —"this isn't real. Seeing her or not seeing her doesn't matter." He didn't care about silly traditions, anyway.

In a low voice, she said, "I'm treating this as I would any wedding. Well, any wedding where I've been given a day's notice." The eye roll at the end surprised him. "There will be video and photos."

She checked the large watch on her wrist. He hadn't noticed it before, so it must be her wedding-day watch.

"Now, let's get this show on the road. We have twenty minutes until Go."

He swallowed. Cassie was right. The wedding may not feel real to either him or Bella, but it had to be real to everyone else. Especially his grandfather.

On Cassie's cue, he went to the back of his yard and stood under a flower-covered arch. How had she managed that in one day? Rows of white folding chairs lined either side of a path that he guessed Bella would walk down. Ribbons and flowers decorated the end of each row of chairs. Everything coordinated in pink and yellow, which weren't colors he would have chosen, but he had to admit it was pretty. Cassie had pulled off a miracle.

Music rose from somewhere, so she'd set up a speaker system.

Bella stepped out the door as the bridal march played.

Another miracle had transformed the mess of a dress that he'd hit with the fire hose into one that took his breath away. *She* took his breath away. He reached out to grip the fence behind him.

Did he have feelings for Bella?

The gloriously hideous dress had been transformed into something out of a magazine. It turned the already attractive woman into one who enchanted him completely. As she drew nearer, he spotted hot-pink shoes under the dress and chuckled.

The appealing package of beauty and spunk had him watching her every move as she drew closer to him. His thought from the moment before grew as she took the last few steps. He couldn't be interested in her as a woman, could he?

No. Not at all. But he did like her spunk.

That was all she was. A beautiful woman with spunk.

What. Was. She. Doing?

Bella kept her focus on everything but the man at the end of the aisle. The man waiting to *marry* her. In a few minutes.

She noticed yellow roses, probably a nod to her Texas roots. They coordinated nicely with the hot-pink shoes she'd chosen at the last minute. Any details beyond that were lost on her. Perhaps other brides felt that too. But their focus would, of course, be on the groom. Hers, not so much.

Each step grew harder as she thought over the situation. Thought over the actions that had brought her here. She could turn and run. Cassie had done that, and look where it had gotten her. Greg and the new life in Two Hearts that she loved. She scanned the crowd, searching for her friend. When she found her, Cassie gave her an encouraging smile.

Continuing walking, Bella had to remember the many reasons she was doing this. She was here because her employees needed her, *and* she would have lost everything in the next thirty days. Everything. Business and home.

As she neared the area where Micah and the mayor stood, she looked at her groom. His terrified expression mirrored her own, but instead of making her more afraid, it calmed her down.

They were in this together. No matter what, she'd support him in this year of marriage, and he would support her. A man who loved his family as much as he did, and who seemed to be loved by the townspeople as well, should be good husband material. *Temporary* husband material.

She smiled when she stepped up to face him. That seemed to relax Micah, and he grinned back.

The mayor began the ceremony. "Dearly bereaved."

Gasps went up from the guests.

Micah spoke softly. "Mayor, that's 'dearly beloved.'"

"Of course, it is. Thank you, young man."

The mayor cleared his throat and began again with the correct words. Continuing, he said, "I've known Micah since he was born. I've seen his choice of girlfriends over the years." The man rolled his eyes.

Micah went beet red.

Bella bit her lip to stifle her laughter.

"He seems to have done well this time." The mayor winked at her, and soft laughter sounded through the group. After words of wisdom that included a mention of his own long-lasting marriage, and a couple of Bible verses, Bella had started to relax.

Their officiant whispered to them. "It's time to say your vows." When neither of them responded, he asked, "Do you have them with you?"

Right. They had agreed to write their own vows. Only in all the hustle of getting ready, she had forgotten. She hoped they'd both forgotten and could laugh about it.

Micah pulled a folded sheet of paper from his pocket. Clearly, one of them had remembered.

She could ask for traditional vows, but the mayor probably didn't have those with him. Someone could look them up on their phone. That wouldn't be disruptive to the ceremony at all, would it? She tamped down the hysterical laughter that threatened to bubble to the surface. Her one solid choice was to make it up as she went. They were filming this for his grandfather, so she didn't want to look too crazy or he'd have the whole thing annulled.

Times had changed, so maybe the mayor would start with Micah, and she would have time to think of beautiful things to say.

"Ladies first."

Of course he'd say that. "Micah, we haven't known each other long, but . . ." She hesitated. What could she say about a man she barely knew? She went through every time they'd been together and pulled out good things. "I have come to appreciate your kindness, your love of family and your town, and . . ." She gulped.

After attending dozens of weddings, she'd thought this would flow easily. Then she remembered one of the last weddings she'd been at.

"We will treasure today as the years march forward, not as the best day of our lives, but as the day that began all the wonderful days of our marriage to each other."

There. That should do it. The smirk on Cassie's face from where she now sat in the front row told her she remembered those vows too. The vendors had talked about them after the ceremony, so she wasn't surprised.

Micah began speaking. "Bella, I'm honored to have you as my wife. I enjoy laughing with you and how you care about others. Today and every day will be a joy with you nearby. I promise to be the best husband I can be."

Short and sweet. Those sounded like vows he'd found online. But who was she to complain?

Whew! They'd gotten through the most intense part of the ceremony.

Bella looked into Micah's eyes, waiting for the next step.

"Give her the ring, my boy."

So much for formality at her wedding.

"Right." He reached into his suit coat jacket and took out the ring he'd shown her. It sparkled in the sunshine as he slid it on her finger. She felt definite tugs on her heartstrings as she looked down at the gold bands and gemstones. The *wedding ring* on her finger.

The mayor said, "I now pronounce you husband and wife."

She was married. They were married.

"You may now kiss the bride."

Her startled eyes met his. Micah smiled encouragingly—at least she'd take it for that—placed one hand on each of her shoulders, and leaned in for a kiss. His lips touched hers, and fireworks exploded around them. She would thank Cassie later for adding fireworks to the ceremony.

When he stepped away, silence met her, and Cassie sat exactly where she had been. It had been the kiss. *Oh my goodness.*

His expression probably mirrored her own. Shock.

"I now present Mr. and Mrs. Walker." Neither of them moved, so the mayor dropped his voice to say, "You're done here."

"Right." Micah put his arm through hers, and they walked down the aisle to the well wishes of townspeople. She recognized a few of them. Those would probably be all she'd ever know since she'd be in the car and on her way back to Nashville soon.

Inside the house, Micah closed the back door and glanced around before saying, "I think we're alone. We did it." He grinned.

She rolled her shoulders to get them to relax. "I'm so glad that's over."

He looked out the door to where she saw people standing and talking to each other. "I guess we'd better speak to guests as they leave."

"Micah, I barely know some of them. The rest don't know me at all. I think I'll be on my way."

Cassie came inside. "That went off well." She rubbed her hands together. "I had to call in some favors."

Bella said, "I'm in awe of what you accomplished. It will look great in the photos."

"I agree. Now, if—" Micah stopped talking when the back door opened.

"Simone!" Bella hurried over and hugged her friend. "I'm so glad you made it."

"A little late for the ceremony. I'm sure it's recorded, so I'll watch later." To Cassie, she said, "Where do you want the cake?"

Bella gulped. "The cake? That's for a reception, and we don't—"

"Over to the side. I have a round table set up." Cassie turned to face the backyard and pointed as she spoke. "I see Dinah. She's catering the reception, so I'll talk to you two lovebirds later." She fluttered out the door, and Bella heard her saying, "Dinah, over here" as it closed. Cassie waved her toward what Bella now saw was a long, empty table with a centerpiece of the same yellow roses that had graced the ceremony. How could she have missed seeing that?

"Did you agree to this, Bella?"

"None of it."

They watched as the cake rolled in on a cart and was transferred to the table. Three layers of pale-pink perfection with yellow roses cascading down the side. Platters and bowls of food were brought in. Something about the punch bowl being filled seemed to cross a line for Micah because he said, "We could cut and run."

"That's your best suggestion?" There was no way she'd leave when her friends had gone to so much effort for her.

"That's my *only* suggestion." He tugged on his collar.

"Simone somehow managed to make a gorgeous cake on short notice. Dinah prepared food for a crowd. My friends and your friends came together."

"I see your point. Would you mind if I took off my tie? I'm normally fine with it, but today with the summer heat, humidity, and . . . everything else . . ."

She laughed. "I don't care what you wear." And she really didn't. She'd never liked men who were sloppy, but she'd only seen Micah in things that fit him well. "You'll find that I'm an understanding wife."

He loosened his tie and pulled it off. "For that, I'm grateful. Let's go to our wedding reception. I sure didn't think I'd say those words anytime soon."

Bella laughed. "Me either."

Cassie opened the door and peered around it. "It's showtime." She peered over her shoulder. "Remember to touch each other." She winced. "That may not have sounded as I'd intended. Lean close; put your hand on the other's arm. That's what I meant. And smile. Remember that this is the happiest day of your life. Or so my brides tell me." She shrugged.

Micah ushered Bella forward. "After you." As they walked, he said, "I love those shoes."

She grinned. A man who liked her hot-pink high heels was a keeper. Realizing what she'd thought, she chuckled. *For a year.*

CHAPTER ELEVEN

By mid-afternoon, Bella's feet wanted out of those shoes, and her face hurt from smiling. The last guest had just left. An older man. Albert something. Only Cassie and Simone were still here.

Simone called to her, "Did you get a slice of cake, Bella? Micah?"

When they both said no, she made plates and brought them over. Smiling, she stood in front of them as they raised their forks.

"Why are you staring at me?" Bella held her fork ready to take a bite.

"I want to know if you like it. I had one of my chocolate supreme cakes in the freezer, so I used it."

"Oh. I wondered how you'd baked and frosted and delivered this on such a short timeline." Bella slid the cake into her mouth. With a sigh, she said, "Heavenly."

"This is wonderful." Micah scooped up another bite. "Do we get to keep the leftovers?"

Simone laughed. "They're all yours. You had a hungry bunch, so there are only a few slices left."

"Mine," Bella and Micah said in unison.

Laughing, he added, "We'll share."

When Simone and Cassie pulled up chairs, each of the women holding a slice of cake, Bella slipped off her shoes to relax.

Cassie said, "You two were convincing today."

Simone nodded. "I agree. I bought into it." She ate a piece of cake, closing her eyes as she did, something that Bella was used to her doing. Then she opened them again. "This is a fairly large house, so there must be several bedrooms."

"Four," Micah answered.

"Have you chosen yours, Bella?"

Bella laughed. "I don't need a bedroom here. I have an apartment in Nashville."

Simone took another bite of cake, closing her eyes again.

Micah watched her. "Why did you do that, Simone?"

"Huh? What?"

He tapped beside his eye.

"Oh. I only want my taste buds involved. If I look, then I get other sensory input."

"We're used to it." Bella leaned closer to Micah. "But I will admit it looks strange. Other than that, she's normal."

"Hey, you're talking about someone who's sitting here."

They all laughed.

Simone wasn't letting go of her question. "You can't keep staying with Cassie."

"But I don't need to be in Two Hearts."

Simone turned toward Cassie. "She can't be that clueless, can she?"

Cassie shrugged. "She can." To Bella, she said, "You're married."

Bella huffed and held up her left hand. "That much is obvious."

"Apparently not. Married people share a home."

She rolled her eyes. "Not these married people. I did this"—she glanced around to make sure they were truly alone—"to keep my business. It's in Nashville."

Micah watched the exchange between the women without interrupting.

"What do you say, Micah?"

He took a step back. "Can I say all of you are right?" His worried expression concerned her.

Cassie asked, "Are you only saying that because three emotional women are waiting for an answer?"

His shoulders relaxed. "When you put it that way, I'm fine. I grew up with twin sisters and a mother. When Grandma was there, their numbers completely overwhelmed the men in the room. To answer the question, I want Bella to do whatever makes her happiest."

Simone and Cassie sighed.

Bella grabbed his hand and squeezed it. "Right answer." To her friends, she said, "But I appreciate your concern." She stood. "Ladies, let's get this cleaned up, and then I'll be on my way."

"I have a team coming to help with that. You two do whatever it is newlyweds do," Cassie added a cheeky grin.

Bella waved then went into the house with Micah behind her. Inside, she said, "I am so glad that's over. I'll gather my things and be on my way."

He didn't say anything, so she went down the hall to the room she'd used today.

Back in her summer dress and sandals, she felt good but somehow let down. She had to admit that there was something about a wedding dress that changed a woman. She'd had her day and gone from bride to married woman. Mrs. Walker. Or would she keep her maiden name? Or hyphenate the two?

What a week this had been.

With her dress in its carrier and her small suitcase packed, she went back down the hall. Micah paced back and forth, whirling around when he heard her footsteps.

"You have to stay."

She took a step back. "What happened?

"Three people called saying they're excited to see you at church tomorrow."

She waved her hand at that. "Tell them I can't be there. It's simple."

"Not in a small town in the South."

His phone rang. He frowned when he picked it up. "Yes. Thank you. We're talking about it now. I'm sure you make a wonderful peach cobbler. Thank you." He hung up. "They heard about the wedding and are dropping off a cobbler tonight. See what I mean? How can I say that my brand-new wife is spending the night in Nashville?"

She did see what he meant. "I don't have anything business-wise to do tonight or tomorrow."

His expression turned hopeful. "You can stay?"

She shrugged. "I guess so. Cassie keeps a room for me. I've been here so many times that I've left basics there. But I will have to wear this dress again, or workout clothes." She did have a box of clothes in the car, but those were to be donated to a charity whenever she remembered to do it.

"I'm sure the dress will be fine."

She headed toward the door. "I know Cassie will be going, so I'll see you there tomorrow."

"Wait!" He yelled, and she jumped back. "You can't go out there now, especially with clothing in your arms. Someone might see you."

"Why does that matter?"

"We're married."

She gave a slow nod.

"You're supposed to live here."

She gazed longingly out the door. That way took her to

comfy clothes and a bowl of ice cream, two things she could use right now. But the man was right. “I’ll wait until dark.”

“Great. And I’ll drive you over and drop you off. Then no one will notice your car there.”

She felt like she’d stepped into the middle of a spy drama. “Your skills for avoiding detection must come from the law degree.”

His sideways smirk said “yes.” “I have had to work with challenging situations—always within the law, of course—to resolve clients’ problems.” He took the dress carrier from her. “I’ll hang this up. Get comfortable on the couch. Or you could change into those shorts and the T-shirt you wore a week ago—washed, of course—if you’d rather wear that.”

“I would. Then this dress can be fresher tomorrow.” Walking down the hall, she asked, “You wouldn’t happen to have any ice cream, would you?”

“Only peanut butter fudge.”

She dropped her suitcase. “Seriously? You wouldn’t tease a girl about that, would you?”

He stood still. “Uh, no. It’s my favorite, so I always keep some in the freezer.”

She ran over and hugged him. “That’s my favorite flavor too. Getting lost in a bowl of peanut butter fudge ice cream sounds wonderful.” She picked up her suitcase and carried it into the bedroom. Then she stopped.

Had she just hugged Micah? Yes, she had.

That probably shouldn’t happen again.

CHAPTER TWELVE

Micah woke up early Sunday morning and got ready for church. When he stepped into the kitchen to make a cup of coffee, he stopped. Wedding cake covered in plastic wrap took the place of honor in the middle of the counter, almost like a centerpiece reminding him he'd gotten married yesterday.

Woohoo! And he'd spent the night alone. Because he wasn't really married. But he was.

What a mess he'd made of his life in a short amount of time.

He filled the coffee maker, then went to shower and get dressed. He returned to the kitchen after that, and stood, mug in hand, as he considered the day ahead and pictured the two of them sitting side by side on the church pew. They had to act like everything was normal. That they'd just had a first night here as a married couple.

That would be a tough sell, considering that their one kiss had taken place during the ceremony. As the memory of their wedding came to life, he remembered that he had to pick Bella up from Cassie's. They'd been able to drop her off at night. Now he would have to drive there in broad daylight. It was probably too much to hope that no one would see him. That couldn't happen, but he also needed her to be there. That was the only reason she'd stayed overnight in what she'd say was a tiny town in the middle of nowhere.

Whistling as he walked to his car, he tried to envision how he might retrieve Bella without anyone seeing. How many people would he, a man alone in a car without his new wife, pass on the way? Maybe none. Maybe half a dozen.

They couldn't take that chance. But how could he fix this? When the beginning of an idea took root and grew, he spun on his heels and went back to the house. This should only require a few minutes.

When Micah passed Albert on his way to Cassie's house, he waved, then turned the car away from him and down the nearest road to avoid closer inspection by someone he knew had great vision. It was the long way to his destination, but that would have to do. As he came around the block, Mrs. Myers was in her front yard, close enough to see his car but too far to see inside it clearly. He waved at her and continued on his way.

Up ahead, Randi was walking a dog. When had she gotten one? And she was on the right side, so she'd have a clear view of the passenger seat. He did a U-turn, hoping she wouldn't look back. Circling the block from the other direction, Cassie's yellow Victorian house was a beacon of light in the distance.

Relief rushed through him when he pulled into her driveway and found no neighbors around. Stepping out, he scanned the area. All clear.

Micah rushed to Cassie's back door and pounded on it so he knew he'd be heard.

Cassie pulled open the door. "Micah, what—?"

He slid through the opening and into the house. "Whew! Made it."

"Are you being chased? Greg will be here any minute." Cassie grabbed his arm and pulled him farther into the house. "He texted a couple of minutes ago that his mother had something to do before she'd be ready to leave,"

"Where's Isabella?"

"Bella."

He rolled his eyes. "I forget when I'm stressed out. We have to get her out of here before the very astute Mrs. Brantley arrives."

After a second's pause, Cassie gasped. "It can't be known that Bella spent her wedding night here. That could ruin everything for you."

"What's all the racket?" Bella asked as she entered the kitchen.

"We have to leave. Now." He towered over her, and that seemed odd. "You're much shorter than I realized."

She scrunched her mouth into a frown. "And people wonder why I wear heels all the time?"

"Not that being shorter is a bad thing." Petite women often caught his eye.

If anything, the frown deepened.

Cassie's phone pinged. "Greg's on his way now."

"Grab your shoes, Bella."

"Not until you tell me what's going on." She crossed her arms and planted her feet firmly on the ground.

Cassie pointed to the table. "She brought her shoes down earlier."

Micah scooped them up.

Cassie nudged her friend. "Hurry, Bella."

"Now you've both lost it. What's going on?"

"Greg's on his way with his mother."

"So?" She raised her hands.

"She doesn't know this isn't real."

"We're here together. Why does it matter?"

Cassie tapped her phone. "I told him to take a scenic route to buy us another minute." To Bella, she said, "You shouldn't be here this morning."

"I came over to see my best friend." She shrugged. "That makes sense."

He leaned close. "Bella, last night was our wedding night. You wouldn't have wanted to be anywhere then or first thing this morning but with your new husband."

She blushed bright red to the roots of her hair.

Cassie strode over to the kitchen entrance. "I can see out the living room windows to the street from here. We're clear, but, Micah, hurry!"

He grabbed Bella, tossed her over his shoulder in a fireman's carry, and ran for the door as though flames were licking at his heels. At the car, he set her down. "Get in. Quick."

"I'm only doing this because Cassie says to." She opened the door. "What is *this*?"

"Oh, I forgot to take it down." He reached into the car, grabbed the stack of pillows he'd used to make it look as if someone was in the passenger seat, and tossed them into the back.

Cassie ran out. "She forgot her purse." She threw it through the open door as Bella climbed in.

He raced to his door, started the car, and slammed it into reverse, making it down and out of there before anyone arrived. The rearview mirror showed Greg's car pulling into the driveway seconds later.

After Micah turned the corner and was no longer visible from Cassie's house, he stopped at the side of the road and leaned back on the seat with a sigh. "That was close."

"I guess I'm being dense."

He turned toward her. She really did look confused. And adorable. *Don't go there, Walker.*

"The good people of this town know we got married yesterday. They're excited for us. They're talking about us."

"Gossip. I've never liked it and always tried to avoid it."

"Not so much gossip as sharing general excitement about us. We're the hot conversation right now."

"Isn't all this a little extreme? That was a dummy in the front seat, wasn't it?" She raised an eyebrow.

He checked his watch, then started driving. "We were close to my grandfather finding out."

"Your grandfather?"

"If anyone in this town knows the truth—besides Greg and Cassie because I completely trust them—then word can get back to my grandfather."

She laughed. "From the middle of nowhere?"

"Do you want this all to be for nothing?"

She swallowed. "Absolutely not. I guess I'm on Team Stealth now. At least I'll be back in Nashville tomorrow, so we won't have to be so careful."

He blew out a slow breath. "I hadn't thought of that. You have a business you need to run."

"I'll go home tonight so I can be there first thing in the morning. See? Problem solved."

He wondered about that. Married one day and his wife runs off to the city?

Maybe he was getting worked up over nothing. It was possible that people weren't watching him as closely as he thought they were.

Micah listened to Greg. Or he tried to. His friend was filling in for the vacationing minister and was giving it his best. But Micah had trouble focusing on anything right now.

He'd gotten married.

Bella, his wife, sat beside him.

He caught some words about truth and honesty from the sermon. Those were qualities that hadn't factored into his decision to marry Bella. He added guilt to his list of recent emotions.

Cassie leaned forward from where she sat on the other side of Bella. When he looked at her, she whispered, "Sorry."

So now he felt guilty about sitting here with the woman he'd married. Sort of. He'd married Bella, but not with the intention of being married *to* her. Not in any definition of the word he'd known up until this week.

People rose to sing, and he joined in, something he always enjoyed. He heard Bella beside him with a beautiful high soprano that didn't surprise him. Everything she did seemed larger than life. Even her petite, shoeless figure this morning had seemed a little dramatic—and adorable.

Then they sat again. When everyone rose at the end of the service and started filing out, he realized he hadn't heard a word that had been said after "Amazing Grace."

"Micah," Cassie said, "Greg wrote that sermon over the last couple of weeks. He had no idea—"

"It's okay. Besides, when the man's right, he's right." He rubbed his hand over his face.

Bella set her hand on his arm. "Don't worry." And somehow, a little of his anxiety faded away.

Dinah walked up to them. "I have a surprise for the two of you." She turned to Cassie. "I didn't think of doing this for you and Greg. Now that I've thought of it, you'll get your gift soon." She rubbed her hands with glee. "Can you believe it? We have two new couples in Two Hearts?" Facing Bella and him again, Dinah said, "My gift of a basket filled with lunch is ready. The two of you can have a wonderful picnic alone."

Bella gave her a gracious smile. "Thank you."

"I guess we're going on a picnic," Micah said to Bella as he watched the café owner walk over to a friend and stop to chat.

"That's good. I think." Bella scrunched up her face. "I'm not sure that I've ever been on a picnic."

Cassie asked, "Never?"

He wondered the same thing. How could you get to adulthood and never have had a picnic?

"My parents were too busy. Much too busy for things like that." To him, she said, "My mother is a renowned plastic surgeon, and my father is a respected psychiatrist. Fun childhood memories include things like hanging out with the nurses in the ER and last-minute babysitters. It went that way when my parents were married to each other and not."

That was the opposite of growing up here.

"Don't get me wrong. I wasn't neglected. All my needs were met."

Bella had made no mention of love. Maybe that was another reason why she'd agreed to yesterday's ceremony. Why bother finding someone you loved to share your life with when your own family hadn't shown you such things?

As they made their way to the exit, Levi and Cherry hurried over with their new baby girl.

Cherry introduced them. "My husband and I own the flower farm."

"Of course!" Bella said. "The one where Carly and Jake got married. Your fields of flowers are so beautiful!"

"We already have two more weddings scheduled." Cherry's voice had a satisfied note. She gestured with her head toward the outside. "Dinah's waiting to give you the food basket."

Did everyone know about their lunch? Probably in this town.

"Have you chosen a place to have your picnic?" she asked with a note of hesitation in her voice.

Micah shrugged. "I haven't even thought about it yet."

She smiled widely. "Good. I have the perfect place picked out. It's in the middle of the rose-cutting garden. I put a bench there—well, I had Levi put it there. Did I mention that it's perfect?"

Bella's face lit up. "That sounds wonderful. Thank you!"

He liked the idea, but also didn't. It sounded like a romantic setting. He and his new wife weren't in this for the romance.

Driving down the road to Cherry and Levi's farm took longer than Bella remembered from the other time she'd been there. She watched the farms and houses pass by. City living offered so much. Why would anyone choose to live this far away from everything wonderful?

She glanced at Micah when she heard the turn signal. He wore a determined expression that deepened when they reached a parking area next to the barn.

"Are you okay?"

"Huh? Why do you ask?" He ran one hand over the back of his neck.

"Let's see. We're in a beautiful place. You're stressed out."

He stared straight ahead. "I'm wondering what they're expecting from this."

"Expecting?"

"Yes. They're being so nice to us."

Bella grinned. "Micah, they like you. You got married."

His sheepish expression told her she'd said the right thing. "I'm not used to this level of interest. By the way, you do know your love life just got put on the front page of the newspaper."

She gulped. "In an actual newspaper?"

"The *Two Hearts Times* won't miss a story like this." Stepping out of his truck, he stretched. "I enjoy getting out of town."

Now it was her turn to laugh. "You say that like you live in a big city and need to find peace and quiet."

"I guess it's whatever you're used to. But honestly, I love it out here. They've made great strides with this farm in a few short years."

"Levi must be driven."

"Ha." He snorted a laugh. "He's driven by Cherry. She's the force behind the business. But her ideas are so good that he's happy to do whatever she comes up with."

"They're a cute couple."

He watched her for a moment.

Were *they* a cute couple? She shook herself out of her thoughts. They were in this for a year. She had to keep her distance from emotional entanglements.

Picnic basket in hand, he said, "I wonder where this special place is?"

Bella pointed to a piece of paper with an arrow on it that was tacked to the barn. "I think they've left us breadcrumbs to follow."

They went to the side of the barn, then turned left at another arrow and entered a field of snapdragons in yellows, pinks, reds, purples, and whites. Bella gasped and stopped to take a photo.

Down the path, they entered an area overflowing with rose bushes blooming in many colors. A moment later, they entered a small clearing with a bench surrounded by those flowers. "Oh, my goodness! This is prettier than I could have imagined." She hurried over and sat down. Then she patted the seat next to her. "Join me, Micah." Leaning her head back, she inhaled slowly, a heady rose perfume filling her senses. "And it smells heavenly."

He spread the blanket Dinah had included on the ground and opened the basket.

"What do we have for lunch?" she asked.

"Let's see." He pulled out containers. "Cold fried chicken, potato salad, watermelon, and slices of two kinds of pie." He held one container closer. "Pecan and something fruity, maybe peach."

"Yum. I'm hungry."

"Bench or on the blanket?"

She eyed the two. "I think we should sit on the blanket. That's more traditional. We can take a selfie or two to show Dinah and Cherry we enjoyed it."

"That's a nice thing to do."

She shrugged. "I can be a nice person." When he started to speak, she held up her hand to stop him. "I know I may seem a little pushy."

Micah seemed to understand when to keep his mouth shut. He silently watched her.

She blew out a big breath. "Okay, maybe a lot pushy. I come from a high-achiever world."

"That makes sense. But as long as you're in Two Hearts, you can simply be yourself."

Be herself? She'd learned early on to control the situation or it controlled you. Her parents had taught her that. She let down her guard for close friends like Cassie and sometimes Simone, but for few others in her life.

"I'll try to remember that." The mood had turned too serious. "Are you planning to share this food or eat it all yourself?"

He laughed, and the feeling shifted. "I'll be nice and share." He handed her a plate. "Take whatever you want. We may have to fight over the pie, though."

She rolled her eyes. "You can have either kind. When it comes to dessert, I'm open to almost anything." She tore off a piece of chicken and popped it in her mouth. "Yum!"

She was enjoying today more than she would have expected. They could be friends for this year, couldn't they?

Bella stretched out on the blanket when she'd finished eating. "That was so good!"

"I pictured you as a caviar-and-champagne woman." He took the other side of the blanket, lying on his side to face her, but his feet hung off the end.

"Are you kidding? I love homestyle foods." She rolled onto

her side, too, and braced herself with her hand on her chin and an elbow on the blanket. "I tend to cook hearty things."

His jaw dropped. It actually dropped. He opened his mouth as though to speak, then closed it again. Then he said, "Tell me what you like to cook."

She smiled and nudged him with her arm. "You wanted to ask about the fact that I know how to cook." She rested her hand on his arm.

Micah covered her hand with his, and she missed whatever he said next. She picked up the conversation, hoping he hadn't told her anything important.

". . . problem is that we barely know each other. Let's go back and forth with things we like and dislike."

He left his hand over hers, and she found it . . . distracting. Pulling her eyes off of that and the warmth oozing through her, she focused on his words. To buy herself time, she said, "You go first."

"I like bacon and don't like tomatoes."

This sounded easy. "I agree with your bacon, but you don't like pizza?"

"It's fine. Just don't chop tomatoes up and put them on my salad."

"That's fair. Let's see. Lasagna and marmalade."

"I love the first one. Can you make it?"

"Absolutely. I'm a good cook."

"That's a relief. I'm a master with a microwave. I think we will be eating better when you're in Two Hearts."

She had forgotten that she now had ties to Micah, his house, and small-town America. She slid her hand away from his, immediately regretting the loss.

"Now what's wrong with marmalade? Toast slathered with it is delicious."

"I'll take strawberry jam every time." She tugged on the tie he'd loosened. "You're next."

He watched her hand on his tie. When she pulled her hand away, he put his over it to trap it. She didn't try to pull away.

"My turn." He pursed his lips. "I know. Salmon and snails."

Laughing, she said, "I agree to both."

His grin made her so fluttery inside that she was glad she was already lying down. "I'll go next. Strawberries and strawberry ice cream."

"Seriously? The berries, but not the ice cream? It's good."

She shook her head. "No. It's kind of an artificial pink. Very little flavor."

"Ah. You haven't had homemade strawberry ice cream."

She shook her head.

"Greg's mother makes ice cream often in the summer. We can put in a request for that. Any other questionable flavors?"

"Peach."

"Oh, my. Making disparaging remarks about anything peach in the South is serious."

Had she actually offended him?

Micah pulled her into a hug, and she felt laughter rolling through him. Pure happiness rushed through her. The mood shifted to something she couldn't define, and their laughter stilled.

Fighting against attraction to this man—because she had to do that to survive a year with him followed by walking away—she put her hand on his chest to push herself away. And she did move a few inches back.

Cupping her hand with his, he gently rubbed it, and she felt swoony to her toes. She could *not* be interested in Micah Walker.

His gaze moved to her lips and she sighed.

This isn't a normal marriage. This isn't a normal marriage. She kept repeating the words in her head. *No kissing allowed.*

When he leaned closer, she met him in the middle. His lips whisper-touched hers, barely a feather across them. Then he leaned back to look into her eyes with a questioning expression that probably mirrored her own. What were they thinking? Should they be doing this?

She closed the space between them, and their lips met for a kiss that could have set the surrounding fields ablaze.

Something touched her ear. She reached up to brush it away. A wet, rough swipe across her cheek followed. Bella broke apart from the kiss and scooted closer to him. "Micah!"

"Huh? What?" He blinked, and they both looked up at a black-and-white cow the size of Texas.

"Move slowly, Bella."

They rolled over, grabbed their picnic basket and blanket, and backed away from the animal.

In the car, Bella asked, "Could a cow hurt you?"

"Since I've never been in that situation, I have no idea. I just know it's much larger than we are. I guess you should have told me to *mooove* over."

She said, "That's terrible," but grinned.

Laughing, they drove back to town.

CHAPTER THIRTEEN

Bella flopped down on the couch in her apartment, immediately wishing she hadn't. "Ouch." She shifted on the cardboard-like cushion. Micah's soft couch had spoiled her, but the furnished studio apartment she'd moved into a few weeks ago to save money hadn't been designed with comfort or style in mind.

Stacks of boxes in the corner of the room screamed, "This isn't a home! It's a storage unit you're living in!" She had to admit the truth in that. So far, she'd unpacked nothing more than the essentials. The trunk of her car still had a couple of boxes in it that she hadn't bothered to bring inside.

If only this place had solved her problems, but even it was too expensive. She'd have to move her worldly possessions into an actual storage unit—paid for with money that needed to appear and soon. Hopefully, Micah's grandfather would come through with the money he'd promised.

Her phone rang, offering a blessed distraction. "Cassie, anything new?"

Her friend laughed. "Nothing. I wondered if you and Micah would like to stop by for dessert tonight."

"I'm home."

"As in with your husband? Or that shoebox-sized apartment with the bad furniture and the upstairs neighbor who plays the drums?"

"The second one. But it's quiet right now." The tap, tap, tap of drums was followed by the crash of cymbals. "I take that back." A trumpet blast shot her off the couch.

"What was that?"

"The guy upstairs must have musician friends over again tonight. I've usually heard guitar with the drums before. That wasn't too bad." Bella didn't mention the evening they'd played Latin music. The tango had gone on for hours, accompanied by the wild clicking of heels on the floor above in what she assumed was the dance. She'd eventually concluded they were practicing for a gig, because it hadn't happened since.

"Well, I wish you were here."

Bella's depressing surroundings almost made her wish she was in Two Hearts too.

The next morning, she went to work early—why not, when the band had started practice again around dawn? Quiet sewing machines were a peaceful change, but sitting idle, they also reminded her that she still had financial problems. Neither Micah nor his grandfather had handed her a check. But she hoped she'd receive one in the next few days, by the end of the week at the latest, and she could turn this ship around.

April was the first one in that morning. "Hi, boss," she said as she went past.

"Good morning!"

April stopped. "You're extra happy today."

Was she? "I had a weekend out of the city."

"Sounds fun."

"It was . . . different."

As the next four members of her team entered one by one, she greeted them with a smile, each giving her a questioning glance as they walked past her. Had she been so grouchy lately that smiling stood out? Possibly.

Every Monday, she had a tradition of giving a short summary of the work they needed to complete over the week, followed by the work it would be nice to finish on top of that. At the end, she waved as she turned to leave.

"I guess we'd better get to work," April said, then asked, "Do we have any new projects like the Michelson's coming up? The dress was over the top, but I had a blast adding embellishments to it."

Bella fought a grimace at the mention of that bride's last name. "None like that. We have more average dresses." She considered the question. "Two mermaids and a ball gown." April's eyes lit up at the mention of the last dress. "Before you get too excited, the bride chose the ball gown to please her mother, but she wants it clean and simple, without embellishment, to please herself."

Bella moved the attention away from the upcoming dresses that needed supplies but wouldn't pay enough of her bills. "Have you found your dream house yet?"

April's eyes filled with tears. "Everything we see in our price range needs so much work. I mean a lot." She sniffed and swiped at her cheeks. "Sorry about the tears. Pregnancy hormones." April grabbed a tissue. "We couldn't move into any of them unless we paid someone to fix it first. One had a bathtub that looked ready to fall through the floor."

"I didn't realize it would be that bad. Even being married to a nurse practitioner? That's like a doctor, isn't it?"

"Sort of and sort of not. Everyone thinks those working in medicine are raking in the money, but he chose general practice nurse practitioner, not brain surgery doctor. They're the ones who make more. We're doing fine, but . . ."

Her defeated tone made Bella wish she could help.

"Maybe if you look further out of the city?"

April rolled her eyes, but at least she wasn't crying anymore. "The prices stay high for any commutable distance, and Daniel works on the other side of town." Her lip quivered again. "I'd like to be in a house before the baby comes." With a watery smile, she added, "I love my work, so that takes my mind off of all of it."

So Bella had a weepy, pregnant employee who needed steady employment and a business that needed an influx of cash. Now. She hoped she'd hear from Micah soon so she could solve the last part.

The soothing sounds of sewing machines and chatter among her employees soon filled the room. Bella continued her detailed inventory. Every dress project needed to use existing fabrics and embellishments as much as possible to save on spending.

CHAPTER FOURTEEN

The moment he'd dreaded all weekend had arrived. Micah stopped at the glass doors to the building to check his appearance in the reflection. His grandfather expected men to be well turned out. No lopsided ties or pocket handkerchiefs out of place. He entered the building, and the receptionist waved him through.

When the elevator opened on the eighth floor, he steeled himself for the meeting. His grandfather had won, but maybe not as he'd expected.

"My boy, so you've decided to join us here." His grandfather's gleeful expression would have made him laugh at another time.

"No. I haven't."

"Then our deal is off." The man turned to walk away.

Micah took a deep breath and rushed his next words. "I chose the second option."

His grandfather turned back. "The second . . . You got married?" His incredulous expression was soon replaced with suspicion. No one got much past a shrewd lawyer.

"Yes, sir."

"Whom did you marry?"

"Bella Bennett."

Suspicion deepened. "You said you weren't dating anyone."

"No, I said I wasn't *seriously* dating anyone. We moved it up to serious." Boy, had they.

When his grandfather smiled slowly, goosebumps chased up Micah's arms. This man was as wily as a tiger. Without giving enough thought to what would happen next, Micah had entered into his lair.

"Then I'd like to meet Ms. Bennett—or is she calling herself Mrs. Walker now?"

Micah hesitated. Of course his grandfather would want to meet his wife. How had he not considered that? He ignored the question about Bella's last name. She'd probably keep her name since this was a one-year agreement. At least, he assumed so since they hadn't talked about that, but what if he was wrong and she said the opposite later?

"I'm sure she can join us for lunch someday." He certainly hoped so. He'd said the words with the confidence of a man who knew his new wife's schedule. Because he was sure most men would know what was going on with their wife two days after the ceremony.

"Noon." His grandfather checked his watch. "I have an appointment now." With a nod, he turned and left, leaving Micah in his wake.

As soon as Micah left the building, he called Bella. Mechanical noises in the background almost drowned out her "hello." "Bella?" he shouted above the din.

"Just a minute." The noise faded and then stopped. "We're running all-out for an upcoming wedding. Someone was working on a sewing machine next to me. Micah, I have special embellishments I'd like to buy for the dress. Imported lace." She needed the money they'd agreed to.

"My grandfather wants to have lunch with the two of us today."

"Micah, I don't know if—"

"You seem to be under the misconception that you can say 'no.'"

"You're right. I have to impress him, don't I?"

"It's more than that. You have to make him believe—" He paused for a few seconds to gather the nerve to say the next words. "That you love me. That you married me for *love*." He tugged on his collar.

"Of course. I'll do my best."

He hoped her best convinced the old man.

He texted her the name of the restaurant. "I'll see you there at noon. My grandfather will have a table reserved. And Bella, I've never known you to be late for anything, but I'll add that he appreciates it when everyone is on time."

With that finished, Micah drove to a favorite coffee shop for a cup or two of his favorite brew. He did miss that about living in a small town. Maybe a coffee shop would come to Two Heart's Main Street if the town grew more. He laughed as he parked his car. That was about as unlikely as . . . him getting married.

The door to Southern Somethings opened as Bella walked up. A couple left, and the man held the door open for her. When she checked her watch as she entered, she found she was five minutes early.

A distinguished, gray-haired man in a tailored charcoal suit and conservative striped tie sat alone at a table across the room. A table set for three. She watched him as she waited for Micah. There was no way she would approach him without Micah at her side.

She whipped around when a hand touched her shoulder. Her new husband appeared as nervous as she felt.

"Ready for lunch with the lion tamer?"

"The what?"

"A nickname he earned. He can tame any jury. His cool logic makes you think everything was your idea to start with." As they were led to the table by the host, he whispered, "Smile. And act like a woman in love."

She widened her smile to something she hoped looked correct. "Right."

The man rose when they approached him. "Edmund Brooks. And you must be Isabella."

"Yes, sir." She used her polished and practiced attitude. "It's an honor to meet Micah's grandfather."

"Please, sit down." His expression felt warm and welcoming, what she'd expect from a grandfather.

She beamed at Micah as he pulled her chair out for her. "Thanks, sweetie."

She felt his small jolt as he touched her arm at the same time she spoke. Words of endearment should be used, shouldn't they? She didn't have much of an example beyond Cassie and Greg and a few other married friends.

Micah kissed her cheek and whispered, "I'll see your 'sweetie' and raise you with a kiss." Then he sat beside her.

Holding hands seemed appropriate, so she reached for his hand and folded her fingers through his. When she looked up, his grandfather wore a puzzled expression. They probably looked less like a loving couple and more like two people trying to sort out their parts for a theatrical play.

The server came to take their drink orders. Bella went with unsweet tea, Micah had sweet tea, and his grandfather ordered nothing other than the water already in front of him.

Mr. Brooks tapped the menu in front of him. "We need to order quickly. I only have an hour for lunch."

There went a piece of the sweet-grandfather image.

Bella did as she was told. Knowing she probably wouldn't be able to eat much, she ordered a small salad. Micah apparently had no such concerns because he ordered a steak and a loaded baked potato.

As they waited, the older man's gaze turned steely. "I'd like to see photos of your wedding."

Did he suspect it had never happened? Bella took out her phone. "The photographer sent over a few, but we don't have the full package yet." Micah watched as she flipped through, passing quickly over one of her tripping. She continued, stopping on a photo of them saying their vows. They seemed to have suitably loving expressions. She passed the phone across the table.

"I expected a ceremony at city hall." He handed the phone back to her. "How did you manage this?"

Bella looked at the photo again. "I'm not even sure. My best friend, Cassie, is a wedding planner who apparently sidelines as a miracle worker. My only job was the dress." Glancing up, she added, "I don't think I said what I do. I own a custom wedding dress business."

He didn't say "interesting" or another platitude; he simply continued his questions. "Tell me how you met."

Bella smiled sweetly at Micah. "Our best friends are getting married, so our meeting was unavoidable."

"Who is that?" the older man took a sip of his water.

"Cassie Van Bibber."

"Greg Brantley."

He seemed to be listening carefully. Almost as though they were suspects, and he was waiting for a hole in their stories.

Bella gave what she hoped was a fond glance to Micah. "Our first meeting was, however, not a good start."

"Maybe I should tell it, sweetie, since I'm the one who had the accident."

"Accident?" Mr. Walker asked.

"It was at Cassie and Greg's engagement party, under a tent at the city park. Bella and Cassie wanted punch. Greg and I volunteered to get some. A stray dog raced through and knocked into me, which sent punch flying."

"And onto my dress. End of dress. End of story."

"But the beginning of us, right?" Micah stepped in to bring the story where she should have.

She lifted their locked hands and kissed the top of his. "Right."

"And what moved you from that first meeting to getting married Sunday?" A note of mockery colored his words. She didn't think they'd won him over yet.

"Saturday," they said in unison.

Bella thought through possible answers as quickly as she could. *Be bold.* She rested her elbows on the table. "Honestly, I was going to lose Micah to the city if I didn't, because of your offer."

Micah squeezed her hand, probably to tell her to be less forthcoming. But she suspected that his grandfather would see through a Machiavellian scheme, so talking this way would throw him off.

"Ah, I see. You're from Two Hearts." His sniffy tone told her he didn't like the small town much. That raised the town's value in her eyes.

"No, I'm from Texas, and I live in Nashville—or I did until last weekend. But I know that Micah belongs in Two Hearts. I think he'd lose his soul in a large city."

She felt her husband's eyes on her.

"So you married him to keep him safe? Is that right? You didn't think he could survive in the big city?" Mr. Brooks's words oozed sarcasm. He'd probably thought he'd get off without following through on his side of their arrangement.

"I married him because I care about him. I want him happy.

Did we speed up our timeline? Yes. Would I have married him in the future if he'd asked? In a heartbeat." She was surprised to realize that those words weren't as far from the truth as she would have expected when she'd met him at Cassie's engagement party.

She felt Micah go still.

Their food arrived with perfect timing, taking the attention off them, but Micah's grandfather looked up every few minutes, first to Micah and then her, as if he were assessing his opponents in a courtroom. This was a game she could easily play. Her parents hadn't been guided by love either, but had appeared to care about each other to everyone outside the family.

By the end of a mostly quiet lunch scattered with small talk about the weather and family she didn't know, his grandfather sat back with a satisfied expression.

"Now that you're married, I will talk about financial matters with the two of you. Couples need to share these things."

His grandfather *would* hand them a check today. Micah had emphasized his grandfather's family loyalty and sense of honor. It seemed his assessment was correct.

"I'll pay for your sisters' education, as promised."

Tension in Micah's hand lessened. "Maisie and Margo will be relieved."

"I've decided to give you and Isabella a month to settle in before I add the burden of money."

Bella's arm jerked, and Micah's grip tightened again.

Micah spoke slowly. *"Burden?"*

"Some people don't handle a large influx of cash well. I think it helps a couple to live completely within their means. I never handed cash to you unless it was a birthday, Christmas, or graduation. You always worked for it."

"That's true."

Micah's grandfather smiled. Was that positive? "I will give

you the first piece of your inheritance thirty days from your wedding date."

Her heart pounded. No money for thirty days?

Another smile. "I'll stop by to visit you in Two Hearts soon. I want to see your happy abode." He stood. "Until then. Give my best to your sisters, Micah."

Micah's comforting warmth pulled away from her as he rose to his feet. Then he shook his grandfather's hand.

She wasn't sure she could have stood so quickly, so she was grateful when the older man gave a single nod in her direction before leaving.

Bella's head spun as they left the restaurant. Micah seemed to understand, because he held onto her arm.

Outside, he turned her to face him. He leaned close and looked her in the eyes. "We'll get through this."

She tried to speak, but only a whimper came out. She leaned against the building and focused on him. "How?" One word, packed with meaning.

He ran his hand through his hair, leaving it standing straight up. Even now, she had to acknowledge that she'd look like a clown if she did that. He looked good all the time. "I'm not sure."

"Micah, I'm in financial trouble."

"I know. I feel guilty because my reason for getting married has been resolved, but yours hasn't. Is there anything we can do to cut your expenses? I could sell my motorcycle and get a few thousand. That would buy you time."

Wanting to feel more powerful, she put her shoulders back, but the movement bumped her head on the building's rough brick exterior. "Ouch." Rubbing where she'd probably get a bump, she realized she had to *choose* to be brave,

"Are you okay?"

"Just not focused on what I should be. I'll figure something out."

"Bella, we're married. *We* can figure things out."

"We aren't really married." She glanced around after she said the words, hoping that no one who shouldn't hear her had.

"Even though we aren't, we are." He blinked. "You know what I mean."

Did she? He was being so understanding. Checking her watch, she realized she had to hurry, or she'd miss an appointment. "Micah, I'll talk to you later."

"Are you coming home tonight?" The way he said "home" made her want to lean into it, to take in everything that could be meant by the simple word. But she couldn't.

"The commute is a bear."

"Yeah. That's why I didn't want to do it. Or one of the reasons. Now that you've met—"

"I see much more clearly why working for him wouldn't be easy."

"He calls the shots, and his employees have to fall in line. The thing is that he's usually right when it comes to the law."

"Maybe not when it comes to life?"

"Not always. He said he would visit us next week."

"Will he?"

"I assume he will. Then again, his comment may just be to keep us on our toes."

"Does that mean I have to move to Two Hearts?"

He took too long before replying. "I'm not sure. Maybe."

Another check on her watch showed she had to race back. "Listen, I have to go, but I'll call you later to check in."

He smiled, and it warmed her to her toes.

That smile kept her happy all the way back to her office. She chose not to analyze why.

CHAPTER FIFTEEN

She had hoped to start the week on a happy note. That had not happened.

Bella ran her fingers through her hair as she raced through the door to her studio. She'd made it with thirty seconds to spare. A small group of women stood in the entryway listening to April. Bella made eye contact with her employee as she approached.

"Ladies, it's a pleasure to see you here." Bella made her apologies, sizing up who the bride would be. Years in the business had her guessing right every time. "You must be Alice." She focused on the young woman who showed the most nervousness.

"I am. Can you help me choose a dress today? I have been to five shops. I know what I want, but I haven't found it."

Bella steered them back to her seating area. "Then you're in the right place, because I take your vision and make it a reality."

The girl beamed.

"Ready?"

She nodded.

An hour later, Bella had done eight sketches. Each time, she showed the girl a drawing, it wasn't right. She'd started to wonder if they could find what Alice wanted when the girl leaped to her feet and pointed at the sketch pad. "That's it!"

This was why she did wedding dress designs. "Let's piece together some of my sample dresses to see if you like the look of this when it's more real."

Alice soon wore a satin mermaid gown with the top of the dress folded inside, and a beaded top Bella sometimes styled as a jacket. The woman stared in the mirror. A small hiccup told Bella she was having her bridal moment. Bella reached for a box of tissues she kept nearby, then moved them toward the bride as tears started flowing down her cheeks.

"You've done it. My idea is a reality."

They soon had a signed contract, a deposit, and Alice back in her street clothes with a promise to return in two months for a first fitting. That would buy Bella time. The real crunch would come when she needed the actual dress materials after that, but unless Alice made huge changes—and Bella would be more cautious about that in the future—this dress would help her instead of hindering her. Besides, she'd either be able to manage that dress then with no problem because her financial issues were resolved—or she'd be out of business and would have refunded the deposit.

Feeling on a high, she went into her office, sat down, and saw the neatly stacked bills on the corner of her desk. She'd find a way. She had her studio, even if the payment was overdue.

More optimistic than she had a right to be after that disastrous lunch, she answered her next phone call with a smile.

"Ms. Bennett?" At her confirmation, the man continued. "This is Charles from your business's leasing office. I wanted to let you know that I'm bringing by a potential lessee of your space in about an hour."

Had she heard him correctly? "Excuse me?" That sounded polite, didn't it?

"The letters we sent notified you that unless you can make your full payment of past-due funds immediately, then we will be finding a new tenant."

How had she missed that? Her eyes moved to the stack. She'd seen the *Past Due* on the envelope and done her best to ignore it. So much for being the consummate businesswoman.

"I'm sure we can work something out. Please?" She hated the desperate tone in her voice.

"You've been an excellent tenant, Ms. Bennett."

She breathed a sigh of relief.

"But at sixty days, we take action. Today is that day. I'll be there on the half hour with the client."

She wandered out of her office and between her seamstresses, checking on jobs to pass the time until Charles and another man arrived. He appeared exactly when he'd said he would. The company did apparently value timeliness. She'd failed there.

As the two men toured the area, the other man's apparent glee increased as he viewed each of the spaces that made up her studio. She went to a clothes rack near the door as the men talked, trying to hear some of their discussion. "Exactly what I need," "rent good," and "contract" floated over to her. Charles shook the man's hand near the door, and she knew she was sunk. The man not only liked it, it sounded as though he was willing to pay for it.

Bolts of fabric, machinery, furniture, and everything else that went into making a business filled this place. They had to go somewhere while she figured out her future. Back in her office, she pulled out a pad of paper and started writing ideas for saving Wedding Bella. Then she crossed off each one after considering it. No money or family connections in Nashville meant she had few options.

Her parents wouldn't welcome her back with open arms.

She rubbed bleary eyes.

A tap on her door was followed by April opening it and peering inside. "Everything okay? We haven't seen you for a while."

"Huh?" Bella squinted at her.

"It's mid-afternoon, and you usually check to see if we have questions."

Bella put her hands on her desk and pushed against it to rise. She did not want to upset her employees, but she would need to make changes and soon. She just didn't know what changes yet.

"Tell everyone we're closing early tonight. With pay."

April seemed poised to ask why, then turned and left. Bella heard her telling everyone and the happy responses.

When everyone had left, she stood at the side of the main room to take in the large space that had seemed perfect the first time she'd seen it. That day, *she'd* been the enthusiastic renter. She considered taking photos to remember it by. Her employees were what made the business work, though, so any photos needed to include them.

She flipped the light switches off.

Driving toward home, she pictured the studio unit, and herself eating dinner alone on the bed that doubled as a sofa. Loneliness overwhelmed her. Maybe Simone would like to come over. Bella pulled into a parking lot and called her friend, jerking the phone away from her ear when Simone answered with what sounded like kids screaming in the background.

"What's going on?"

"A birthday cake decorating class for ten-year-olds. The mom was a wedding cake client's sister and asked me if I'd consider doing it." The background noise seemed to escalate, if that were possible.

"How's it going?" Simone would have heard the sarcasm in her voice if she hadn't been overrun by kids.

"Fine."

"I'll leave you to your fun, then."

They hung up after agreeing to have lunch together soon. Bella would have to get the full story when they met.

Bella pulled back into traffic and drove, not caring where the road took her as long as it wasn't to her empty home. Maybe she'd stop for dinner somewhere. Of course, that took surplus money, money that was better spent on something for her business.

Buildings became less frequent and trees more. Then she realized that she'd pointed the car toward Two Hearts.

There were worse places to go. The drive would be long, but she had Cassie, Greg, and Micah there. Her husband. Maybe he'd have something in his fridge that she could make for their dinner.

An hour later, she slowly drove down the street toward his house. Should she surprise him?

She took out her phone, and he answered on the first ring.

"Bella, I was just thinking of you."

She grinned, feeling better for the first time in a while. "Why?"

"I had to take a class on firefighting. As soon as they talked about water pressure, I saw you being pummeled."

Her dark day felt surprisingly lighter. "What are you doing for dinner?"

He paused. "I guess I'm going to make a peanut butter sandwich."

She knew he had food in the freezer and on the shelves that she could work with. His grandmother had left the kitchen well stocked.

Unsure of how he'd react, she hesitated. Should she go to Cassie's and not say anything? "I seem to be in front of your house."

The sound of footsteps pounding on wood floors stopped just before she saw the front door open.

"What are you doing here?" he asked as he came outside and

stood on the porch. He motioned with his hand toward the driveway.

She pulled in and turned the car off. "It was a long day. Can I make you dinner?" Other words hovered on her lips—*Are you okay with my being here?*—but she didn't say them.

"You're always welcome." She saw him tap his phone, and the call went dead as he approached her car.

Bella opened the door but didn't get out. That felt like it would take too much effort.

He crouched beside her. "I'm sorry about what happened with my grandfather."

She studied his face. His green eyes were gentle, and his eyebrows had knit together a little with worry. She'd showed up in his driveway with no warning, but he didn't seem annoyed or even all that surprised. Instead, he was ready to comfort her.

"You know, you're a good guy."

"Thank you. I think. Did you used to consider me a not-so-good guy?"

Being able to make her happy right now made him even better. "I had little to go on. Leather jacket. Motorcycle. Pink punch on me, soon followed by water. Lots of water."

"It's possible I didn't make my best first impression." His thoughtful but teasing face made her smile.

Memories of her day wiped it away. She hadn't told anyone about her lease, and she didn't think she could talk about it yet.

Her car's clock reminded her of the time. "I think I need to eat before I do anything else."

He stood and held out his hand to her. "Let's go inside. Unless you'd rather go to Dinah's Place. She closes in less than an hour, so we'd have to hurry over there now." He quickly added, "Maybe that isn't your style, though."

Hearty homestyle food sounded perfect. "Will you buy me pie?"

He chuckled. "Of course."

"I may need two slices tonight."

"Consider it done." His lopsided grin made her smile again in spite of her day. "Stay here a minute. I'll be right back."

She heard the roar of a motorcycle. A minute later, a leather-jacket-wearing Micah pulled up beside her car. He held out a helmet. She'd never been on a motorcycle before, but it sounded freeing after her long day.

He shouted over the engine, "Climb on behind me and hold on. There's nothing better than this for relaxing on a day like today."

She did as instructed, but as her arms wrapped around his waist, she knew this aspect of the ride might be anything but calming. Closing her eyes as Micah zoomed down the road lifted some of her burden.

The motorcycle leaned to the left, they turned, and came to a stop. She looked up to see Dinah's Place. "That was too short," she shouted, the motorcycle turning off halfway through her sentence.

He explained how to climb off, then did so himself once she had. "I didn't peg you as a motorcycle fan."

Bella pulled off the helmet and handed it to him. "I didn't know it until now." She already missed the sense of freedom and the feel of him in her arms. That counted as a hug, didn't it? "Can we go for another ride soon?"

Micah laughed. "I'm happy to get on my bike any chance I get."

That sounded more fun than she would have realized.

Bella spooned in another bite of the chicken and dumplings Dinah had set before her. Warm chicken, broth, and the chunky noodles they called dumplings in the South soothed her from the inside out. She stopped when she realized Micah was watching her reach for another bite.

"What?" She dabbed at her chin with a napkin.

"For a tiny woman, you can pack in a lot of food."

"I keep moving. I'd quickly be in trouble if I slowed down for long."

He shook his head and stabbed another bite of the chicken fried steak drenched in gravy on his own plate.

"I could say the same about you," she added.

"I'm not tiny."

She had to agree. "Six feet tall?"

"A half inch under." He took a bite of his mashed potatoes and swallowed before continuing. "When I was a teenager, I wanted to be at least six feet tall. That sounded manly to me."

"And now?" She was curious; Micah Walker was all man. She couldn't imagine any woman thinking otherwise. At least no one she knew would.

"Now, I'm fine with who I am. I also wanted to be an astronaut."

"The program turned you down?"

He shrugged. "I went a different direction with my career when I realized that job wasn't what I'd expected. I first discovered you couldn't take a shower while you were in space. That was a huge plus. Then I found out I couldn't take my dog with me. That ended my love affair."

Why would any man expect to take his pet with him into space?

"I was ten at the time."

She swatted his arm.

"By the time I was twelve, I knew I wanted to be a lawyer. What about you?"

"I wanted to be a clothing designer from the moment I learned to sew. I was five, and I made a dress for my doll."

"A wedding dress?"

"Nope. I didn't know that was my calling for a while. It was a surprise when I found out I loved designing dresses for a bride's big day."

"Life can have great surprises."

And some not-so-great ones.

"Ready for pie?" He leaned to the side to try to see what remained of the pies in the glass-covered displays. "Your choices are more limited this time of day."

An older woman got up from a table across the room and came straight to theirs. Bella nudged Micah and raised her eyebrows in question.

He quickly assessed the situation, and quietly said, "Joanie Dunn, a friend of my grandmother's."

With a glance at Dinah, Joanie leaned over and spoke. "I have tonight."

That made absolutely no sense, but Micah gave a single nod to acknowledge her comment.

Bella wasn't one to sit and be silent. "For what?" Maybe that was the benefit of not knowing everyone here. You weren't afraid to jump in and ask.

Joanie stared at them. "You don't know yet, do you?"

Dinah went back to the kitchen, and that seemed to light a fire under Joanie. She spoke quickly in a low voice. "To bring food to the newlyweds. Tonight's my night. We can bring anything—main course or dessert, but I know you like my chocolate pie, so I'm making one just for you, Micah." She pointed to his empty plate. "That's best anyway since you've already eaten dinner."

After that, she scurried away, leaving Bella staring at her husband with her mouth hanging open. She shut it and asked, "The whole town is going to bring us food?"

He spoke slowly. "That's my guess. One night at a time. Maybe the other night's cobbler was the first of it, and we didn't know. It's possible that the picnic was the second day's meal."

"They want to be kind. And, as Mrs. Brantley pointed out on Sunday, we're the first young couple living in the town itself to get married in a while. We're unique."

"This could be nice. There are a lot of fine cooks in Two Hearts. We'll get a delivery every evening."

They both seemed to realize what that meant.

"I need to be here" Bella blurted at the same moment Micah said, "You need to be here."

"Oh, my goodness. I have to commute from Two Hearts to Nashville."

"It looks like it." His eyes grew big. "With people dropping by every day, you need to live—"

"With you."

CHAPTER SIXTEEN

Micah and Bella faced each other just inside his house. She had the strap of a tote bag filled with what she'd called "gym essentials" that was always in her car, and he had just set the second of two boxes he'd brought in from her car's trunk on top of the other.

Bella had tried to make the case again for staying with Cassie from now on, but he'd argued well that she needed to be on site for possible visitors, including his grandfather. His experience as a lawyer in a courtroom had apparently come in handy.

"I guess you're sleeping here from now on." Micah cringed. Those weren't the most insightful words he'd ever spoken.

Neither of them moved. They were married, but . . .

Then Bella rubbed her eyes. "With the day I've had, and everything else, I'm feeling a little overwhelmed." She stared at him. "I guess I do need to be here now, and it will save me money to live here for as long as this marriage lasts. I need to move the rest of my things from my apartment, but—"

"Don't worry about it," he interrupted. "I'll rent a truck, and we can load everything into it. It will be easy." Helping was something he was good at. "Let's get you settled in the room you used on our wedding day." Wedding day. Those strange words slipped out easily.

Offering a faint smile of encouragement, he reached for a box, but she put out her hand to stop him. "I can get this." Bella hefted it into her arms. "Wedding dresses, bolts of fabric; it can all be heavy, Micah. I may be tiny, but I'm mighty."

His parents would say they'd raised him better than that. He needed to find a way to help her. Micah grabbed the other box before she could say she'd be back for it and led the way down the hall. "I put on clean sheets, and fresh towels are in the bathroom. The floral ones are all yours."

That got a grin. "You don't use towels with flowers on them?"

He shook his head. "Not a chance. That was one thing I had to buy when I moved in."

She rolled her eyes. "Dinner guests don't know your bath towel choice."

"I'm not a floral guy. Or pale pink."

"Is that the other option?"

This time, his mock-serious expression made her smile. "Grandma likes those girly colors. I bought gray towels."

She turned and went down the hall. "Your secret is safe with me."

Bella woke while it was still dark. She reached for her phone on her nightstand and found a lamp base instead. When her hand finally landed on the phone, she turned on the flashlight.

Micah's house. She'd been so tired last night that she barely remembered getting under the covers. She turned off the light and set the phone back on the nightstand.

Strange sounds echoed outside the house. She froze, listening. Then she remembered the summer camp her parents had sent her to when she was ten. What she'd later learned were crickets had kept her up all night. She settled again into the covers and the surprisingly comfortable bed.

Birds singing woke her the second time. Sunlight poured into the room through an open curtain she'd definitely pull closed tonight. *Sunlight*!

"Oh, no!" She jumped out of bed. Both her phone and the clock on the nightstand told her she had twenty minutes to get dressed and be on the road to the city. With her robe on, she grabbed her purse and tote bag for toiletries, opened the door, checked the hallway to make sure Micah wasn't around, and dashed across the hall to the bathroom. After the fastest shower on record, she brushed hair she hadn't had time to wash, put on the barest of makeup, and returned to her room.

Well, the closest she'd come to her own room for the foreseeable future.

Opening the box she'd brought in yesterday, she found a dress she rarely wore on top. The good news was that it matched the shoes she'd worn yesterday, which were sitting beside the bed. She pulled it on, zipped it, and checked her appearance in the mirror, immediately remembering why she never wore this dress.

Bold gold and brown stripes circling her body made her look like a bumble bee. The dress probably wouldn't flatter anyone, but it had looked good on the hanger at the store. A glance at her phone told her she should have left by now. As long as she didn't stop to check her appearance in any mirrors today, she could pretend she was wearing something attractive.

She grabbed another garment out of the box—this one no more familiar. As she held up the boldly patterned dress, she realized that this box was full of to-be-donated items. She really should have taken time to label everything when she'd moved. But what were the odds that this box would be the one that ended up here?

With the week she'd had? The odds had been against her.

Another quick check of the time on her phone told her it would have to do for now.

~

Micah measured coffee beans, ground them, then added them to the coffee maker and waited for perfection. If he did say so himself.

He might not have been able to cook to save his life, but he could make a great cup of coffee. He wouldn't have a homemade meal waiting for Bella after her drive back—unless it was made in someone else's home—but he could give her coffee for her commute.

Bella dashed between the hall bathroom and her bedroom, finally emerging dressed . . . as a bee?

All the words he shouldn't say popped into his mind. *How are you, honey? Will you be buzzing around the office today?* He choked on laughter he knew he'd better keep to himself, and coughed to cover it. He held out the mug to her as she rushed down the hallway. "This will help you on your drive."

"Thank you!" She tilted the cup back, took a sip, and swallowed. Staring at him wide-eyed, she said, "This is *coffee*."

Maybe she hadn't slept well. "Of course it's coffee."

"Water." She raced into the kitchen with him behind her. He pulled a glass out of the cupboard and handed it to her. She held it under the tap, filled it, and chugged it down. Then she filled it again and drank half of the glass before stopping. He'd never seen anyone drink that much water at once.

When she'd finally set the glass down, she said, "Thank you for making that for me." Then she grimaced. "Have you noticed I only drink tea when we're out?"

He shook his head. "I must admit that I didn't." But he was a guy. Guys were known for missing details like this. "Wait. Are you telling me you *don't like* coffee?"

"It's nasty." She winced. "Sorry."

"Have you tried good coffee?"

"I once challenged the barista at a well-loved café to give it his best shot to convert me. I had a tiny sip and handed it to Cassie, who pronounced it so weak she could barely tell it had coffee in it. I still thought it tasted bad."

"Okay. Noted. No coffee."

"It's bigger than that. I need tea in the morning. I've stocked Cassie's cupboard with favorites. I'll have to get some for your house too." Bella wrapped her arms around him, hugged him tightly, and gave him a quick kiss on the lips before she ran out the kitchen door. Then he heard the front door slam.

Wow. What would happen if he served her tea?

As she drove out of town, minding the speed limit because getting a ticket here would not be good, she knew she'd made a mistake. She had kissed Micah as though they were in a relationship. Grinning, she said, "We're married."

Bella watched the reflection change in her rearview mirror. This time, seeing Two Hearts felt . . . comfortable. She'd spent the weekend and then last night in Two Hearts. It had all gone better than she'd imagined.

The people were surprisingly friendly and kind.

And Micah had been, well, Micah. He was a good guy. He just wasn't her guy.

All in all, she hadn't hated being in Two Hearts.

Towering buildings on the horizon told her she'd be back in the city soon.

Bella had been tired many times. Everyone had. But she had now found a new level of exhaustion. It climbed up every limb, sucking energy from each part of her body. Even her limp and lifeless hair had succumbed to exhaustion.

She'd gotten married Saturday to a man she barely knew, but she had to admit she found him intriguing. Everything had seemed to be on an upswing.

Monday had been the worst day of her life.

She'd climbed out of bed Tuesday morning with a new lease on life. She'd known she'd find a way to resolve her problems.

Then there'd been Wednesday, Thursday, and Friday.

Now it was Saturday—seven days after the biggest decision she'd ever made. Her shop wasn't open on Saturday unless they had an appointment, and thankfully, they didn't today.

She stared at the ceiling of her new room. Her old way of life had ended.

One week ago, she'd started down a path toward Two Hearts that didn't seem to have any exits off of it. She hadn't been showered with an abundance of options, though.

She'd moved out of her apartment. Micah had gathered some men together, and they'd brought the rest of her things here on Thursday. Or was it Wednesday? And she'd received a letter from her business landlord on one of those days, giving her a week from today to vacate that space.

Rolling onto her side, she stared at the floral wallpaper and felt like screaming. This room was in no way her style. If she was going to live here, she'd have to do something about that.

Wait. She *did* live here.

Bella sat on the edge of the bed. Two solutions to her present mood presented themselves: Cassie and ice cream.

A completely honest conversation with her best friend was probably where she should have started before she went down this path.

After what had become a pattern of peering out to make

sure no one—meaning Micah—saw her before she was presentable, she darted across the hall, took a shower, and put on makeup, taking the first steps to becoming functional for the day.

She found a covered mug of tea in the kitchen with a note.

A friend needed help. I may not be back for lunch. Micah.

Warmth spread through her. He had been everything she'd hoped to find in a husband. And now he'd added another layer to his knight-in-shining-armor coating. He helped others. Of course, he'd done that with her too. You couldn't go any deeper to help a stranger than to marry them. Then again, he'd also done that to help himself and his sisters.

With her morning officially open, she called Cassie.

A meow was the first thing she heard.

"How are you today, Romeo?"

Her friend's laughter was exactly what she'd needed to hear. "We're on the couch, and he had his face next to mine. Are you driving here for the day?"

When had she gotten so disconnected from her best friend?

"I'm here now."

"At my house?" Bella heard shuffling sounds and another meow that made her think Cassie had moved Romeo and was on her way toward her window to look out.

"Two Hearts. I, um, moved out of my apartment this week."

Her friend paused a beat before responding. "I've missed important things."

"Yeah. You really have. Can I come over now?"

"Of course. Greg's working today, and I have time before I need to go anywhere."

"See you soon." Bella reached for the button to end the call.

"And Bella—"

She put the phone back to her ear. "Yes?"

"I want the whole story."

"That's my plan." Bella grabbed her car keys as she spoke. "Cassie, if I lock Micah's house when I leave, I can't get back in."

Cassie laughed. "Don't worry about locking doors in Two Hearts. Wait! *Where* are you?" After a two-second pause, she said, "Are you living with Micah?"

"I'll be there in a few minutes." Bella hung up the phone. Her current situation was best explained in person.

Cassie was standing at the edge of the driveway when Bella drove up. The moment the car engine stopped, Cassie pounced. She leaned in through the open car window. "What is going on, Bella?"

"Let me at least get out." Bella dropped her keys in her purse and opened the door.

Soon lounging in an Adirondack chair and staring at the trees overhead, Bella started on her story. "I had some problems."

"I knew that."

"You only knew part of it." Bella began at the beginning with Honoré's dress.

Cassie checked her watch before she could finish that part of the tale. "I don't want to stop you. Greg's mother invited me to lunch. Let me call her to say I can't come."

Bella held up both hands in a *stop* motion. "Don't do that."

Cassie tapped her phone. "Are you kidding? It's just lunch with—"

"Your future mother-in-law." Bella moved to stand. "Please don't cancel because of me."

"Mrs. Brantley? My friend Bella is here, so I'll need to reschedule lunch."

Bella flopped back on the chair.

Cassie turned to her. "I'll ask her." She tapped her phone again. "She's on mute. She invited you to lunch with us."

More than anything, Bella wanted to crawl into a hole and hide until this was all over. She could step back out a month from now—or better yet, a year from now—and she'd have a normal life again.

"She might be someone good to bounce ideas off."

Bella stood. "Why not? I haven't done well with this on my own."

"I don't know; you married a nice guy." Cassie shrugged. "You may not know him well, though."

"And there we have the downside to my plan. I married someone barely above a stranger."

Cassie told Mrs. Brantley they'd be right over. "It isn't far, so let's walk."

Bella pointed to her feet and the high heels she wore.

"Why do you insist on wearing those everywhere?"

"I'm starting to wonder that myself." Stepping forward, one heel slipped into the grass. As she yanked it out, she said, "I may have to switch to the sneakers I've only used at the gym."

Cassie rubbed her ear. "I must need to have my hearing checked. My friend Bella in flat shoes?"

"If you were barely above five feet tall, you'd wear heels all the time too."

Cassie walked toward Bella's car. "Actually, I wouldn't."

"Yes, you would."

"I value the lack of pain in my feet."

Bella laughed. "There is that."

It took barely three minutes to reach Mrs. Brantley's house, and when they did, Bella couldn't help admiring the front garden. Even the house seemed welcoming to her today, which was a surprise since it was another older home.

Greg's mother greeted them at the front door. After waving them inside, she led them to the kitchen table. "Sit. Sit. I'll only be a minute."

"Where's Cookie?"

"The little scamp got into a potted plant I have—had—this morning. She's doing a timeout in the backyard."

Bella wondered if the dog felt punished when she was allowed to run free and chase squirrels.

A minute after they'd sat down, Mrs. Brantley brought over bowls of a creamy soup and green salad.

Bella said, "I hope my being here didn't put you in a bind."

Mrs. Brantley laughed. "I make more than I should every time. If Greg said he was free for lunch, there would be enough for him too."

Bella scooped up a spoonful of what appeared to be potato soup with bacon and parsley on top, but paused with it just above the bowl when the older woman leaned her elbows on the table and seriously said, "Now, tell me what has happened."

"Could I wait until after lunch?" Her appetite usually vanished when she talked about her current mess.

"Of course."

Bella took a bite of the soup. "Mmm. This is delicious." Maybe everyone would forget about her problems by the time they'd finished.

When Mrs. Brantley had removed their bowls, Cassie said, "Bella has some problems. You're good with solutions."

So much for that hope.

Mrs. Brantley glanced at Bella. "Let's take tea and cookies to the backyard to relax and talk it over."

Bella asked, "What kind of cookies?"

"Peanut butter."

After soup, salad, and light conversation, she knew the time had come. They marched outside, each with a mug in hand. Mrs. Brantley also carried a container filled with cookies she'd suggested might still be warm.

When they were seated, Cassie said, "Bella has some financial problems."

Mrs. Brantley took a sip of her tea before responding. "I wondered if it was something like that when you suddenly married Micah."

Bella gasped. "You guessed?"

The older woman shrugged. "Why else would you marry someone you barely knew?"

Bella felt heat rising in her face. "Has the whole town figured it out?"

"I don't think so. And don't worry. Your secret is safe with me." The way she said it made Bella wonder how "secret" this was. "Tell me what's going on."

She started at the beginning. Even Cassie gasped when she went into details about Honoré's dress. Then she told them about her employees.

"Oh, my." Mrs. Brantley put her hand on her chest. "A pregnant woman on top of everything else?"

"It kept getting worse and worse. To save money, I gave up my apartment and moved in with Micah on Monday." She didn't mention the extra incentive of being there to receive the meals townspeople were bringing. That would make her seem ungrateful. "Now, I'm commuting back and forth to Nashville every day."

Mrs. Brantley winced. "That's a lot. We've had people from Two Hearts give the commute a try. It only lasts a month or two before they have to move closer to their jobs." They sat in silence for a moment before she asked, "Why did Micah agree to help?"

That launched Bella into the story of college money and Micah's grandfather.

"Well." Mrs. Brantley huffed out the one word. "You've been struggling alone. Let's see what we can do together."

Bella felt like she'd been hit by a truck. She'd been alone with this—not even wanting to burden her best friend—but now a stranger wanted to help. She looked away and blinked to hold back tears.

Mrs. Brantley patted her arm. "We're on your side."

"I hope you have ideas beyond those I thought of when I was

awake in the night." Over and over again.

"Let's look at this logically. You have a place to live."

Bella snorted laughter. "Right. With Micah."

Cassie raised an eyebrow. "Your husband."

That put her in her place. She had married the man.

"He's treating you well, isn't he?" Cassie leaned toward her with concern.

Bella waved a hand away from her. "He's great. Now that I'm commuting, he has a mug of tea ready for my drive every morning. I chose a winner, even if it was a quick decision." Micah really was going above and beyond with this whole "husband" thing, even if he was just playing a role.

Mrs. Brantley leaned back. "Now, it seems like the first thing you need to do is reduce expenses."

"That would be nice. The problem is how to do that." She studied her fingernails for a moment. "And, uh, I may have neglected one important detail." She swallowed hard and looked at the two women. "I've lost my business's lease. I have a week to get out of there."

"Bella!" Cassie stared at her. "That's an important detail."

"I know. I think I expect it to fix itself if I ignore it. It hasn't."

"So you have to move." Mrs. Brantley focused into the distance as though she were pondering solutions. Then she smiled. "I have it."

"You know somewhere I can move in Nashville?"

She shook her head slowly from side to side, the smile widening. "Here."

Bella's brow furrowed as she focused on the word. "What do you mean?"

"We used to have a bridal shop."

Thankfully, Cassie jumped in to diffuse the idea. "But that was decades ago when the town was flourishing."

That told Bella everything she needed to know about it. Two

Hearts's biggest fan didn't like the idea. They clearly needed a Plan B. Or was it Plan H for *Help!*?

Mrs. Brantley wouldn't be dissuaded. "Cassie's clients are driving out here to see her."

Cassie shrugged. "Yes. Only because they want country weddings planned."

"That isn't completely true. Didn't you win over someone who had planned to get married in Nashville?"

Cassie shrugged. "I did. Her friend dragged her out here—her words, not mine—and she fell in love with the church."

"That means that people are willing to come to our charming small town."

Bella considered the idea. Tears threatened again. Focusing on the idea at hand, she pushed them away. "What's the old bridal shop building like inside?"

Cassie's eyes widened. "You're considering it?"

"Give me more options."

When her friend said nothing, Bella continued. "Would I have to spend tens of thousands of dollars to make it usable?"

"I was inside almost all the buildings on Main Street when we cleaned up the storefronts for the country music star's wedding. I know that nothing in that one was falling down or caving in. I would remember something like that. In fact, most of the buildings are in surprisingly good shape when you consider they've been shut for years."

A bubble of excitement grew. "I *could* move the business." Then it deflated as though a pin had let the air out. "But I can't ask my employees to move." Bella threw her hands in the air. "I'm back to square one."

CHAPTER SEVENTEEN

Bella stood in front of the abandoned wedding shop on Main Street.

Mrs. Brantley's calm wisdom had prevailed: "Look at it. Then decide." When Bella had agreed, the older woman picked up her phone and got to work.

An hour later, a brick building with the faded and broken sign above it was before her. The only clues to its former life were the word *wed* and the outline of a ball gown in what she was sure had been white. Once.

She'd seen the sign before but not paid much attention. It was, after all, in a small town that she'd had no intention of spending more time in than it took for a visit with Cassie or to do last-minute fittings on a dress for one of the weddings her friend managed.

In short, Bella had planned to live in a city. Always.

Plans sometimes changed, and this change was huge. Bella Bennett was about to become a small-town girl. If the idea hadn't terrified her, she might have found it funny. She did not.

But she refused to be defeated. If Cassie could make her business a success in Two Hearts, so could Bella. Then she remembered that Cassie was still working on it, so even that was an unknown. Besides, her friend liked living here.

She probably should have allowed Cassie to come with her as she'd offered, but Bella had run her business herself up to this point. She could take this next step. If there was one.

A deep voice caught her attention. "You must be Bella."

She turned to see an older man. "Yes. I'm waiting for the owner to let me inside."

"She's getting up in years, so she asked me to meet you here. I'm Albert." He put out his hand to shake hers.

"I'm glad to see you, Albert."

"You're a friend of Cassie's, aren't you?"

"I am."

He stared at her. "I remember now. You're the one at their engagement party who had the pink splash on your dress."

"That's me," she muttered. So many people had first met her that day.

He unlocked and opened the door. Stale, warm air poured out. When she followed him inside, she found a room with metal racks for dresses against either wall and a pedestal for a bride to stand on and show off her dress in the middle. The mirrors behind the pedestal were so covered now with dust that they showed no reflection.

Glancing up, Bella saw what could be a pretty chandelier under the grime and cobwebs. An old-fashioned cash register perched atop a wooden counter to the rear of the room.

This had been a fancy store in its day, and many parts of the business had been left. The problem was that she made custom dresses. She didn't have ready-made dresses to buy, so she didn't need a big inventory for people to browse.

Since this was a possible next step, she decided to be positive.

Facing the front window, which had, at least, been cleaned recently, she found that sunlight filled the area. Bella knew downtown had been fixed up for Carly and Jake's celebrity wedding.

As she pictured a customer entering, possibilities rushed in. The room would be inviting, with white walls and bright pink accents. Maybe she would only see people by appointment, as she currently did. Customers would walk in and see her sample dresses displayed. That could be a nice improvement. Right now, they were crammed into a too-small room.

Albert had stayed silent. "What do you think?"

"I think . . . I like it." Surprise whooshed through her. She actually *liked* it.

"The oak floors should clean up nicely." He crouched and rubbed an area to reveal the brown wood under the grime and other things that had once crawled or flown and which she'd chosen to ignore.

"That's great. I don't want to replace flooring." She barely had a budget for paint, but she wouldn't share that information with him. "Let me see what the back room has to offer." The employees-only area held shelves with wrapping paper from another time, along with stacks of blank, yellowed invoices. Bella opened and closed the door to a small bathroom quickly. A grimy bathroom was far worse than dust on a mirror.

"Would you like to see the upstairs?"

At her questioning look, Albert pointed to a door she hadn't opened yet. "I know every building in this town." With a chuckle, he added, "I will admit that I never set foot in this wedding shop when it was open, though." He started up the stairs, and she followed him.

Bella crossed her arms over her chest to keep them from touching walls that made the cobweb-covered chandelier downstairs seem clean. At the top, Albert waved his hands to brush aside more webs, then motioned for her to stand beside him. A large room, empty except for some shelving against the right wall and a couple of big, old, wooden desks, featured several large windows to the front overlooking Main Street. Unlike downstairs, these had not been cleaned recently or, she guessed by the lack of light penetrating through them, at any time in the last decade.

Albert continued his tour. "This building has a lot more natural light than most of those along here. It will be bright and cheerful on a sunny day."

Standing in the room where she could barely make out the details made her question that premise.

He pointed behind her. "There are windows on both ends."

When she turned, she did see what could have been a row of windows almost completely hidden by shredded orange curtains.

"There's also a bathroom in the corner. I believe this upper story was once rented as a separate office, so that's probably why there are two. Rare in an old building," he said the last more quietly, probably more to himself than her.

The two levels combined had more square footage than her current location. A surge of excitement shot through her. She could make this space what she wanted it to be. This floor could also have white walls for brightness—because she didn't trust Albert's assessment of the light—and maybe yellow and teal accents. She went to the wall and flipped a switch. Nothing happened.

"The power's been off for years."

"That makes sense." The yellowed plastic of the light switch plate made her wonder about the wiring. "Albert, I often have multiple heavy-duty sewing machines going and need strong overhead lighting for my employees to work. Can this old electric system handle that?"

He frowned. "There's no question—"

Her hopes rose.

"That it can't."

And fell.

He tapped his chin. "I seem to remember that Howard—he was the county's favorite electrician for decades—did work on this place. I may be wrong about what I said." He held up a finger. "Yes, the details are coming back to me. A business was planning to move in here but backed out. Another of the hopeful things for this town that didn't happen. They had the electric in this building and the one next door upgraded to code. That was probably twenty years ago, but it would be more modern than a lot of the buildings in town."

"So, I'm safe to work here?"

He wavered his hand back and forth. "Probably. I'd have someone come out to check it."

She muttered, "More money," not realizing she'd spoken loud enough for him to hear.

"Squeezed tight?"

She blinked and stared at him.

"Money squeezed tight?"

"Oh, yes." The second she said that, she knew she'd revealed too much. The good people of Two Hearts couldn't know about her situation. They had to assume she was doing well and married for love. "We're newlyweds, and I'm moving my business. It's a lot."

Albert nodded thoughtfully. "I can see that. Herb owes me a favor."

"Herb?"

"The electrician now that Howard has retired. I found unusual supplies he needed and rushed them to his job site."

When she didn't say anything, he added, "I own the hardware store."

Now it made sense that he knew so much about construction and the building itself. "I would appreciate any help."

He perked up at her words. "You're going to rent the

building?" He seemed to be holding his breath as he waited for her answer.

Being in the middle of the filthy room, with its dust motes floating in the air and questionable wiring in the walls—all in the small town of Two Hearts—made her wonder what rabbit hole she'd fallen down.

Among every option, this one was best.

"Yes, I am." Determination and optimism rushed through her. She wouldn't be a victim to everything that had happened. This would work. A year in Two Hearts wouldn't be the end of the world.

Would it?

He gave her a long stare. "If you don't mind my saying so, you look more big-city than small-town."

She chuckled. "It's the high heels, isn't it?"

"That may be it. You could try sneakers."

She felt her eyes widen.

Micah waited beside Bella as she unlocked the door to what he hoped would be her future business location. His plan was supposed to have pulled her out of her financial nightmare by now, but it hadn't. Now he wanted to help any way he could to make up for that.

He should have anticipated the move his grandfather had made, but even after thirty-plus years of dealing with him, that had come as a complete shock.

He followed her inside. The now-clean windows had given him a false impression from the street. He started to gasp, then put his hand over his mouth, not wanting to take in any of the dusty air in this place.

She linked her arm through his and pulled him forward. "I'll set up my shop as it was last time this place was open for business, with dresses hanging to the side and . . . well, everything pretty much the same. It made sense in 1960, and it makes sense today." Gesturing at the room in general, she added, "Of course, the walls will be freshly painted white. I think the cash stand may be hot pink. Or teal." She stared at it for a moment. "I think the pink."

Bella could clearly see a picture he could not.

"And then"—she tugged him forward—"upstairs is quite wonderful."

He hoped it wouldn't be any more "wonderful" than the downstairs.

It was.

Cobwebs must have been knocked away downstairs when they'd cleaned the windows a few months ago. Here, they flourished. Both the webs and the cause of them needed to be removed, along with the other insects that were probably lurking in the dark. Maybe he'd surprise Bella by getting someone to do that. If a friend asked, "What was your wedding gift to your wife?" he could answer "Pest control." He knew Bella would not appreciate the humor right now.

"This will be the office. Customers won't come up here. It's painted white too."

There she went, saying that in present tense, as though it already existed.

"The accent colors are yellow and maybe teal. What do you think?" She cocked her head to the side as she looked at him.

He could only think that she looked adorable when she did that. Focusing on her words, he said, "Bella, I'm not a color expert. Choose colors you'd like to live with. Ones that bring a smile to your face."

"Yellow it is. There isn't a happier color anywhere, in my opinion."

"My grandmother will appreciate that thought. Yellow is her favorite color."

"I can see that. Curtains. The room I'm staying in. All yellow."

"The main bedroom is too. If you spend time in there, you'll notice the yellow wallpaper on one wall is intense."

He watched her face turn fiery red. When she turned away and headed toward the front windows, he realized what he'd said. There wasn't much chance of *that* happening.

She turned to face him, all thoughts of his last words seeming to be gone. "Should I take the place?"

Her hopeful expression said she'd probably already made the decision. Or maybe she just hoped he'd encourage her in that direction.

"It does make financial sense."

The excitement faded. "You're right."

He wanted to bring it back. "Can you see Wedding Bella here?"

She lit up again. "Yes. It surprises me to say this, but I believe I can. The electrician Albert mentioned said the wiring is good, so that's a relief."

"Then let's sit down with Hector Holton and hammer out the terms of your lease. I'll draw up the contract."

"Can we do that today? I don't want anyone else to get it first."

It took him a moment to process her words. "Bella, you're in Two Hearts. Look around you. There is no chance—and I do mean zero chance—that anyone wants this place but you."

"I guess I fell in love with what it could be. My heart said I had to hurry."

His heart wondered if there could be more between them. If she could fall for a building . . .

"Are you ready to go?" She tugged on his sleeve.

Grinning, he said, "Let's go to my office. If that's okay?"

She hugged him. "That's better than okay."

When he slid his arms around her, he had to agree.

CHAPTER EIGHTEEN

Now, she had to tell her employees that they were either commuting, moving, or losing their jobs.

This would be the most difficult conversation of her life.

When she arrived at her business, a man in uniform was measuring the door and the area next to it that had her sign on it. "Can I help you?"

He turned to face her, and she read the name on his uniform, *Best Signs*. "I'm measuring for the next tenant."

Her stress level ramped up another notch, surprising her that it was possible. "I see. And when will you be installing the signs?"

"Friday." He smiled, seeming oblivious to her distress.

He opened the door for her, and she marched inside.

A building in Two Hearts that desperately needed to be cleaned and painted—oh, and the power turned back on—was her only option.

Her employees had arrived before her.

April pointed to the door Bella had just entered. "What's with the sign guy?"

Bella put her hands over her mouth and took a deep breath.

Why ease into the discussion? Standing straight, she tried to appear confident of her choices. "I have some news for you." She bit her lip for a second, then continued. "Due to some problems that were my fault and some that were not, I've had a financial glitch."

"I knew it! I told everyone you were closing as soon as I saw the sign man." Gertie tended to be a bit dramatic.

"Is that right, Bella?" April put her hand on her belly.

"I'm not closing."

A collective sigh went up.

"I'm moving the business." She stopped for a beat. "To Two Hearts, Tennessee."

"Where?" Dora gave her a puzzled expression. "Is that a place, or are you saying you now have two hearts beating as one?"

Definitely not the second option. "It's a place, and it's about an hour and a half west of Nashville."

April asked, "Is Two Hearts nice?"

Bella winced. "It was nice. And I suppose it could be again. But right now, the town has fallen on hard times."

"That's too bad. I love watching TV shows where they go to small towns. Don't you?" April turned to the other women, and they nodded agreement.

"There's one show that makes me want to move to their small town every time I watch," Dora said with a wistful tone.

Two Hearts definitely wasn't like that place.

Her employees looked at each other, and Gertie spoke first. "You expect us to drive ninety minutes back and forth to work?"

"You can move with me or not. I won't be angry with anyone for leaving. I know this is a big thing to ask."

Conversation exploded around her.

April's quiet voice broke through the chatter. "Is it expensive to live in Two Hearts? Could we buy a house?"

Could she? "My friend Cassie—"

"The wedding planner?" Dora asked.

Of course, they knew who Cassie was. She funneled a lot of clients to Wedding Bella.

"Yes. She moved there. I know her house cost a lot less than the condo she owned in Nashville."

April's face lit up. "Then count me in. Us." She put her hand on her belly again.

"Won't your husband have a say in it?"

"Daniel is ready to move to a new place. We've talked about living in a small town." She sighed. "This is great."

"I'm single. Count me in too." Dora grinned.

Gertie said, "I'm sorry, Bella, but my husband has a couple more years at his job until he's vested for retirement. We'll be staying."

Bella didn't like the unkind thought that came to mind that her shop might be more peaceful if Gertie found a new job.

The two other women were undecided.

April asked, "Can we drive out there today to see?"

Bella thought over their dresses in production. Nothing was due immediately. "Let's do that." She pulled out her phone and brought up a map. "We can all meet at Dinah's Place for lunch when you arrive." She showed them where it was on the map.

Once her employees had left, Bella stood still in shock. That had gone better than she had expected. Then she realized she'd better get herself in motion. A crew from Wedding Bella was about to descend on Two Hearts.

Bella and Michelle pushed a couple of tables together, and everyone sat down. As they sat, April exclaimed, "This town is like ones on TV!"

Dora winced. "I don't know. April, did you notice the abandoned-looking buildings down the street?"

Bella felt the same as Dora. "Let me tell you a story." She launched into Cassie's run from the altar, how she ended up in Two Hearts, and her decision to move country music star Carly Daniels's wedding there. "The town came together in ways you wouldn't believe."

Michelle paused by their table. "I hope you don't mind my saying something, but I overheard you talking. Are you thinking of moving here?" She glanced around the table.

"I'm moving my business, Wedding Bella, to Main Street."

A crash sounded behind Michelle, and they all turned that direction. Dinah, holding half of a broken plate in her hand, rushed over.

"Did you say you're moving a business onto Main Street?" Her eyes were lit with passion.

"Yes." Bella managed the one word before Dinah shouted.

"Glory be!" She raised her arms in praise. "We haven't had anything there in . . . well, so long that I can't tell you exactly when. Except for the sometimes-open consignment shop." She glanced around and leaned closer. "Which isn't much, if I'm being honest."

"And you're all moving here?" Michelle circled her finger around the group.

"I'd like to." April pointed to herself. "My husband would need to find work, though."

Dinah shook her head. "That's the problem. There aren't a lot of jobs here."

"I suppose he could open his own office. He's a nurse practitioner."

"Is that like a nurse?"

"It's more like a doctor. He can do most of what a doctor does."

Dinah and Michelle looked at each other. Then Dinah shouted, "Glory be!" again. "Honey, we haven't had a doctor in this town since old Doc Evans met his maker ten or fifteen years ago. The vet does what he can in emergencies, but humans aren't horses." She shook her head. "That's led to some interesting situations."

April asked, "Is there a real estate agent in Two Hearts?"

"Are you thinking of buying a house?"

The young woman nodded. "We're having a baby around Christmas. I'd like to be settled before then."

"We'd welcome you here. There isn't a real estate agent—"

Michelle jumped in. "Randi got her real estate license a month or so ago."

"How did I miss that?"

Michelle smiled. "I think she felt foolish when she finished the training and no one wanted to buy a house. Plenty want to sell, of course."

April's eyes lit up. "They do?"

Michelle and Dinah looked at each other, then Dinah spoke. "Two Hearts hasn't had its best decade."

"Or two," Michelle added.

Dinah shrugged. "There haven't been many home buyers."

"Like none."

"Michelle, let's not scare them off." Dinah frowned at the waitress.

Michelle added, "It's a nice town. I didn't move away." A second later, she added, "Cassie bought her house."

Dinah lit up. "See. There is a market for houses. I'll call Randi, and she can show you some houses today, if you'd like."

April looked over at Bella. "Do we have time?"

"After we have lunch and tour my new building, I'll give you all the rest of the workday off to explore the town."

Dinah hustled toward the kitchen. "Then I'd better get busy making lunches. It's all on the house today."

Michelle held her pen over her pad. "Everyone know what they want?"

Dinah shouted, "Michelle, please call Randi as soon as you've given me their orders. Tell her to be at Bella's building in an hour."

Bella wasn't sure if that was enough time to eat and get over there, but in what seemed like record time, their food had arrived. Happy sounds went around the table as they tried what they'd ordered. Once they'd polished off the last of their pie, with April asking for a half slice of both chocolate and pecan and Dinah obliging because of "her condition," they walked to her new store.

Coming from this direction, she could see that she did need a sign that sat away from the building or else the building next to it would block its view. She didn't have money for that or anything else, so she hoped Micah was handy with a saw and paintbrush.

Happy conversation carried them down the street and into the building. Quiet fell over the group when they stepped inside. Bella glanced from them to the store. "It was a little overwhelming when I first saw it."

Dora asked, "What about when you saw it the second time?"

Bella laughed. "That was better because I could already see it as it could be."

"Show us what you see." April gestured to the room.

Bella shared her vision as they walked through the lower level and upstairs. By the time she ended the tour, Bella could almost see those pink and yellow accents. Based on the happy sounds coming from her employees, she felt like this would actually be happening.

CHAPTER NINETEEN

She'd signed the papers. The store on Main Street was all hers. They'd negotiated a deal where she paid a small amount of rent the first six months as she settled in. When Micah had proposed it, she'd felt like that would be taking advantage of the owner. Then Hector had suggested an even lower price, saying he hadn't earned a penny from the building for years and had to pay property taxes, anyway. He'd do whatever he could to help her get started.

Then he'd said words that made her both weepy from the sentiment and scared stiff because of the responsibility: "Two Hearts needs you."

As the first shop opening on Main Street, she would have to work hard to bring in clients. Those clients would hopefully stop at Dinah's Place to eat. More money would be brought to town. She might even have a bride who liked the town enough to plan a visit and stay at Randi's motel.

Minutes later, she and Micah had walked out of the man's home with signed documents.

The new Two Hearts location of Wedding Bella was a reality. Or at least it would be once decades' worth of grime had been successfully removed, and everything from her shop brought here.

According to both Micah and Albert, her new shop would be exactly what she needed when it was done. And she could almost picture the finished result with fresh paint and a lack of dust. What she had problems with was the effort it was going to take for her to transform everything.

The next day, Bella got ready as usual, with the notable exceptions of shorts instead of a dress and sneakers instead of heels. Then she went toward the kitchen, her smile growing because she knew Micah would be waiting there with her tea, as usual. That joy was quashed when she discovered an empty room with a mug, accompanied by one of her pink sticky notes, on the counter.

The note from Micah simply said he'd meet her at her new shop this morning. Disappointment washed over her. When had he become the thing she looked forward to in the morning? She didn't want to consider that for a second.

Since she had on comfortable shoes—not that high heels weren't comfortable—she decided to walk in the cooler morning air. Micah could drive her home later.

Everything had been moved from her old location and into the corner of her new shop in anticipation of having the building cleaned, painted, and ready for business. She'd have to spend every day for a week or two here to do that.

Cars lined Main Street on both sides, but the streets were empty of people. Nearing her new shop, she noticed a container filled with pink and yellow petunias on either side of the entrance. The town had been fixed up and flowers placed here and there on the street for Carly and Jake's wedding—Cassie had pointed out the work the town had done—but Bella would have noticed these flowers earlier, wouldn't she?

Mrs. Brantley stepped out the door as Bella reached to push on it.

"Micah told me the town would be happy about my store, but having you here is surprising," Bella said.

"I'm not the only one who came to help."

"That's great!" Every person who helped would get her to her goal of opening more quickly. "Let's go inside so I can see who's here." She reached for the door again.

"Wait a moment. I have to tell you something." The woman gave a furtive glance over her shoulder—toward what, Bella didn't know, but her concern was growing.

"There's an issue." She put up a hand to prevent Bella's questions. "You need to see it, but I don't think it's all bad."

"*All* bad?" Bella stepped around her, and Mrs. Brantley didn't stop her this time.

A dozen or more people busied themselves in the shop, some on the floor level, some on scaffolding cleaning the upper walls and ceilings.

"Surprise!" Mrs. Brantley said, and the group turned to face her, everyone grinning. "I wanted to build suspense."

Bella put her hands on her face. "I don't know what to say. Thank you!" With the grime gone, a brick wall to the left of the room stood out in a good way. Maybe she'd keep it rustic and not paint it.

Mrs. Brantley surveyed their progress. "I must admit that painting isn't my favorite activity. What do you think about the bricks?" She gave a nod toward the wall Bella had been admiring.

Bella nodded. "I love it that way. I'll need to be careful not to put delicate fabrics near the rougher texture, just in case, but it adds warmth to the space."

Mrs. Brantley stared at the wall in question for so long that Bella thought she disagreed. "I think that's wise," Mrs. Brantley said at last. Pointing to the back wall, she continued, "I have an idea. I was talking to Jason Fulbright's son Jordan and discovered that he's an artist. I mentioned your project."

Bella inwardly groaned. Could it ever end up good when someone's kid drew on your wall? She was about to say "thank you" and move on when Mrs. Brantley made an excellent point.

"You do, after all, need a sign. I think he could do one for outside and also paint a similar image on that back wall."

With no other free options in sight, she agreed and was told the "young man" would be over shortly.

Bella toured her almost-but-not-quite-ready shop. The decorative old tin ceiling and brick wall downstairs added charm. The white paint had freshened everything up. She ran her hand over the register stand. The hot pink here had brought the room to life.

Cassie stepped over. "This is better than I expected. A lot better."

"I think so too. I almost hate to say it out loud, but this location is nicer than what I had in Nashville."

"How?"

"The layout works better. The workroom upstairs is much larger. And Albert was right when we toured the building the first time. I love the light pouring in through the windows." Even with much of the building far from ready, the place made her smile.

Micah found Bella downstairs with a paint roller in her hand and a satisfied expression on her face. Volunteers had worked all day yesterday and come back today after church for more.

"It's coming together nicely. It's what you described and better than I could imagine."

"It is." She dropped her voice. "I haven't gotten up the nerve to clean the bathrooms, though. Painting is my avoidance tactic." She put the roller down.

"Someone else can clean it for you." He motioned to the

townspeople who had showed up this morning. Albert swept cobwebs from the ceiling upstairs, Mrs. Brantley sprayed the mirrors behind the bridal pedestal with glass cleaner, and Levi was mopping the floors.

Micah leaned against the wall. "Learn to accept help. Small-town people like to help. Your neighbors want to see you succeed."

Bella frowned. "Micah, I can't let other people clean these bathrooms. And I need to have every single room ready for my employees tomorrow. It's my job." Dread oozed from her words.

"I'll do it." He held out his hand for the cleaning materials. "I'm your husband, so I'm allowed to help."

A glimmer of hope lit her face. "Are you sure?"

"I may change my mind if you don't hurry."

She picked up a bucket with supplies stuffed into it—spray cleaner, scrub brush, and paper towels—and handed it to him. "Do you want the disposable coveralls I bought?"

Dread now moved over him. He hadn't looked in the room he'd offered to clean. "Do I need that?"

"I wouldn't set foot in there unless I was covered from head to toe and was wearing goggles."

A few minutes later, armed only with the bucket full of supplies, he entered the room. He'd be in and out of there in a few minutes, so he'd decided against the coveralls.

It was worse than he'd anticipated. Worse than he could have imagined. He backed out, donned the coveralls and goggles Bella provided, and entered again. He sprayed everything within sight, then closed his eyes to clean first the toilet followed by the sink. Once that was done, he felt like he could get in there and scrub the rest.

What seemed like hours later but probably wasn't, he emerged. Bella hurried over as he lifted his goggles. When she peered around him to see inside the small room, she squealed.

"Thank you! I'd hug you, but I don't want to touch you right now."

Warmth rushed through him. Would she push him away if he tried to accelerate their relationship a notch later? "I will take a rain check for that hug."

She started to say something, then stopped herself. Starting again, she said, "I'll give you that rain check." She gave him a cheeky smile before walking away. "Oh, and there's a second bathroom upstairs." Her soft laughter had him shaking his head.

Micah adjusted his goggles and went up the stairs. When he opened that bathroom door, he took a step backward, slamming into the wall behind him. The things he'd do for Bella. Closing his eyes, he aimed the spray around and down. He could handle this.

When he finally finished, Micah stripped off the suit and debated burning it, but ended up stuffing it in a trash can. Both bathrooms sparkled. And he would seek out that hug—or hugs—when they were home tonight.

CHAPTER TWENTY

Bella approached the door to Wedding Bella. The gorgeous sign overhead was nothing short of perfection. Jordan had turned out to be a forty-something skilled artist. He'd painted her business name and a wedding dress in gold and pink on a sign Albert had cut from wood and hung when it was completed.

Standing in front of the building, much as she had slightly over a week ago, she couldn't stop the wide grin on her face, but she did stifle the urge to do a happy dance right there on the sidewalk. Not that anyone was there to see her. As usual, this part of Main Street looked abandoned, with the exception of her shiny new shop.

Using the wonderfully old-fashioned key to open the door, she stepped inside, and more perfection greeted her. The townspeople had put many hours into helping transform this from a cobweb- and dust-covered abandoned building to a shop that could stand up to anything in the city. Several shades of pink from pale to magenta, all in small doses, brought the lower level to life without taking over the room with bright colors. Jordan's matching design on the wall behind the cash register stand added a custom touch.

A vision of brides coming here to try on sample gowns, the room bustling with laughter and happiness as they found their perfect dress, filled her mind. She could see the vision so clearly that she was surprised the women weren't here right now.

The front window displayed the dress she'd recently worn for her own wedding and an adorable flower girl's dress her team had made from left-over fabric and lace. Today, most of those employees would be making the drive to Two Hearts for work. And she'd be able to pay them herself until Micah's grandfather gave them the promised money.

How could he find fault in a relationship that had made this dream come true?

She went upstairs to her new office and started on some dress designs using the fabric they had available. She knew two brides-to-be had appointments tomorrow and—she hoped—would give her the down payment for their dresses that would allow her to buy materials.

Everything seemed on track.

The door chimed, and April called out that she'd arrived. Soon the other three women were here and at work on their tasks. But the doorbell stayed silent after that.

People weren't going to magically appear. She had potential brides who were willing to drive from Nashville, but she needed a steady stream of customers to help this business take off. With very little money for paid advertising, what could she do? Even then, what would she say? "Drive an hour and a half to the middle of nowhere to shop for a wedding dress"?

Her beautiful new store could still fail.

The phone rang, pulling her out of her sense of gloom. For the first time in a while, she could answer without fear of it being a bill collector.

"Wedding Bella."

"Miss Bella? I'm Penelope Bowen. I'm at your business's door, but it looks closed."

Bella went to the front window and looked out over the empty street. No one was there, so Penelope must be in Nashville. "There should be a sign there saying we've moved."

"No, ma'am. There's only a sign saying that a graphic design company will be moving in soon."

Bella closed her eyes in frustration. She'd have to call her old landlord to see if he would kindly put her sign back. Until the new guy moved in, it shouldn't matter to him.

"That's no matter," Penelope continued. "Please give me directions, and I'll come right over."

Bella checked her schedule. "I don't have any appointments scheduled for right now. Are you sure you made one?"

"I actually hoped I could stop by to see your dresses. We set the date for our wedding last night," Penelope said gleefully.

While Bella often couldn't have helped a walk-in customer before because they were too busy, she certainly could now. "I'm in a small town outside of Nashville. Are you willing to drive?"

"Franklin? Spring Hill?"

"Two Hearts. It's about ninety minutes west of Nashville."

"An hour and a half?" Penelope's incredulous tone told Bella that she wouldn't be making the drive. "I'm going to have to think about that. Why there?"

"I married a man who lives here. I have a brand-new, beautiful shop." She hoped to entice her with the *new* factor.

"I have today off work. Let me see if I can talk my mother into driving there with me. Wait! You do have appointments open, don't you?"

So many available appointments. "We opened today, so we haven't had a chance to book many yet."

"I'll talk her into it. I'll see you about two."

That went better than expected. She had . . . one appointment booked for this afternoon. A business couldn't run on a single appointment in a day, or even the two she had for tomorrow.

No. She needed a second miracle. The shop existed, but now she had to find a way to entice brides to Two Hearts to browse through her samples. She went online to find ideas. Nothing free or close to it appeared in front of her.

Maybe Cassie would have an idea or two.

Bella picked up the phone and dialed her friend, which felt odd, considering she lived and worked a block or two away.

"What are you doing this afternoon?"

"Busy, busy, busy. I have two weddings to work on. I'm taking a trip to Nashville at the end of the week to choose flowers with clients and meet with bakers. I wish we had everything here."

"Maybe you will eventually." If they could come up with a great plan. "I need to bounce ideas off of someone."

Cassie chuckled. "Bounce away."

"I thought I'd stop by your house."

"I'm still not used to you being so close. If you're driving, stop and get coffee and pie from Dinah's. For future reference, you're welcome to come anytime if you arrive with those." She paused for a moment. "Well, to be fair, I'd love a visit from you whenever you wanted to stop by, but the coffee and pie would be a bonus."

Bella laughed, feeling lighter than she had for a while. "I'll be there shortly."

She felt strange going to Dinah's alone. As she entered the door and all eyes focused on her, she felt like backing out and driving away as fast as she could. Before she could do that, Dinah herself said, "Welcome, Bella. Is it Bella Walker or Bella . . ."

"I kept my maiden name. Bella Bennett has a nice ring to it."

"It does at that."

"Cassie sent me here to get coffee and pie for us. I know that she adds cream to her coffee, but I don't know her favorite flavors of your pie."

"She tends to favor the fruit or chocolate pies when those are options. I made it easy for you today with chocolate chess pie." Dinah got busy boxing up a large slice, while Bella eyed the desserts.

"I'll have the lemon meringue and unsweet iced tea."

"You're a tea drinker, aren't you?"

"I am. Never coffee."

"I'll remember that. We have some nice flavors of hot tea, too, when the weather turns cooler." Dinah rattled off a few.

The odd thought that she'd still be here during the winter months didn't upset Bella as much as it would have in the past. With everything bagged and paid for, Bella left feeling almost like a local. Even the restaurants in Nashville that she frequented most didn't remember her favorites.

Bypassing the front, she went around to Cassie's back door with a bounce in her step. She did wonder when, if ever, she'd become accustomed to the use of a back door instead of the more obvious front. Another small-town quirk, apparently. Of course, the apartments she'd lived in during her adult life had only had the front door.

Growing up, her parents had both owned large houses in Texas—her mother's in Dallas and her father's in Houston—except for the years when Bella had been ten and eleven, when they'd remarried and then quickly divorced again after realizing they shouldn't have married either time.

With her background, it was a wonder that she'd gone into the wedding industry. Of course, her own married life hit quite a few unconventional notes, but it had started with a beautiful ceremony.

She tapped on the door, then opened it. "Cassie?"

"Come in. I'll be just a second."

Bella stepped through the kitchen and into the living room.

Her friend came down the hall from where Bella knew she had her office. "I see you brought goodies."

Bella held up the bag and cup holder. "I come bearing gifts."

"Yum. Let's go sit outside. I've needed a break. Romeo, you ready to go outside?" Her gray and white kitten zoomed around the corner and skidded to a stop.

Laughing, Bella trailed after him. "He seems to know what you meant."

"Either that, or he knows we take a break almost every afternoon and he gets to go outside. When it isn't raining, that is."

She opened the door, and Romeo shot outside.

Once she and Cassie were settled on chairs with their pie containers on their laps, drinks on the table between them, and Romeo happily chasing a butterfly, Cassie said, "I hope this isn't as monumental as the last conversation you wanted to have."

"Nothing like that," Bella said between bites. "Dinah's crust melts in my mouth. I'd love to be able to walk into a kitchen and make a pie this delicious."

"You're sounding uncharacteristically domestic. Is that what I have to look forward to with marriage?"

"It's probably more that I lost all my favorite restaurants, and I can no longer phone for delivery." She might also like to surprise Micah with great food one of these days. "I'm actually a good cook, remember? My grandmother taught me how to make everything from roast beef to soup."

Cassie frowned. "Why have you never cooked anything like that for me? You've only made simple meals."

"Again, we had restaurants. And I was super busy." She popped the last bite of pie in her mouth. "Mmm."

"Before we get on a food tangent—which with us is perfectly normal—you were going to tell me what you wanted."

"Right." Bella set the empty pie container next to her iced tea. "We need to drum up business for Main Street."

Cassie laughed. "Are you just now figuring that out? The town has been trying to do that for decades."

Bella winced. "Right. And I have a new shop on Main Street. The *only* shop on Main Street."

"Do you have any ideas?"

"I hoped the two of us would come up with something. Maybe something bridal or wedding-related since we both work in that industry."

"I honestly wish I had ideas. The bridal fair didn't go over too well a few weeks ago."

Except that Bella had gotten to spend time with Micah, which had led to her marrying the man. "What did you do to promote it? I stayed out of it until the day it happened."

"I sent an email to brides who had contacted me, but not scheduled anything yet. I thought they might be interested."

When her friend didn't say anything else, Bella asked, "That's it?"

"I hoped it would be enough. We only had, what, four people show up?"

"That was my count too. The space was small, though, so we couldn't have managed a much larger group." The park she'd passed earlier would be a better size for an event. "What if we held another fair in the Two Hearts Park?"

Cassie's face scrunched up. "It's a mess, and we'd still have to get people to drive here."

"We need to put it all over social media, send emails, and ask friends in the industry if they'll tell their clients. I think we could get enough people to come to make it worthwhile."

"We know a lot of people in Nashville. There's still the problem of the park. By the way, I have walked around the block a few times. I've caught glimpses of something in the back corner in that overgrown area. I'm not sure, but there might be a gazebo or bandstand under all those vines and weeds. It's probably half fallen down, but it could be something good if it's uncovered."

Bella started to smile. "Do you think we can do this? Bring in clients for our businesses? Maybe Simone would like to come, and a couple of other vendors, so it isn't just us sitting at a picnic table with brochures."

"Agreed. If we're going to do this, we should turn it into a real bridal fair. Let's talk to every vendor we know."

"Will the mayor like the idea of us using the park?"

"We're planning to bring people with deep pockets to Two Hearts, *and* we're going to improve the park? He'll be thrilled." Cassie shrugged. "He liked the paparazzi from Carly and Jake's wedding."

Bella stood. "Seriously? No one wants paparazzi."

"The mayor loved the attention to the town."

An image of hoards of paparazzi showing up and being welcomed by the high school band and a parade made Bella grin.

"The mayor has supported everything I've done, but I know for certain he wanted to retire a decade ago. No one else will take the position."

"He made it through the wedding ceremony, but there were moments when he seemed to forget what he wanted to say."

"I was worried a time or two. He's done good work, but I think he'd happily step down. You know, Mrs. Brantley took charge of getting Two Hearts cleaned up and ready for Carly and Jake's wedding. She'd be perfect."

"Greg's mother?" At Cassie's nod, Bella continued, "Should we ask her to help with our bridal fair?"

"Now that you mention it, before we go any further with this, let's get her feedback. She knows this town better than I do. She'll be able to tell us if this is a good idea."

Everyone knew Two Hearts better than Bella did. "I sure

hope it is, because it's the only idea I've got. Wedding Bella has to succeed."

Cassie hugged her. "Don't worry. My business is picking up. If I can make it here, so can you. Do you want to go to see her now?"

Bella checked her phone. "I have a new client who says she'll be here at two o'clock. It's a quarter till now, so I'd better head back."

"Come back here when you're done. Then we can go to Mrs. Brantley's house together."

Bella parked down the street from her shop so she could leave room for customers, as silly as that seemed when she walked down the sidewalk to her business. Every parking space was empty except for the one she'd just taken. Her employees had parked in the small lot behind the building.

Inside, she checked to make sure everything was ready for Penelope. The dressing room with its satin robe would welcome her. One dress in several sizes in each of the major silhouettes—ball gown, mermaid, fit and flare, A-line, sheath, and even tea-length in case she wanted to go short—hung from the rack to the left side of the shop.

Bella caught herself overdoing the preparation when she straightened the same dress on the hanger a second time. Would Penelope drive from Nashville? Would anyone, especially clients who hadn't met her and established a relationship, make that drive?

At exactly two, a car pulled up into the space directly in front of the store, and two women got out, one about twenty-five and bubbly looking and the other twice her age, and, from the frown on her face as she looked up and down the street, none too happy about their destination. Before they could leave, Bella hurried over to the door to open it for them.

"Welcome!"

The older woman said "Thank you?" with her rising tone at

the end making her hesitation clear. She smiled when she stepped inside. "This is lovely!"

"May I show you samples of different styles of dresses? Please keep in mind that these are only samples. Your dress will be custom made for you, Penelope."

"Nice. Nice. Very nice." The mother oohed and aahed over them.

"I told you Miss Bella was known for making pretty dresses."

CHAPTER TWENTY-ONE

Bella and Cassie tossed ideas back and forth as they walked over to Mrs. Brantley's.

"We're going to get advice, but I'm starting to realize that we can't do all of this on our own, Bella." Cassie waved the list of tasks she carried. "You and I are still newcomers to Two Hearts. Not only that, but this event is going to take a lot of work. Top of the list is cleaning up the park and bringing it back to life."

"We'll need to see what's in all that brush in case there's a building we can use for the event."

"Well, if there's something that's been hidden in the underbrush for decades, it probably isn't in good enough shape to use two weeks from now."

Bella started a to-do list on her phone. "So there's clearing the park out. That will take money, and the town doesn't seem to have much of that."

"I have considered that this afternoon. We will have to pay for everything."

Bella spoke slowly, "Did you forget that I don't have much money right now?"

"If we're frugal, I can pay for it."

She didn't like owing money to a friend, but this felt like their best plan. "I'll pay back my half as soon as I can."

"I know you will."

After adding this to her list of bills to be paid, Bella mentally shifted to the event itself. "Our first job will be to find out who's willing to attend the event as a vendor. Do you think anybody in this town would want to come?"

Cassie shrugged. "I suppose there's Dinah. She did cater your wedding. Granted, it was a simple event—"

"But we keep hearing from everyone how much they loved the food. Sometimes people just want traditional foods instead of caviar."

"I know I always want foods other than caviar. Something about fish eggs does not appeal to me no matter how high-end it is."

"So, Dinah. Anyone else?"

Cassie thought it over. "Maybe Randi from the motel. She could do a bridal or weekend package that includes breakfast at Dinah's."

"That's good."

Cassie tapped her finger on the notepad. "It seems to me that the first step is getting approval for this."

"It seems to *me* that the first step is to talk to someone like Mrs. Brantley to see if they think it's possible in that park. And if it could be pulled off in a couple of weeks. I really need to drum up some business—and in a hurry. Here I am with a shop on Main Street in the same place where one failed decades ago."

"Don't talk that way. It will all work out. If brides are willing to come out here for me, they'll be willing to come out here for you."

"Wedding dresses are different. If they know they want a dress from me, it's easy. They will come. But you know how many brides want to try on dresses in several stores before they choose one. Will they go to two stores in Nashville and then drive all the way out here for a third?"

"They will if you have a reputation that draws them out here."

"The Michelsons trashed my reputation, so that isn't going to happen."

"They didn't. They made some whispers that can't undo all your good work. Ignore them and move forward. You had that bride today."

"Penelope."

"She drove out here. If you get a couple of wedding dresses done and people talk them up again, everything will be back to normal."

She certainly hoped it would.

They stopped in front of Mrs. Brantley's house. "I called earlier to confirm she would be home and was up for company. She's excited that we're coming. She loves people so much that it's a shame she's sitting alone all day long."

Mrs. Brantley let them inside, while Cookie bounced around them. Mrs. Brantley said, "Cookie, sit." The dog's rump hit the ground. But her tail swiftly swished back and forth on the wooden floor.

Laughing, Cassie said, "You're being a good girl, aren't you?" She crouched and scratched the dog behind her ears.

As she stood, Mrs. Brantley said, "Bella told me about her wedding, then we discussed having a shop in town. Is there monumental news today too?" She looked from Cassie to Bella.

Cassie answered. "We have an idea, and we wanted to run it by you first to see what you think of it."

"Let's talk in the kitchen. I have hot-out-of-the-oven peanut butter cookies."

It was like the woman had a sixth sense allowing her to bake right before someone stopped by. She had whenever Bella had visited in the short time she'd lived here. "How do you always have something warm from the oven?"

Mrs. Brantley chuckled. "Sometimes, it's just because I baked, as it was with the brownies. Today, it's because I had frozen some cookie dough, and I was able to pull it out and put it in the oven for you." She leaned closer. "Now that you know my secret, you have to keep it to yourself."

Cassie and Bella were both grinning as they sat down. Once Mrs. Brantley was assured that they had the cookies and beverages they needed, she took her place at the table. "What do you have in mind?"

"Our idea is to hold a bridal fair in Two Hearts," Bella explained. "We would invite as many vendors as we could think of to have tables there, and then we'd get brides to come here to attend it. They'll see Two Hearts, which may make them want to come back, and hopefully both Cassie and I will get more weddings scheduled."

Mrs. Brantley shrugged. "It sounds great in theory. In fact, I love the idea. Where are you planning to hold the event?"

"Here you have our problem. The one idea we have is to use the park. To clean it up and use that whole space with tables. If the weather is forecast to not be great, we could put up tents."

She nodded thoughtfully. "It's possible that we could use the band stand if it's still in good shape."

"I knew there was something tucked back in there!"

"It hasn't been touched in decades, so it has probably fallen down. You know, I'm not sure how the town got so lost. We didn't have any hope left until you rode in here, Cassie."

Her friend turned bright red. That was a sight to behold on a fair-skinned redhead. "It was easier for a stranger to see the potential."

"You may be right. Now I see potential all around me. I just have to figure out how to get the people and the funds to make it happen."

Cassie asked, "Have you talked to the mayor?"

Mrs. Brantley rolled her eyes. That surprised Bella because she was always so reserved and in control. Never a bad word about anyone or anything. "He's a good man. And he did a good job with what he had at the time, but it's time for someone else to step up and assume the role."

Cassie and Bella looked at each other. Cassie broached the subject. "Has anyone expressed an interest in the position?"

She shook her head. "No one. One man considered it a few years ago. Let me think. More like five or ten years ago."

"What about a woman?"

Mrs. Brantley pursed her lips as she pondered that. "I don't see any reason why not. The town's never had a woman mayor, but she would certainly be as good as any man."

Bella opened her mouth, the words *What about you?*—on the tip of her tongue, but Cassie nudged her and shook her head slightly. She was right. Mrs. Brantley needed to let the idea of a female mayor sink in before they said anything more.

"Is there anywhere else that we could do the event?" Bella asked instead.

"There's the lake. We used to have a picnic area out there and a dock for the town."

Cassie said, "I've heard the lake mentioned a time or two, but I've never seen it. You say there's a park out there?"

Mrs. Brantley got a faraway look. "There was a park. You remember that we had hot springs. The water from the springs flowed into the lake, so they were close to each other, and both had recreational areas. We had picnics out there and July Fourth celebrations." She sighed. "The lake's shoreline is overgrown and inaccessible except for cleared areas around the few cabins on the shore that are still maintained. The man who owns the grocery store goes out there to his cabin every weekend and fishes. He pretty much has the place to himself."

Bella considered the idea. "I'm not sure that's the location for a bridal fair."

"I think we can do the park more easily, if I understand the situation."

"Oh, you're understanding it correctly, Cassie." Mrs. Brantley gave them a rueful smile. "The lake area would necessitate bringing all the public grounds back to life, probably redoing the dock because it would be unsafe, and replacing the picnic tables. That would take a lot more work and money."

Bella shifted in her seat. "It does sound expensive." A trace of panic swept through her.

"There are—*were*—some pretty houses on the lake. I used to notice one every time I passed it. When I last saw it, I could tell it needed a lot of work." After another lengthy sigh, she added, "I think for what you ladies are interested in, the city park is easiest. We can get Justin on the cleanup soon. I'm not sure about the expense even for that, though, to the city's coffers. We probably can't manage more than a very small amount."

Cassie held her hands up in a *stop* motion. "Don't worry about that. We're going to take care of the expenses. We need to keep costs down, of course. But we hope and pray that this will be a way to bring in business and that it will more than pay for itself in the end."

"In that case, let's get started." Mrs. Brantley looked down at the table in front of her. "Once we finish our cookies. Always go with the pleasant things in life first."

Words to live by.

Once they'd eaten every crumb of what turned out to be some of the best cookies Bella had ever had—this woman could open a bakery—they started on a walk over to the park.

A minute or two into their walk down the sidewalk, Mrs. Brantley suddenly stopped. "The more I think about this, the more I realize that we do need to run this past the mayor first. He is getting older and is perhaps not as capable as he might have been in the past, but he's still the mayor, and we ought to bring something like this in front of him."

Disappointment rushed through Bella. "That means we won't be able to take care of this today then, doesn't it?"

"Not at all. I happen to know that our good mayor is at the diner every day at this time. He's a fixture there." Mrs. Brantley took off at a pace that had Bella and Cassie hurrying to catch up. When this woman was determined, there was nothing stopping her. They arrived at the diner with Bella wiping the sweat off her brow.

Inside, they found the mayor, exactly as Mrs. Brantley had said they would. He had dozed off in his chair across the room with a cup of coffee in front of him. The older woman paused for a moment with them just inside the restaurant. "There was a day when no man could best him, but I think it's time for him to retire."

Dinah stopped clearing the table that she was working on. "Are you here to see the mayor?"

Cassie answered. "We are."

"Someone"—Dinah leveled her gaze at Mrs. Brantley —"needs to step in to take over the job." She leaned closer to them and lowered her voice. "Last week, Michelle happened to catch him as he fell forward into his soup. The man might have drowned in my restaurant."

Mrs. Brantley turned toward her and spoke with excitement in her voice. "You're a strong woman, Dinah. I bet you'd be an amazing mayor."

Dinah put her hand on her hip. "If you think I've got time to take on anything else, you are mistaken, Emmaline. This place keeps me busy all day long. I am so glad when the Lord's day comes around and I can relax."

"Are you unhappy with your business, Dinah?"

She laughed. "I love it. But it does keep a body busy. No, what we need for a mayor is someone who has free time. Maybe their children are grown, and they're looking for the next interesting thing to do in life."

Bella hid her grin behind her hand. Subtlety, it seemed, was not Dinah's strong suit.

"We need to think about that. For right now, we'll head on over and talk to him." Mrs. Brantley started on her way and added, "Oh, my. Once we've woken him up."

Dinah turned toward Bella and shook her head as Mrs. Brantley crossed the room. In a quiet voice, she said, "You know, she'd make the best mayor the city's ever seen. She'd help us."

"I'm starting to see that myself. Has anyone asked her?"

"No. Emmaline needs to come to the idea on her own." Still shaking her head, Dinah went back to gathering up the plates and glasses from the vacated table.

Bella hurried to join Cassie and Mrs. Brantley.

The mayor was now up and awake but still groggy. "Ladies, to what do I owe the honor of this visit?"

"There's a project we would like to talk to you about, Mayor." Mrs. Brantley seemed to want to lead the conversation. That was fine with Bella. "Everyone, please be seated." She motioned to the table.

The mayor rubbed his eyes. "Emmaline, explain the concept."

When she began by saying Cassie and Bella would be paying for the expenses of the park's renovation, the mayor's eyes lit up.

"I've started to get up in years," said the man who had to be approaching ninety or might have already passed it. "I think it would be best to have someone else spearhead projects like this." He focused on Mrs. Brantley as he said that.

She leaned forward, interested. "That sounds like a good idea to me. Take some of the weight off your shoulders. Did you have someone in mind?"

The woman really had no idea of her actual worth in this town, did she?

"There was someone who stood out when we had to prepare the town for that country music star's wedding. She went above and beyond. Everything was tracked and kept in order. In fact, I can say that the results wouldn't have been as successful if she hadn't taken the reins and brought the preparation for the event all the way to its beautiful conclusion."

Mrs. Brantley sat quietly as she listened. Then she sat up straight. "Are you talking about me?" she asked in an uncertain voice.

"I am. If you would take care of this, I would be eternally grateful."

"I'll do it. I'm a natural-born organizer."

The mayor clapped his hands with happiness. "That you are. I knew I could count on you." They started to get up, but the mayor put his hand on Mrs. Brantley's arm. "Emmaline, I'd actually like to give the whole job of mayor to you. Would you be willing to consider that?"

Mrs. Brantley dropped back into her chair. "You can't be serious?" Some of her usual fire was back now.

"I've never been more serious. I want you to consider running for the position."

"I'm sure there are many good people in this town who would be better suited to it."

"I don't think there's another person who could lead us the way you would into what seems to be the rebirth of Two Hearts. We have Cassie and Bella here. Two young ladies who are doing great things for the town they've just come to."

Bella thought about her motivation, and shame flooded her. Right now, she needed to survive. Maybe she could do something nice for the town later when her life settled down. People here had been nothing but kind to her.

"Mayor, I will certainly consider that idea." This time Mrs. Brantley did stand.

"Talk it over with Greg. He has a good head on his shoulders. And your daughter too."

She gave a nod. "I will." She looked at Bella and Cassie. "It's time for us to get started on a bridal fair, ladies."

Bella wanted to shout with joy. If they could pull this off, she might finally be able to bring her business back to life.

Bella and Cassie were soon seated in Cassie's office. Bella sat on the other side of the big wooden desk, watching as her friend emailed all the vendors she'd worked with, which was not just dozens but hundreds when you considered every business large and small.

Bella tapped her fingers on the desk. "I feel like I should be doing something too. I don't have vendors like you do. Should we invite brides we've worked with? They are married—well, I hope most of them are still married—so they don't need a bridal fair."

Cassie stopped with her fingers on her keyboard. "Many of them are in their twenties and thirties. They probably have friends or relatives tying the knot."

"Very true." Bella opened the laptop she'd brought and powered it up. An hour later, she let out a massive sigh.

"How are you doing? This is my last one to send." Cassie tapped a key. "I don't want to look at my computer again today." She stretched her arms over her head.

"I have some more." A few minutes later, Bella sent the last message. "You know, Cassie, I went through my entire list of clients. I wonder if I sent one to someone who went with another designer in the end."

"Don't worry about it. Unless they hated you, you're just inviting them to an event."

"I like the way you think." Bella shut off her computer and closed it. "It's probably too late today to hear back from anyone. Maybe we'll check tomorrow morning and find replies saying yes."

"I'm so excited I can barely stand it. Where are you off to now?" Cassie began tidying up her desk.

"I'm going back to my shop to see where we are on a couple of dresses. Then I'm going home."

"To Micah?"

Bella shrugged. "It's strange, but his home is mine right now. There are perks."

"Like a kiss in the morning?"

Bella swatted at Cassie's arm. "Like dinners and desserts being dropped off. I wonder what tonight's dish will be."

They walked out of the office and down the hall.

"I had so many sweets and other food when I moved here that I shared them with everyone who stopped by," Cassie said. "I got to know Greg better when I fed him lunch."

Bella nudged her. "That worked out well." She checked her phone. "Micah's been getting home before me. No calls from him, so dinner hasn't been dropped off yet. Last night's was tuna noodle casserole."

"Yum. That's one of my favorites."

Bella grimaced. "I *hate* tuna noodle casserole. To be fair, it was probably a world-class meal, and Micah enjoyed it."

Cassie laughed. "Tonight's should be better."

Bella pictured her former tiny apartment in Nashville. Even it had multiple restaurants she could walk to or that were a short drive away. "I miss being able to go to a restaurant on a whim. Small-town life has been okay, but there's nowhere in Two Hearts to have dinner out after a long day."

CHAPTER TWENTY-TWO

Micah watched out the window, waiting for Bella to arrive, and becoming concerned when she wasn't home by 5:30 when he expected her. A few minutes later, she pulled into the driveway and parked.

He opened the door as she came up the sidewalk. "I have a little surprise for you."

"Recent surprises haven't always been pleasant, but since you're smiling, this must be a good one." Bella stepped into the house and set her purse on the side table.

"You know that restaurant we had lunch at with my grandfather?"

"Yes," she said slowly. "Southern Somethings."

"The chef grew up in Two Hearts and is a friend."

As his smile grew, hers dimmed. Had he said something wrong?

"Did you drive to Nashville for takeout? Please tell me you don't have food that sat for a couple of hours in your vehicle."

Laughing, he said, "No—"

"Micah! I forgot to bring the paprika. Do you have any?" his friend called from the kitchen.

He didn't even know what paprika was. "I only have that if my grandmother bought it."

Bella loudly said, "There's a fresh bottle in the cupboard to the left of the stove."

He heard a door open and close.

"Thank you."

To Micah, she said, "Some of the herbs and spices had been there a while. I bought a fresh batch at the store the other day."

"If you know how to cook, how come . . ."

Exhaustion seemed to pull her down to the couch. "I've been too busy to think about anything but surviving, Micah. I got a lot done today." Then she perked up. "But this has been an excellent day."

"See! I said you'd do well. How many customers did you have?"

Before she could answer, his friend stepped out of the kitchen carrying a loaded tray along with some small plates. "Appetizers are ready. Dinner will be in about twenty-five minutes."

Micah took the tray from him and set it on the coffee table in front of Bella. "Thank you, Nick. This is my wife, Bella."

The plates slipped, but Nick grabbed them before they went too far. "You said you wanted me to cook for 'Bella.' You didn't mention you'd married her!"

"I guess that was an important detail I forgot to share, wasn't it?"

"Perhaps. Could you help me in the kitchen for a moment, Micah?"

Since he was completely useless anywhere near a stove and Nick certainly knew that, he knew this had nothing to do with food preparation.

As soon as the kitchen door swung shut behind him, Nick said, "You said you wanted to impress a woman with a meal from my restaurant. Didn't you already impress her enough to marry you?" A flicker of knowledge seemed to hit his friend. "Wait. Your marriage is in trouble, and you're trying to use food to save it? I mean, my food is good, but—"

"Wait! No. You jumped to conclusions. It isn't that I'm trying to win over my wife." Well, actually he kind of was, but for different reasons. "It's that we got married so quickly that she doesn't really know me very well."

Nick put one hand on his hip. "You're saying you don't know your wife? I've always known you to get along quite well with the ladies. What happened with this one?"

"Let's say that I asked her to move to Two Hearts, and she's always lived in a big city."

Realization dawned in Nick's eyes. "Oh, now I see. You want to make the small town feel familiar. You want it to seem like the city."

Micah grinned. "Exactly!

"Micah, I hate to burst your bubble. I mean, you've been my friend for most of my life. Two Hearts isn't the city. During dinner, it may feel that way. With the unique addition of your grandmother's flowered couches and chairs. You have to make Bella fall in love with Two Hearts."

That wasn't good news. Probably because every word was true. "You're right. But how do I do that?"

Nick shook his head. "I'm not sure. Two Hearts is a good place, but it's not Nashville. You're going to have to figure that one out. A small town has things to offer. I have to say that I kind of miss it sometimes."

"Maybe you could open a restaurant here." Micah meant it as a joke.

Nick nodded thoughtfully. "I'm seeing changes. Just driving down Main Street tonight. Wow! Cleaned up, it seems to have a new lease on life."

"I'd better get back to Bella."

"She must be a winner if she managed to get you to the altar. She's a special woman."

Micah glanced over his shoulder with his hand on the door. "I've started to realize that."

A moment later, he was back in the living room with Bella and hoping she would enjoy the meal.

"Micah, how did you talk him into coming over here to cook? It's a long drive from the city to make dinner for a couple." She didn't voice the next words that came to mind: *And very expensive.*

He looked down at the floor for a moment and then into her eyes. "I knew that you were missing the restaurants. Dinah's a great cook—"

"She really is."

"But it's just her. In the city, you can pick and choose where you want to eat day-to-day and go to more than one place in a single day. Not in Two Hearts. At least not until now." He sat on the couch, but not too close to Bella, per her rules.

She leaned closer to him, completely breaking the rules. "What's on the menu?"

Micah did his best to appear unaffected by her nearness. "I have absolutely no idea. But he said it would be delicious."

Bella laughed. "Well, if the wonderful scents are anything to go by, he is correct. I know I enjoyed the lunch we had there. What little of it I remember after the bombshells your grandfather dropped on us."

"I am sorry about all that."

She waved his comment away. "That wasn't your fault. Besides, I think we're figuring things out anyway. Don't you?"

"Yes. I've been surprised at how well we've done."

Bella cocked her head to the side as though she were thinking about something. "Micah, your grandfather didn't stop by when I wasn't here, did he?"

"I haven't seen him since our lunch." He blew out a breath. "I hope we aren't going to get an unexpected visitor in the near future. My grandfather is wily enough to want to keep us on our toes with the mere mention of visiting."

"Maybe that's all it will be then? A threat." She quickly corrected herself. "I mean a promise."

"No, you probably got it right the first time. I've obviously known him all my life, and I'm still not sure if he will or won't show up here."

"Well, I like the pattern we have for our lives. We're still getting the nightly food deliveries from the townspeople. Life is good here."

She thought life was good in Two Hearts? *Focus, Micah. Focus.* "We got off track. How many clients did you have today?"

"One." Her flat tone of voice told him all he needed to know. She hadn't done well today.

"That's not normal, right? Don't you need more to succeed?"

She nodded.

"But you looked happy when you walked in the door. I'm a man, and we don't always pick up on those details, but even I know those things don't go together."

She smiled. "Cassie and I had an idea. We pulled Greg's mother into it, and the mayor agrees, too."

Micah's eyes grew wider as she went on. "You have been busy. What are you planning to do?"

"We're going to have a bridal fair in Two Hearts." Excitement bubbled in her voice.

Micah leaned closer to the tray of appetizers. "Tell me all about it while we eat what looks to be something delicious."

"I've tried everything, and it's all wonderful." She pointed at a small square. "I believe it's brie baked into puff pastry."

"I love brie." He grabbed one and popped it in his mouth. "Yum!"

"We have a lot to do in the next two weeks."

He paused with another bite halfway to his mouth. "Two weeks!"

"Yes. I need business to pick up and to do that in a hurry. If we can bring all this together quickly—and it works as we hope it will—then I'll have new clients for the future."

He could read the panic in both her voice and on her face. Building her shop was one thing, but they had to figure out a way to get people to come.

"We want to hold the fair in the city park. It's going to take a lot of work to get it ready. The area around the swing set is being maintained, but grass has grown high in some areas."

"So, the area where Greg and Cassie held their engagement party needs to be mowed? That shouldn't take too long. I could borrow someone's riding lawn mower and get it done one day after work."

Her eyes lit up, and he knew he would do anything—within the bounds of the law—to make that happen again.

"That's so sweet of you!" She chewed on her lip for a moment. "But Cassie, Mrs. Brantley, and I were talking. We'd like for the whole park to be refurbished. Have everything beautiful before the event."

"I don't think that's possible. That back side of the park has been a tangle of weeds and brush since I was a kid. I'm not sure about the current condition of anything under that."

She leaned forward excitedly. "After I talked to Cassie, I went by to look more closely. I think there's something wooden in there. Maybe it was white at one time. Mrs. Brantley remembers a bandstand or something like that."

A picture formed in his mind from long ago. "I don't know how I forgot about this. We must have been about ten years old, Greg and I and a few other guys." He looked up at her. "We didn't bring the girls along for adventures we considered to be rugged and manly."

"But of course you're more open-minded today, aren't you?"

She gave him a look that said there was one safe answer to that question.

He grinned. "Of course. But on this particular day, we decided to find out what was under all that brush. We tried to come in from one side and then another. It was thick, and so tangled that none of us could get through. It must have been a spring when we'd had a lot of rain followed by sunshine, the perfect formula for plants to grow. Finally, Greg pushed through a hole between some of the brush. And disappeared."

"He's alive today, so I have to assume nothing ate him."

Micah chuckled. "No. We didn't find any wild animals inside. Thankfully. We found that building you're talking about. Parts of it were still white then. It had a base and columns, at least from what we could see. Sunlight barely filtered through, and vines covered most of the building too."

She shuddered. "Sounds creepy."

"It does sound scary, but we loved it."

"What happened?"

"We all ran into the center of the building and were horsing around. Then Greg's foot went through a board, and the boy next to him also went down. I jumped out of the way. But they were stuck."

"You went to get help?"

"Are you kidding? We were a bunch of preteen boys. We were in a place we probably shouldn't have been. No, the rest of us pulled the two of them out. The one guy was limping, so we dragged him through the hole in the brush and *then* called for help."

"So, from that moment until this, you haven't been back inside?"

"We fixed it up. And it became our fort."

"But you broke it."

"Albert over at the hardware store—"

"He was there even when you were a kid?"

"I suspect that Albert must have been born in that hardware store. He's been there so long. His father and his grandfather also ran it. Anyway, Albert gave us a scrap piece of wood when we asked for one. Having been a boy himself, he didn't ask what we needed it for." Micah grinned. "We made the tunnel through the brush big enough to bring that through. After patching up the building with a few nails and a hammer borrowed from my dad, we had one of the coolest boys' forts I've ever seen."

"Then what happened?"

"Girls."

"Girls found your hideout and took it over? What did they do, paint everything with flowers? Something had to make you run away from that place."

"No. We discovered girls. I doubt any of us have thought of that place since then. It was standing—more or less—" He wavered his hand back and forth. "About fifteen—no, make that twenty years ago."

Her face fell. "Parts of it had already rotted away then. I had really hoped we could set something up on it, maybe the table where we greeted brides for the event. Or we could have a musical group playing there if it turned out to be a decent place for that. Something to make the park so appealing that brides would be interested in staying longer in Two Hearts. I want them to come to my shop for their dresses and consider having their weddings here with Cassie."

He considered who he could call to try to salvage the old building, and then he remembered that Emmaline Brantley was on the job. "Do you want my help, or is this all taken care of now?"

Her face lit up at his offer. She needed to stop doing that, because it tugged at his heart too much every single time.

"We would love help. Mrs. Brantley is going to recruit Justin and the teenagers to pitch in by mowing and maybe plant some flowers. But I don't think they would be the people to work around a possibly rotting structure. I think we need someone who's older than that, someone who's going to be more observant because they know about buildings more. I don't want anyone injured."

"Good point. Then I am going to get on the phone and call a bunch of people to see who we can gather together." As he thought about it, the list of boys who had been part of the original fort crew came to mind one by one. Unfortunately, half of them had moved away for work. "I'm on it. You know, I wouldn't have thought doing this in two weeks would be possible until miracles were accomplished for the country-music wedding. And you said you had Greg's mother on board with this?" At her quick nod, he continued. "She certainly proved herself to be a good leader at that wedding."

"It's funny you should say that. The mayor asked her today if she would take over for him."

"On this project?

"Yes. He put her in charge of this, but he also asked about her becoming mayor of Two Hearts."

"We would need an election."

"I don't know the laws surrounding it, but I get the impression that if she volunteered to do the job, no one in town would argue. She'd get every vote. Am I wrong about that, though? I'm new to Two Hearts."

When she said she was "new" to the town and not "temporarily here," his heart did a funny leap into his throat. Did she feel like she belonged here?

"Micah?"

"I guess I should look at the law first."

"Naturally so."

"But you are absolutely correct. If someone competent was on the ballot, she or he would be elected." He chose another of the appetizers. "I've always loved cantaloupe wrapped in prosciutto. Delicious." Micah popped it in his mouth.

"Don't sound so surprised. You did hire the man and ask him to come here. You must like what he cooks." Bella leaned back in her seat.

"You seem to be happy."

"This is a real treat." She put her hand on his arm, and he turned toward her. Staring into her eyes, he wanted to kiss her. But he thought that so many times during the day when she was nearby. If only they were really married.

She lifted her hand off his arm and put it on his cheek. "Thank you," she whispered.

He leaned forward.

"I'm sure you're hungry. Dinner will be in a few minutes now," his friend called from the kitchen.

They sprang apart, and Bella moved over several inches on the couch.

"Oh look! The mail arrived. Was there anything for me?" She jumped to her feet and went over to check.

When Nick announced the food was ready, Micah directed Bella to sit at the table, pulling out the chair for her first. Then he went into the kitchen and came back with a plate in each hand. "Is there anything else I can get you?"

His nervousness was adorable. "I can't tell yet because I haven't taken a bite of the food. But it looks lovely." She smiled at him, and he hurriedly took his chair across from her. "I want to thank you for doing this. I know we will have a food delivery, but it's wonderful to have a full, gourmet meal after what turned out to be a very long day of work."

He unfolded the cloth napkin he'd found in his grandmother's linen closet, having placed one beside each of their place settings, and put it on his lap. "I do takeout brilliantly. I may have to look into making some meals myself, though. My mother did send me a slow cooker last year for Christmas, or maybe it was the year before."

Bella took a bite of some chicken with sauce. "Oh my, this is wonderful."

They ate in silence for a few minutes, occasionally exclaiming over the wonderful food.

"Dinner was superb, but I don't want you to think that I need a meal like this every single night. I often came home from work and made a salad with whatever I had on hand. Easy is fine with me. Besides"—she grinned at him—"that slow cooker is probably still in the box, isn't it?"

"Good guess. But it does make me a little nervous that you know me that well already."

She laughed. "It isn't just you. It's so many men. Some men venture into the world of cooking. Like your friend. But the rest of them . . ." She shook her head. "So many survive on whatever they can find. One thing I do not miss is fast food. So don't help me out with a bag of burgers."

He chuckled. "I promise I won't do that."

Nick stepped out. "When you're ready for dessert, let me know."

Micah said, "Nick, this is absolutely fabulous. But I know you've got a long drive back into the city tonight. If you want to leave—"

"No. I'm staying the night with Mom and Dad. They still have my old room locked in time. There's a poster with a famous chef taped over my childhood desk." He winced. "Most teenagers wouldn't have done that, but I knew what I wanted to do with my life."

"I remember that. He had his own TV show, didn't he?"

"He did. I would still like to follow in his footsteps with that."

"'Still'? You're only in your early thirties. I think you've got some time to figure that one out."

Nick took off his apron. "I think I will take you up on

leaving now, though. I have enough dessert to share with my family, so I'm going to go over there and visit with them. I need to get up early to be back to work in the morning." He sighed. "I wish there was something I could figure out to do in this town. I love my job, but sometimes the stress . . ."

Bella knew what he meant. She wouldn't have been able to identify that a year ago, because she'd loved the life she'd led. But she was already starting to enjoy the slower pace of a small town. It wasn't that no one worked. Sometimes, they worked very hard. They just didn't seem to be doing it in a frantic, running-around sort of way.

An idea came to mind. "Nick, do you cater functions?"

"You mean like this one?" He gestured toward their table. "No. I did this for a friend."

"No, I mean like a wedding. Have you ever done that?"

Micah turned toward her. "I see where you're going with this. Cassie uses caterers, doesn't she?"

"Every wedding has at least one."

Nick shook his head. "The event would have to be large to make it worth my while. More than the standard Two Hearts fare."

Micah chuckled. "Her best friend is a wedding planner. You know who Carly Daniels is, right?"

A look of realization came over Nick's face. "Are you telling me she's the one who arranged that for Carly? I know I saw something about it when I was at the grocery store one day. They love to plaster celebrity weddings on the front of the magazines they tempt you with near the checkout."

"Not just that. It was here in Two Hearts."

"Are you telling me that was held in this middle-of-nowhere town that died decades ago?"

Bella shrugged. "And it was gorgeous."

"I couldn't survive by catering an event every once in a

while. It's something to consider, though. We may have to get together and talk about it sometime."

Nick gathered up his things and left while they ate what he called a plum tart. It was similar to a pie with a crust on the bottom and sides, had a layer of creamy custard, and was topped with thinly sliced plums arranged in a circular pattern and a clear glaze. It was one of the most beautiful and delicious desserts she'd ever had.

"Micah, I wonder how Dinah would feel about someone coming into town to cook."

His fork clattered onto his plate. "I hadn't thought of that. She has been the one person in town for years."

"Cassie has brought in caterers, so nothing would change if that was all he did. Besides, I think we could use a second restaurant. Something that was open in the evenings would be very nice."

"That is true. You have to get to Dinah's Place for an early dinner or you're out of luck. But I never have blamed Dinah for doing it that way. She's serving breakfast in the wee hours of the morning and must be exhausted by the end of the day."

CHAPTER TWENTY-THREE

After a busy morning, Bella brewed a travel cup of Irish breakfast tea and walked to Cassie's house for an update. They sat outside, and Romeo chased a butterfly. "I hope you have replies to your emails, because I don't have any."

"Not a one. I have checked for responses so often that I'm not getting anything else done today."

"I guess it's still early in the day. If this doesn't work, I may have to have a barely-there business for the next year. Then I can move back to the city after—"

"Don't think that way." Cassie checked her phone. "Wait, Bella, I just received confirmation from two vendors that they'd like to attend. Check your messages."

Bella took her phone out of her purse. "Cassie, I have a text from Honoré Michelson."

"The woman who started all this?"

Bella gave a slow nod. "One and the same."

Cassie was looking through the emails. "What does she say?"

Bella set her phone on her lap. "I have no idea. I am not going to open anything from her. Ever. That ended so badly that

I ended up getting married to a man I barely knew and moving here. To a small town."

"I do see your point. But I'd have a hard time not opening it to see what she wanted."

"I have no such problem." Bella changed subjects. "Are your vendors willing to put money down on tables?"

"Better than that. One of them would like to be a co-sponsor with us and have a larger sign at the front. Do we want to do that?"

"That probably depends on who it is."

"It's my main vendor for tents."

"Hmm. What if they provide tents for the event and we prominently display their name to say they provided them?" Bella could see their event coming to life.

"Wonderful idea. Then we're protected, rain or shine."

"Exactly. Everybody is happy. And who else confirmed?"

"Someone from a classical music group that I use fairly often at weddings. They even sent a deposit online."

"Does that mean we can have live music set up in the corner of the tent we're getting for free?"

"Oh, my, you are good at this. I'm supposed to be the planner." Cassie tapped on her phone. "I replied to both of them."

Bella checked her phone again. "Now I'm getting responses too. One is the sister of a bride I designed for. Another one is from a bride who came into my Nashville shop but didn't commit to a dress. She wants to know if she can try on wedding gowns at the fair." She frowned. "I hadn't thought about that. How would I manage it?"

"It's easy. You're what, maybe four or five blocks from your business? Anyone who has that much interest can be sent over there to have one of your people show them dresses and let them try on a couple. You could step away from the fair if it looked like you were needed."

"The tent vendor sent an enthusiastic reply." Cassie continued after a moment of staring at her phone. "They'll give us their largest tent for the day as long as they can post their sign next to it. I think this is going to work, Bella. Oh, now I've gotten a couple from brides who want to come out to Two Hearts to consider a wedding here." Her friend glowed. "Every time I get a new bride to visit Two Hearts, it brings me that much closer to making my business succeed so far from the city."

"Cassie, you got approval from the tent guy, and you're waiting to hear from the musician, but what about tables? We're going to have to spend money to rent them."

"I haven't heard yet from any of my table vendors. Let's see if we can get them free too."

Micah parked his truck at the city park. When he looked to the left, he saw the swing set area with fresh mulch under it. Straight ahead, Justin was riding a mower, and some of the other teenagers were cleaning up, apparently under the direction of Greg's mother, who was standing to the side and watching closely. Then she turned and walked away.

He had always respected her as a parent because she explained how to do something and then she expected you to figure it out. That was probably part of what had helped Greg become a man who could think independently as a police officer.

When he looked beyond Mrs. Brantley, he saw the tumble of vines and trees and heaven only knew what else that had accumulated in the back of this park during his lifetime. What must it be like to grow up in a town that would never let this happen?

Mrs. Brantley called him as he stepped out of his truck, now loaded with pruning tools and other gardening equipment. "Bella tells me you're going to be spearheading the cleanup process." She pointed to the mess he'd just been looking at.

Was he? Yes, he'd pretty much volunteered to do that, so he was now in charge of it. *Never say you're willing to do something if you aren't.* "I have Greg and some of the other guys coming. Greg can't get here until this afternoon because he's on duty."

Her gaze narrowed as she approached him. "I know that you boys had your fort here when you were kids, but that doesn't mean that women can't help on this project, now, does it?"

It had never once occurred to him that any adults had known about their fort. It had been their secret place. Only apparently, it had not been.

"You can let it be known that any woman who wants to help can."

"That sounds like a good plan." Mrs. Brantley frowned. "Do you have anything to protect yourself from snakes?"

Micah froze in his footsteps. "You know, we never saw any snakes in there."

She tilted her head to the side as she studied the foliage. "That was fortunate. Maybe today you'll be just as lucky."

He continued walking, but his pace had slowed from before. "I have learned to identify snakes, so the fear of them is gone. Mostly. Here in the South there are the good guys—if you can call any snakes good—and those that are trying to kill you."

"Well, be careful."

In spite of his bold words, he approached the jungle with some trepidation. A couple of the farmers who had helped on the church painting project were there. He wished he could remember their names. One of them had turned out to be quite a good painter. The other one painted like Micah did. Paint got on the wall, but it also ended up on him.

~

After spending the morning with Cassie going over their plans, Bella decided to go to the park to see if she could help. When she arrived at the site, where Micah and some other townspeople were already standing around near the buried bandstand, Bella looked around to make sure there were people watching them. Then she leaned over and kissed Micah's cheek.

Michelle said, "You two are such a cute couple."

Mission accomplished. Michelle worked at Dinah's restaurant, so their cute moment would be shared with diners there.

Micah winked at Bella.

He and a few guys she didn't know were staring at the tangle of vines, weeds, and brush. All the men wore long-sleeved shirts, jeans, and gloves and boots in spite of the heat. Micah said it was to protect them from poison ivy and in case something tried to bite them before they saw it. She didn't want to know what that might be.

When no one began working, she asked, "Are you waiting for something?"

One of the men said, "Yes, ma'am. I think we're waiting for this job to take care of itself."

Everyone laughed.

"Let's get started." Micah clipped a couple of vines, tugged on them and threw them to the side. They all started working, but didn't seem to make much progress. Then Albert arrived with a chainsaw, covered from head to toe with what she guessed must be protective gear, including glasses.

The men stepped back as he pulled on the starter cord. Albert sliced through layer after layer of brush, stepping away so the men could remove the sawed-off pieces and toss them to the side before continuing. It wasn't too long before they had a tunnel of sorts, but what it led to was far from clear.

A small area of white appeared at the end of the tunnel. Bella did not normally believe in luck, but she fought the urge to cross her fingers and toes and everything else she could in the hope that this would be the showstopper of the park. That it would dress everything up and make their event even more special.

"Oh!" went up from one of the men. As she wondered if she should call for help, he added, "We found part of the building intact."

The men pushed into the small opening to see whatever it was.

Micah asked, "Bella, do you want to check it out?"

Did she? "I'm not wearing any of that special protective gear you men are." The shorts and sneakers she'd put on this morning—what had happened to dresses and heels?—left her exposed.

Micah studied what they'd accomplished so far. "Good point. Let's widen this path a bit so we can see what's around us."

Albert cut a wider slot, starting at the outside again, and the other men cleared out the chainsaw's debris. When they got to the building, Bella saw a patch of white and the corner of a sign.

Micah said, "I think you're good if you walk down the middle of the path."

"Michelle?"

"Don't look at me. Your husband is waiting."

Several of the men chuckled.

Bella felt her face flaming as she moved forward, carefully glancing around before every step. What lived in the woods in Tennessee, anyway? Did she really want the answer to that? Deciding it was "no," she followed the path straight to Micah, hoping he was on alert. When she neared what did look like part of a building, she saw a sign painted by a child.

She pointed to it, and Micah chuckled. "I'd forgotten we did that." He grabbed the vines still surrounding it and yanked them back, exposing a boldly painted *No Girls Allowed* sign in red on a scrap piece of wood.

She remembered his saying that girls had pulled the boys away from their fort. "I guess the rules changed, hmmm?"

The men laughed while Micah pulled her in for a hug and swung her around in a tight circle. "Girls can come in here now anytime. Right, men?"

"Absolutely," a voice she didn't recognize replied.

Micah set Bella down. "CJ's the single one of us here. We're grateful he's helping fix this old mess, even though he's fairly new in town."

Bella looked over at the man. He was handsome in a lumberjack sort of way. Tall with a big build that was all muscle. His reddish hair and beard added to the lumberjack vibe.

Taking her eyes off the man she might have to find a woman for—because that's what married women seemed to do, didn't they?—she studied the visible area of faded, white-painted wood.

"Does the structure appear sturdy?"

The lumberjack said, "We're going to have to get more of this off here before we can tell. Then I can see if we can save it."

One of the men she didn't know explained. "He's a carpenter."

CJ shrugged. "Carpenter, tiler, anything to do with construction. Anything *but* painting." He said the last word with disdain.

Micah said, "If you want to go back out, Bella, we'll get rid of the rest of this brush and see what we've got. It's going to take us a while, so if you have anything else to do . . ."

She had a million things to do to get ready for this event. As she walked out of the tunnel, her phone pinged. Looking at it, she saw another text from Honoré Michelson. Her finger hovered over the button, but she left it unread. There was nothing that Honoré was likely to say to solve the situation, and so many things she could say to ruin Bella's day.

Tucking her phone back in her pocket, Bella went over to one of the picnic tables. She wondered if she'd found another project that had to be done before the event. Peeling brown paint didn't present the image they wanted for the park and the town. She may not want to saw through brush, but she could paint.

Then she saw Mrs. Brantley on the other side of the park. That woman had the answers to everything, so she would be able to give her an update. Bella hurried over. When she neared, she asked, "Do you have plans for painting the picnic tables?"

Mrs. Brantley glanced up from her clipboard.

"It's on my list of things that need to get done."

"Could I do it?"

Mrs. Brantley studied her as though assessing whether she actually *could* manage that.

"I just painted inside my shop."

The older woman's shoulders relaxed. "Bella, if you want to take on the project, please go ahead. Are you sure you don't need to be doing something with the planning?"

Bella raised an eyebrow. "You do know that Cassie's on the job, right?"

Mrs. Brantley laughed. "I have noticed that my future daughter-in-law is quite good at organizing events."

"She is a hundred percent in her element right now. I told her to give me any jobs she wants me to do. Right now, my main task is waiting for the guys to uncover whatever is back there." Bella pointed to the corner of the park.

Mrs. Brantley's gaze followed hers. "I've been wondering about that myself. Is it going to be an asset? Or is it going to be something we have to take time to pull down because it's unsafe?"

Bella hadn't thought of that. She'd been hoping for the best case, not figuring out what to do if it didn't work out. "I guess we just need for it to be usable, then, don't we?"

"I do love an optimist. The group of men, including your husband, seems to be making good progress."

Every time Bella heard the word "husband," she felt like looking around to see who the speaker was talking to. It certainly couldn't be her. "They found the boys' *No Girls Allowed* sign, but Micah assured me that the rule has changed."

Mrs. Brantley chuckled. "Micah was on the 'most eligible bachelors' list here for a long time. Many of us didn't think he would ever get married. He seemed to enjoy the single life too much. I guess it took someone from outside Two Hearts to convince him, but it was the same with Greg."

That reminded Bella of the man she'd just met. She described him to Mrs. Brantley.

"He's been living here since early this year. He's actually a very skilled, fine carpenter. He planned to drive through town but decided to stay. I've had him fix a few things around the house."

Bella started toward the hardware store. As she went through ideas for paint colors in her mind, she realized she didn't want to carry a gallon of paint for a couple of blocks. She turned toward home, then drove the short distance.

With her many supplies loaded in the trunk, she went back to the park. Painting the tables had been more complicated than she'd realized. She now had paint mixed in the perfect color, the primer she'd been told to use first, brushes, a paint scraper, and sandpaper.

When she had hauled everything over to the picnic tables, she wondered what she'd gotten herself into. But there was no turning back now, and this needed to be done. Glancing over to the vine entanglement, she saw that the men were still hard at work. Micah threw more debris on a pile that now towered over them.

The man at the hardware store, apparently Albert's protégé, had given her clear directions. She had to scrape off peeling paint, sand the wood, and wipe everything off before painting.

A few hours later, she stood with her hand on her lower back and admired her work.

She had just painted a picnic table, and it was a pretty color. It might not be for everyone, but it would certainly suit their event. She gave a satisfied nod and put the lid on the paint can so she could call Mrs. Brantley over to see what she had accomplished.

When the older woman arrived, she stared at Bella's work. Her jaw hung open, Bella assumed out of surprise that the job had been so well done.

"That's a unique color to paint a picnic table."

Bella beamed. "I thought so too. You always see them brown, but that's ugly. We needed to spice things up a bit for the event and in general. Won't that be a prettier addition to the park?"

Mrs. Brantley hadn't broken her gaze.

Then someone from across the park shouted. The two women turned in that direction. Micah stood outside the weed jungle with his hands on his hips, watching them. Then he started in their direction.

When he was a dozen feet away, he said, "I have to guess that Mrs. Brantley wasn't responsible for color choice."

Bella frowned. Did they not like it? "We're getting the park ready for a bridal fair."

Micah walked all the way around a table with a puzzled expression on his face. "I can see that. But how many men will want to have the family picnic photo taken while sitting at a pale-pink picnic table?"

Bella stared at her handiwork. The man had a point. She had been so caught up in her own event that she hadn't thought about the use of it later as much as perhaps she should have.

"Do you want me to repaint it when it's dry?"

Mrs. Brantley stepped into the conversation. "We don't have time for that now. It's a beautiful color. And it does suit your event perfectly." She seemed to be talking herself into the color. "We will revisit this later when we get some feedback from other people. But for now, pink picnic tables win."

Micah shook his head one more time. He would not contradict the woman in charge, but Bella wasn't sure that he agreed.

"Should I paint the other one the same color?"

They both looked from her to that brown and faded picnic table.

"I already bought the paint."

Mrs. Brantley said, "Then let's do it. Maybe we can put a flower box over near it."

"To make it even more feminine and pretty?" Micah asked.

"Son, when you're on a path, you just have to let it roll."

Bella would have to remember that saying. Micah and Mrs. Brantley both shook their heads another time before walking away. Bella got to work on the second picnic table. She really didn't see what the fuss was about a pink picnic table. Was it an outdoorsy color? There were pink flowers, weren't there? Did everything outside have to be the color of grass or dirt? Then she realized that there was tradition involved too. But it was traditional to date your spouse before marrying them, and she hadn't bothered with that.

When the second table was done, she stepped back to get the full effect. It really did look amazing. She heard another "Whoop!" from the men's work area and was shocked when she turned to find that the weeds were all down and a building now stood there. It didn't look too bad, either.

After replacing the lid on the paint can and putting the brush in a plastic bag as the man at the hardware store had told her to do, she ran over to see what their discovery looked like up close. With every step closer, the building appeared worse and worse.

By the time she was standing near Micah, she realized that time had all but destroyed it.

Albert said, "Everyone, stand back." He and CJ were walking around it, pushing on supports and seeming to be testing it to see if it was sturdy.

"Micah, do you know what's going on?"

"Construction is not my strong suit. But they're trying to figure out if the building can stay up or if it has to come down." He put his arm around her waist and tucked her next to his side.

She started to pull away and then realized she needed to stay there for appearances' sake. A few seconds later, Bella knew she liked being next to him far more than she should. Her heart felt a tug toward him. When had she fallen for her husband? Probably halfway between his having a chef come out to cook for her and his trying to save a building she'd like to use for her event. Either way, he had—and would probably have—her heart forever. She leaned her head on his shoulder, and he responded by rubbing her upper arm.

The problem was that he clearly felt nothing other than friendship for her. He was so good at making all the right moves and thinking about looking like a married couple, but he had never said anything to make her believe he had deeper emotions for her.

CJ returned with a rope from the back of his pickup, tied it around one of the posts, and tugged on it. The building gave a shake but stayed together. He pulled harder, and it still stayed upright. He knelt and looked underneath the building. "I think we may have dodged a bullet on this one. I assumed the posts would be rotten, but the builder knew a fair amount about construction and wood. I suspect these are cypress posts, and that wood is virtually indestructible by time and bugs."

"But what about the boards that broke when we were kids?" Micah pointed at the floor of the building.

"Not cypress."

Micah grinned. "Even a lawyer can figure out what you're telling me now. And the roof?"

They all looked up.

"Unfortunately, only part of it seems to be cypress. The beams going across." CJ pointed at some large beams that seemed to be holding up the roof. "Those must be cypress, but I can't see them from here to get a better look. The roof itself won't be."

Bella frowned. "So what this man is telling us is that we have to scrape together the money to replace the floor and the roof. I don't think we have that in the budget." Bella's bright future with the bridal fair vanished. Now instead of a weedy eyesore in the corner of the park, they had something that was potentially dangerous for people who came to their event. Not what she had hoped for.

Cassie hurried over to them. She clapped her hands together with glee. "You saved it!"

Bella explained what they just learned, and Micah followed up with a question. "How much will it cost, Albert? You know your lumber and roofing prices better than any of the rest of us, I think, except for CJ over there."

The two men conferred and came up with a figure.

Cassie said, "That's not bad. I'm going to pay for this out of money I just got paid for a wedding."

"I can't let you do that, Cassie," Bella said.

"Bella, we need to have something like this event to drum up business, and so far, we haven't had to spend much money on it. It's a good investment in the town."

By then, Mrs. Brantley had joined them. "That is generous of you, Cassie. Thank you." Looking around at the men, she said, "Okay, you heard the lady. Get all the supplies you need. Let's get this taken care of. And I think for this paint"—she glanced over in the direction of the picnic tables—"we'll stick with white. Agreed?"

The men all turned to look where she had, and gasps went up, except from Micah, who had already seen it. Bella heard a whispered, "Pink?"

After they agreed on next steps, Bella returned to her car with the remainder of her painting supplies. Micah must have some sort of storage shed. She remembered a building in the far corner of the property.

Back home, she searched on her phone for how to clean latex paint off of her brush, happily discovered that it was with water, and took care of that. Then she hopped in the shower to get rid of the remaining paint that had ended up on her instead of the picnic table.

Clean and in fresh clothes, she sat down and went through her emails. Most of them were routine. One was a bride inquiring about dresses. She quickly responded to her. And then there was one from Honoré. She was being insistent on whatever she wanted to say, but Bella wasn't in the mood to deal with any of it.

CHAPTER TWENTY-FOUR

Micah helped Bella carry boxes of brochures she and Cassie had made over to their registration table. For this occasion, Bella had been up late every night this week to build a new website that also featured images from weddings that brides had allowed her to share online. It seemed almost everyone was happy to let others see their big day.

With that done, Micah said, "I guess I'd better make myself scarce, then, for the day. This looks like a ladies-only event." He glanced around nervously.

"Hey, you're a married man now. This shouldn't scare you anymore."

He straightened. "You're right. I have seen these as predatory moments, but I don't have to do that anymore, do I?"

Bella laughed as she pulled out a chair and sat down behind her table. "You do not. Besides, these are engaged women. Although, they do often bring sisters and friends "

"This seems to be an event the town is interested in, and you're one of the people in charge." Micah scanned the area. "There will be eyes on you, so also on us."

Bella noted Mrs. Brantley's presence. Of course, the mayor

was nowhere in sight. He had gleefully announced that he would be going fishing during the event since it was under such good care. She spotted Albert from the hardware store helping in one corner and quite a few other people she now recognized but still hadn't put names to. Last minute touches on the landscape and even a paint touchup on the bandstand were being done.

Small town life was so different. She probably wouldn't have known the people doing the work in the city. "You're right."

"We had better look like a happy couple." His voice came from nearby. "Let's make this look real." Bella turned to look at him as he bent over to kiss her cheek, the kiss instead landing on her lips and lingering there.

When he stood, he had a dazed look on his face. "I guess I should apologize that I missed your cheek?"

Bella couldn't say that she needed an apology. She had enjoyed that more than she should have.

She needed to keep her distance from this man. There was nothing forever about their relationship.

Mrs. Brantley stepped over and clapped her hands. "Now, now. None of that while we're here."

Micah's face turned red. "We'll try to be careful from now on."

Mrs. Brantley laughed. "I'm teasing. You are married, after all."

Bella looked up at her husband. Every time she thought of that, her heart did funny things.

Micah got his cocky grin. "We are married, aren't we? I sometimes forget about that." He whistled as he walked away.

Once the event was in full swing, she realized she hadn't put out her fabric samples. So much for being organized. Micah's kiss had distracted her. The unfortunate thing was that she'd like to be distracted more now.

She and Cassie stood in front of the tent and watched the people milling around between the tables. "Bella, this turned out better than I ever imagined it would." Credit cards were out, as more than one sale was being made.

"How did you manage to get twenty-eight vendors on a summer Saturday? Aren't they all busy doing weddings?"

"It's truly amazing." Cassie picked up a business card someone had dropped. "Quite a few must have their second-in-command taking care of everything in Nashville, because almost every vendor here is the owner of the business."

Someone walked over to Bella's table and picked up one of her brochures.

"I'd better run over there and see if I can help her."

Bella walked as fast as her heels would carry her on the park's newly mown grass. "I'm Bella. Can I help you?" As she came around the table and looked at the bride, she froze.

"Honoré?"

She didn't realize the volume of the word until the people at the surrounding tables went silent. She gave her best smile. *Think professional, Bella. Think professional.*

"What can I help you with today?" A few seconds later, the ambient sound rose again, so everyone had turned back to their own business.

Honoré glanced around them. "Could we go over there"—she pointed to the picnic tables—"and talk for a moment?" When Bella hesitated, she added, "I promise I'll be brief."

Bella started in that direction without even acknowledging her words. She knew it was rude, but every fiber of her being was rebelling against kindness. It took everything Bella had to not scream at Honoré for ruining her business and her life.

When they reached the picnic tables—thankfully, no one else was around—Bella turned to face her former client and crossed her arms. "Again, I ask, Honoré. What can I help you with today?" *And how quickly can I get you away from here before I implode or start crying?*

"First, I want to apologize for Aunt Sandy's actions."

Bella's arms dropped to her sides. She tried to speak, but nothing came out.

"And I want to pay you for the work you did. I did not know until last week that you had not been paid for anything. You shouldn't have given the money back, you know."

"I shouldn't have?"

Honoré shook her head vigorously from side to side. "Aunt Sandy almost always asks for her money back. People know not to give it to her. She returns to the store, even if she says she won't."

Everything around Bella started rippling and spinning. She sat down on the picnic bench behind her and leaned forward with her head between her knees.

"Bella, do I need to get help? What's wrong?"

She heard footsteps running toward her, and then Micah was kneeling. "Are you okay?"

Bella lifted her head and looked at him.

Then he turned to look up at the other woman with her. "Honoré?" he said incredulously.

"Micah? I haven't seen you in a year, maybe more. You know Bella?"

He sat beside Bella on the picnic bench. "She's my wife."

Honoré glanced back and forth between them. "I had no idea."

Micah's gaze hardened. "What did you need here, Honoré?"

"I can tell you know our story. I'm trying to pay your wife for everything she did on the wedding dress. Aunt Sandy apparently stiffed her on the bill."

The world was starting to right itself with Micah at her side.

Honoré pulled a check out of her purse and held it toward Bella. "By my count, this covers it. Do you agree?"

Bella took it from her and tried to read it, but the letters and numbers swam in front of her eyes. She held it out to Micah. "Please read it to me."

When he told her the amount, she gasped. "Thank you, Honoré."

"Aunt Sandy wanted me to wear an over-the-top dress for my wedding. That was never what I wanted, but she's known for having excellent fashion taste. When we went to pick it up, I looked in the mirror and thought, 'Who is that woman?' She wasn't Honoré. She was a younger version of my Aunt Sandy. The thing was covered in sequins. You know I wanted something simpler."

Bella sat up straighter. To Micah, she said, "I'm okay now. You can go back to helping if you need to."

He put his hand on Bella's arm. "If you're sure."

"I'm okay, Micah. We're just talking about wedding dresses. That's my favorite thing to do. Other than hanging out with you, of course."

He laughed. Then he got up and went across the park, glancing over his shoulder a couple times as he did so, obviously trying to make sure that she was indeed okay.

"I remember clearly what you wanted when you came in," Bella said. "You wanted a simple and elegant dress. Not without any embellishment, but just added in the right places to enhance your beauty."

Honoré beamed. "See, you're the only one who ever understood."

"I remember that your wedding was sometime this month. Is that correct?"

Honoré looked very young at that moment, but they were almost the same age. That made Bella feel like she had aged a decade in the last month or two.

"It's next Saturday." She said the words in a voice so low that Bella could barely hear.

The pieces started to fall into place. "And you're getting married at a high-end hotel. I seem to remember a ballroom. I'm sorry that I don't remember all the details. I normally would, but a lot's happened since then."

"Can we talk?"

Bella scooted around on the bench so she was facing the other side. "Of course. Have a seat."

Honoré sat down. "These are the cutest pink picnic tables I've ever seen. Not that usual ugly color."

Honoré went up a notch in Bella's esteem.

"I'm getting married one week from today. I don't have a dress. And I don't have a place to get married. I don't have anything for the wedding."

"Honoré, you had everything planned. And when I say planned, I mean *planned*. There was a notebook with every single detail. You even had an online portfolio of all your colors and everything you wanted, didn't you?"

The other woman nodded. "I did. It got so out of control that I didn't even recognize it anymore. Bella, I don't know what to do. I've been trying to reach you because you seemed to understand what I was going for. The bridal bouquets got huge, and they had to be only the most expensive flowers. Everything was over the top."

"Are you eloping?" Bella said the word slowly as that was quite a shock for her to even consider.

Honoré smiled for the first time. "Yes. He's a great guy, Bella. Both of us want to get married, but we have simpler tastes than our parents. I mean, driving through this town, I saw that cute little church. I want simple like that."

"Do you need to keep costs down?"

Bella realized she had never learned what Honoré's groom-to-be did for a living, or his family background.

"I can pay for anything we need. Yes, I am a trust fund baby. But Philip has a great job too."

"Let me get my sketch notebook and bring my friend Cassie over here a few minutes after that. Is that okay?"

Honoré's shoulders relaxed. "Does that mean you can make me a dress, and I can have a wedding in a week?"

"I think we can make it happen."

Honoré grinned. "I hoped you would. Is it okay if I bring Philip over here?"

At Bella's puzzled expression, Honoré pointed toward the parking lot. "I left him in the car because I wasn't sure how this would go."

"Of course. But let's you and I talk about the dress before he gets here so it's still a surprise to him."

The bride-to-be clapped her hands with glee. "I love that idea."

Bella hurried over to her event table, where she pulled her sketchpad out of her bag. Then she went to Cassie and waited for her to wrap up with a bride who was setting a date for a wedding in Cherry and Levi's barn. As the woman walked away smiling, Bella turned to her friend. "How's it going?"

"It's going very well." Cassie held up three fingers. "That's my third confirmed wedding today, and there's a fourth bride who seems to be considering the town."

"Do you have a minute?"

"No one seems to be coming toward my table. What did you need?"

Bella pointed to the picnic table. "That is Honoré Michelson. I'd like you to help her."

"What?" she shouted. The crowd got quiet again. Cassie smiled at everyone. "That's great, Bella," she said loudly. Between gritted teeth, she whispered, "Are you insane? She stole your business."

"She just paid me for everything and more. And now she's

getting married next Saturday. She and her guy are eloping. She wants to do it here."

Cassie said, "Are you sure about this? About working with her again?"

Was she? "Yes, I know she's sincere."

"Okay. Let's get this done."

That was one thing that Bella had always loved about Cassie. She could change on a dime and roll with whatever happened.

"What's that over there?" Honoré pointed across the park to the newly renovated bandstand. "Could a wedding ceremony be held there?"

Cassie and Bella looked at each other.

Cassie the Wedding Planner came on duty. "It would be beautiful for a wedding ceremony, wouldn't it?"

Honoré seemed to be thinking about something. "The little church is cute, though, too."

"They're both nice. Which can you see yourself getting married in?"

"I've always wanted to have my ceremony outside. My mom and Aunt Sandy made the decision, basically without even asking me, for my wedding to be in the huge church in Nashville and then to have the reception at the hotel. Would that bandstand be available for a wedding next week?"

Cassie said, "I'm sure it is. We just restored it. Micah's over there right now doing some finishing up."

Honoré's eyes lit up. "Ours would be the first wedding there?"

"Absolutely. Is that what you'd like?"

"Yes. But we'll have to make sure Philip agrees."

"Often, when people elope, it's a small party with them and

maybe some close friends or family. What did you have in mind?"

"I think just the people who are closest to us. So it will be a normal wedding in a way, but it won't be the wedding that has been planned for me." She pointed to the side of the tent. "I like this tent, and I think this size would be perfect."

"Now that we understand what you want, please tell me what the colors are, and any other details, and we'll get started on it."

Bella held up the sketch of the wedding dress. "And I'm going to get my team on this right now. Would you be able to come out for a fitting on Tuesday?"

Honoré nodded. "Yes. Tell me what time, and I will be here."

They agreed on a morning appointment, and Cassie went to work on the rest of the plans while Bella returned to her table. She called April, and they discussed what needed to happen. Micah was going to run over with the design, and her team would start working on it. They already had all of Honoré's measurements. She didn't look like she'd changed a fraction of an inch since then, so at least that part should be straightforward.

That a day that had started with such uncertainty could end up this amazing made Bella's head spin. She had four more brides as clients, and two of them had already given her a deposit based on her sketches and portfolio. It seemed that the damage Honoré's aunt had done was minor.

When Cassie stopped by Bella's table a while later, her friend still had a stunned expression. "I can't believe I am planning a wedding for the woman who ruined your life."

Had her life been ruined? Bella looked around. Her friend was here. Her husband was nearby. Mrs. Brantley waved to both of them as she walked by with her clipboard firmly in her hands. It didn't seem so terrible right now.

"I was so angry with Honoré. Even when I saw her. But after

she explained, I just felt sorry for her. Even I have people who care about me."

Cassie raised an eyebrow. "Like your husband?"

Bella ignored her comment. "You, of course, will always have me as your friend. More of a sister, really."

"Agreed. But I have Greg now and his mother, and even his sister who I haven't met yet. I don't ever need to feel alone again, and neither do you."

"I realize that now. Micah has been so sweet to me in spite of the circumstances. Your future mother-in-law is amazing. She said to treat her like family, which makes sense since *you* are like family. And Dinah is funny. I like her. In fact, I like almost everybody I've met since I moved here."

"Almost?"

Bella thought about it. "Well, no place is perfect because people are people no matter where you go. But I haven't met anybody irritating yet. It's a place with good people."

"But then there's Honoré."

"I have to say that she has done an amazing thing by breaking free from the plans she did not want."

"From my experience planning weddings, most brides would have gone through with the existing plans and maybe later regretted it or even at the moment regretted it. But they wouldn't have had the guts to stand up for themselves and say that this wasn't what they wanted or needed in their lives."

Bella glanced over at the bandstand. "She's definitely going to have a ceremony there, then?"

"She is. It's exciting that we're getting new places to do weddings. What about the dress? Do you have time to do it?"

"I believe we do. If she'd wanted to replace that thing that got destroyed, I wouldn't have had time. It's too labor-intensive to add all those embellishments, but that isn't what she wants at all. It's not what she told me the first day I talked to her, and it's not what she said today. We can do a beautiful, simple dress."

Cassie said, "I can already see that bandstand draped in lavender roses. They'll entwine the support posts, and we'll make a frame of them so that the photos of the bride and groom during the ceremony are stunning." Cassie started gathering her supplies together. "Lavender and a darker purple are the colors she wants to use, with some white thrown in. I think it's going to be gorgeous."

"This isn't quite my idea of eloping. I really see that as 'the two of you hop in a car or on an airplane, find a justice of the peace at the other end to marry you, and it's done.'"

"It wasn't mine either when I first started in this business. Then I learned that there are planned elopements. She's doing it a week before the real wedding was scheduled in order to get her way. The question is, will she invite her family?"

The sad expression on Cassie's face told Bella she could well be thinking of her own parents, especially her mother. "I asked her that very question, and she still didn't know. No matter what, she'll have an absolutely beautiful wedding next Saturday with seats for fifty guests."

"Who's going to cater it?"

Cassie cocked her head to the side. "I don't think you've ever asked that question. I asked Honoré and Philip what kind of food they'd like, and their reply was very general, no true specifics like 'I must have caviar' or 'Don't ever serve anything with eggs in it.' I've had both of those."

"Remember Micah had his friend come out to cook dinner for us?"

Cassie's expression changed to one of nervousness. "I'm not sure this would be the wedding to try a new chef on. I think we need someone experienced."

"I can tell you were wrapped up with Greg and thoughts of your own wedding when I was explaining this to you. He's the executive chef and owner of Southern Somethings in Nashville."

Now Cassie's eyebrows lifted. "Honoré would love food

from that restaurant! *I* would love food from that restaurant. It's one week's notice, though, and the wedding is on a Saturday. That must be his busiest day."

"I know he doesn't serve lunch. So if this is a morning wedding, and I'm assuming it is since no one would want to be outside in the middle of the afternoon at this time of year, then maybe he could do both. Since you apparently didn't hear the rest of our conversation, I have to assume that you also did not hear me say that he's from Two Hearts. His family lives here."

"Okay. I'll contact him. Just give me his information."

Bella waved at Micah.

When he came over, she explained what was needed, and that put a big grin on his face. "Nick's going to be excited. I told him you planned weddings and that he should think about doing catering." He gave the number to Cassie and went back to his work on the bandstand.

The day was winding down. Bella looked around at the tables, now mostly empty of brochures and samples, and at the last few attendees lingering and laughing near the parking lot. This had been a success on all counts.

When the last of the attendees had left, she helped fold up the tables and chairs. The tent company would take the tent down tomorrow or possibly tonight.

Now she just wanted to go home and relax with Micah.

CHAPTER TWENTY-FIVE

Bella slipped off her shoes when she stepped into the house. This had been a long but oh-so-wonderful day with Honoré and the other brides she'd talked to. She had enough money to get her business on a solid foundation again. That dress of Honoré's had cost so much that it had destroyed her when she hadn't been paid and had restored her when she was. She would never let her business get into that precarious position again.

Today everything had changed. She didn't have to be married anymore. Micah had saved her, but she didn't need to be rescued now.

She was a free woman. Or was she? They'd each had reasons to marry the other. Micah's was because of his sisters. She couldn't run out on them before the year was out. Besides, she'd leave a giant piece of her heart behind if she did. He may not care about her, but she had fallen in love with him.

Bella carried her shoes down the hall to her room. Their bedroom doors faced each other. Hers on the left and his on the right. To say this was not a normal marriage was an understatement.

"Is that you?" Micah called from the kitchen.

Bella laughed in spite of herself. "If it isn't me, there's probably something wrong."

She heard laughter. "I stopped at Dinah's and got dinner for us. I knew you'd be tired when you got home."

And that shot her theory completely to pieces. Micah hadn't married her and then forgotten about her. He'd married her, and he took good care of her. Having somebody thinking of her and being considerate was something that was hard to dismiss.

"Whatever it is, I'm sure it's wonderful."

He peered around the kitchen door. "Are you ready to eat now?"

Her stomach rumbled an answer to the question, and she put her hand on it. "Apparently I am."

He chuckled. "I'll bring it right out then. The special of the day was her famous loaded potato soup and a Reuben sandwich."

"It sounds delicious."

"Dinah said she made it simple since she'd be working at the event all day. So it was really easy for Michelle and that other woman that they've hired to make sandwiches and soup. But she did get up early and make pies. Do not feel like you're going to miss something. I got a slice each of chocolate and pecan. It's your choice."

"Can we share both of them?"

"I do like the way you think."

"I have an idea for after dinner. Would you like to go on a motorcycle ride?"

Remembering the way she'd felt the last time made her answer quickly. "Yes!"

"I hoped you'd say that." He gestured toward a chair. "I left my leather jacket out just in case."

Her world felt settled around her as they ate dinner, and then he brought out the pieces of pie. He set them both on the table, handed a fork to her, and picked up one for himself. "Dive in and eat as much as you want."

There was something surprisingly intimate about sharing a slice of pie with this man, as their forks hit occasionally and she grabbed a pecan before he could.

As they stood after dinner, both getting up from the table at the same time, they ended up directly in front of each other. Micah put his hand on her cheek. "Bella." He all but sighed the word. "Can I kiss you?"

She wrapped her arms around him and pulled him close, kissing him before he had a chance to reconsider. When they stepped back later, they looked into each other's eyes.

Bella put her hand on her mouth. "What have we done?"

"I was rather wondering the same thing. I'm sorry to interrupt."

They whipped around at the same time toward the voice. An older woman stood beside the open door with a suitcase on either side. "I did knock, and I did say hello as I opened the door. But you two seemed to be . . . otherwise occupied."

"Grandma!" Micah raced over to the woman and pulled her into a tight hug.

"Don't squish me."

He laughed. "You always say that."

"I guess I do." She looked around Micah, toward Bella. "Are you going to introduce me to who must be the lady in your life?"

He looked at Bella with panic on his face. So much for having actual feelings for her. "Bella, this is my grandmother, Elaine Walker. And Grandma, this is Bella. My wife."

"Your what?!" his grandmother all but shouted.

This wasn't going well.

"You got married, and you didn't tell me?" Perhaps she was more upset about that than about his having a wife. Bella sincerely hoped so.

His grandmother crossed the room and took Bella's hands in hers. "I am so happy to meet you. I'm not sure why Micah didn't tell the family." She glared at him. "Because you didn't tell anyone in the family, did you? Your mother or father would have been on the phone with me immediately."

Bella hadn't realized he'd kept her that much of a secret. Why would he do that? Unless . . . he was ashamed of her?

"We got married rather quickly—"

"Oh."

Bella was about to give her usual reply when Micah did it for her. "She isn't, Grandma."

His grandmother smiled happily, more happily than she had a moment ago. "Then why the hasty wedding?"

"We just decided we wanted to get married, and we didn't see any reason to delay."

She'd said she wouldn't lie, and he hadn't said a word that wasn't true.

"Well, this has been a long day of travel for me. I think I'd like to freshen up in my room and then come out and sit and talk to you for a while. If that's okay? I did interrupt you."

Her raised eyebrow at the last comment brought back the heat in Bella's face, and she noticed Micah fidgeting on his feet. Then she realized the important part of what this woman had said. *Her* room. That was the room Bella had been sleeping in since the first day she'd arrived. The room filled with all of her things. Not the room across the hall where Micah slept.

"I've been using that as a place for my clothes. My wardrobe is probably bigger than it needs to be, but I can't resist a great sale. Give me a few minutes to move my things into the master bedroom, and then you can go in there." She didn't have time to move the stack of boxes against the wall that they'd brought from her apartment. Those would have to stay. But she had to get any personal items out of there that clearly said she'd been sleeping in that bed.

She hoped that Micah's dumbstruck expression was not caught by his grandmother. Bella scurried down the hall, hoping Micah could distract her long enough to buy her the time she needed.

~

"Grandma. Can I get you something to drink?"

As Micah walked past the hallway, he saw Bella carrying a load of her things. He wished he could stop to help, but he needed to be the distraction right now. Maybe when Bella was done, he would have a chance to walk through the room to make sure she hadn't missed anything. He stopped to retrieve his jacket, which would not be worn on a ride tonight after all, and hung it up.

"I'll take some tea if you have it."

"We have so many kinds of tea." At her confused expression, he added, "Bella's a tea drinker. Not coffee. That took a small amount of adjustment on my part."

"Iced tea then?" She had a hopeful tone to her voice.

"I know she has something called mango hibiscus as iced tea in the fridge right now."

"Sounds delightful. I may love this woman."

Micah hoped she did. Because he certainly had fallen for her. Hook. Line. And sinker.

When he came out, he saw Bella going into the bedroom with her arms loaded with linens. He stifled a shudder. What would his grandmother have thought if she'd walked in there and found out that was where his wife had been sleeping?

They chatted for a few minutes before advice started.

"I don't see any flowers. Your grandfather gave me fresh flowers every week for years."

Would Bella like that? He realized that anyone working with

weddings must like flowers, and he knew his wife did like pretty things.

Bella came down the hall smiling. But he'd learned in the beginning that wasn't her real smile. Of course, it had fooled him at first, but only briefly. By the time they'd gotten married, he'd known.

His grandmother patted the seat beside her. "Sit down. Tell me all about yourself. Now that I've had tea with my grandson, I'm feeling refreshed."

Bella looked up at him with panic on her face. But he saw her take a deep breath and put that smile on again. "I'm Bella Bennett."

"Micah's father is my son. Feel free to call me Elaine, Mrs. Walker, or even Grandma, like Micah does."

"Thank you, Mrs. Walker." She'd used the most formal option.

His grandmother's gaze locked on Bella's left hand. "Is that my ring?"

Bella's face registered shock. "Micah?"

His grandmother continued. "I told that boy to use the ring when he got married. I never expected him to do either of those things." She chuckled. "It's very pretty on you."

Bella relaxed. "Thank you, Mrs. Walker."

"And how long have you two been married?" She glanced from Bella to Micah.

"A few weeks."

"Micah!"

"I know. I know. It just happened so suddenly. We're still getting used to the idea."

"Where did you go on your honeymoon?"

Both he and Bella looked at the floor.

Bella said, "We haven't taken one yet. I needed to move my business to Two Hearts and get that started. So that's where we focused our finances."

He cocked his head to the side and stared at his wife in amazement. She'd made that sound quite wonderful.

"That's very responsible of you." His grandma smiled broadly. "I haven't seen wedding photos yet. Do either of you have any on your phone?"

Bella brought up the photos of that day, and her hand stilled on the phone. It hadn't been that long ago, Micah realized, but it certainly seemed like forever. She leaned over to show her, flipping through the photos one by one.

"Oh, my goodness. You made a beautiful bride. That dress—"

"It's one of mine."

She looked at her, puzzled.

"I make wedding dresses."

"You sewed your own dress? That was a big job to take on."

"Yes. No." She started again. "I'm a custom wedding dress designer."

His grandmother's face registered shock at Bella's words. "In Two Hearts?"

"I think it's going to work. My friend Cassie and I had a bridal fair today in the park."

"The overgrown park?" When Bella nodded, she added, "It seems like a lot has changed while I've been gone."

"It's actually just changed since Cassie rode into town. But that's a long story and one I'm sure Micah will be happy to tell you."

"Getting married and moving a business are a lot to do in a short time. But, at least, you have this house."

"Yes, ma'am. It's very nice that Micah and I are able to live here. Now that you're back, will you want to have your house to yourself, though?"

Micah's stomach twisted. There was an important detail he had not shared with Bella, and he hoped she didn't get angry.

"This isn't my house, anymore. It's Micah's."

She turned to look at him. "It's yours?"

"Ours," he said firmly.

"But it looks like your grandmother lives here."

Mrs. Walker shrugged. "That surprises me every time I come to visit. Not a thing has changed."

"Grandma, I've told you that's because I want you to feel comfortable here."

"That's sweet of you, my boy." She patted his knee. "But this is a rather old-fashioned place for young people." She laughed. "It's actually old-fashioned for me, now. I decorated my condo in 'Florida beachy.' It seems odd to step back into this."

Hope lit in Bella's eyes. "Does that mean you wouldn't be offended if I, er, made a few changes?"

"I'd be disappointed if you didn't. It's your house now." His grandmother yawned. "Oh, my. I flew into Nashville this afternoon after a long delay in Atlanta with my connecting flight, and then I rented a car to get here. I am ready for bed. Would you mind if I left you alone now?"

Micah stood and held out his hand for his grandmother to take, and she stood. Not that she needed help to get to her feet, and she would not for many years to come, but it was something they'd done since he was a little boy.

"I'll grab your luggage and lead the way down to your room."

"I think I know the way to a room in a house I lived in for almost fifty years."

Micah hurried in front of her down the hall with the suitcases. As he entered the room, he looked around. The bed was made. Nightstands were cleared off. He set the suitcases down and opened the drawer in the nightstand as subtly as he could in case Bella had been using it. A romance novel sat in there, and he knew his grandmother wouldn't read that. He grabbed it, held it behind his back, and swung around to face her.

"I'll let you get settled then, Grandma. I know Bella's been using the bathroom across the hall so she could have her own space in the morning. You may find some of her things in your way." He thought he covered that in a satisfactory manner.

"Don't worry about it. I'll be fine. See you in the morning for some of that wonderful coffee that you make."

The door closed in front of him, and he stood there wondering how they were going to make it through the next days, weeks, or months that his grandmother lived here. He went back down the hall to the living room and found Bella looking shell-shocked. She said, "Micah, what?" She didn't even have to finish her sentence for him to know that she was feeling the exact same thing he was.

He sat down beside her on the couch. She leaned close to him and whispered, "We have one bed to share now." Her face turned red.

While he certainly wouldn't mind sleeping under the same covers as husband and wife, he did not want to do that when they were forced together and barely friends. There was only one option that he could think of, and it wasn't very pleasant for him.

"I'm going to have to sleep upstairs."

"Micah, there isn't an upstairs."

"There is. The door at the end of the hall that we've never opened because there was no reason to open it—"

"I assumed that was some sort of closet."

"It's a narrow, steep staircase, the kind they seemed to love in old houses, and it leads upstairs to two rooms. We used to play there when I was a kid, but I know that in the past they must have been actual bedrooms."

She let out a big sigh. "That sounds easy, then. Good."

"Not really. There is neither heat nor air conditioning upstairs. It's going to be hot as blazes. The good news is that there are windows on each end, so I should be able to get a good cross draft once it cools down. If there's a breeze at night."

The next few days passed in a blur. Bella got up and showered in the attached master bath, after having moved her things there. The first morning, Micah looked tired. But they went to church, and everything seemed okay. The second morning, he seemed more tired. By the third morning, he had bags under his eyes.

This wasn't going well. Here she was in a big, comfortable bed, and he was relegated to the hot attic. The fourth morning, she found Micah in the kitchen with his coffee. She leaned closer to him and whispered, "We need to make it better for you up there. I think they make portable air conditioners. And what are you sleeping on, anyway?" She knew she should have gone to check, as any decent human being would, to make sure that he was at least comfortable.

He glanced toward the door. "We can't talk about this here. Grandma will be coming down the hall any second. If you brought lunch from Dinah's, maybe we could meet in the park to eat and talk about it. Does that work with your schedule?"

She thought over her day. Honoré would come this morning for her fitting. Her staff had managed, by no small miracle, to get the dress sewn together. It looked beautiful, and she hoped that Honoré agreed. No matter what she had said, the memory of the last dress they'd made had not been erased.

"If we could eat about one o'clock, I think I'd be done."

His grandmother walked in the door seconds later. "You're having lunch together? That's sweet."

Honoré arrived alone, and that both surprised and relieved Bella. She peered around her to make sure an entourage wasn't about to storm through the door, but the sidewalk outside was empty.

When the bride saw her dress on the hanger, she squealed with delight. "That's exactly what I want. You got the shape perfect. What about all the pretty things that are going to be on it? That little bit of sparkle?" She turned toward Bella.

"This is just for the shape, and we'll make sure that it fits you perfectly now and then will add all those details. I think that's our best plan for getting a custom dress out in one week."

Honoré rubbed her hands together gleefully. "I can't wait to try this on."

A few minutes later, she looked at herself in the mirror as April pinned the dress to get the fit correct. "You are geniuses. I've always felt like my figure was not quite."

Bella asked, "'Not quite'?"

"Not quite thin enough. Not quite busty enough. Not curvy enough. Just . . . not quite."

The beautiful woman in front of her didn't feel good enough. "Let me say that you made our job easy. I'm glad you're happy with the results." Bella would make sure that her narrow waist was emphasized and her bustline made to look a little fuller in the final version of the dress. Those were easy-to-design tweaks. Bella had grown skilled at making the most of a bride's figure.

With a promise to have the dress done by Saturday morning, Honoré was on her way.

Checking her phone, Bella saw that it was 12:30, so she raced out the door and over to Dinah's to pick up lunch for them. When she walked up to the counter, Michelle asked, "To go, or do you need a table?"

"To go." She looked at the menu for today. "I'm getting lunch for Micah and me."

Michelle looked at the daily menu board with her. "That's easy. He gets the soup and sandwich meal a lot."

"And you'd better put a piece of pie in for each of us. I haven't noticed any pattern to his pie eating."

Michelle laughed. "That's because he's just like you with pie. He'll eat anything."

Something they had in common. "Then put in slices of whatever you think are the two best pies of the day."

She found Micah seated at one of the picnic tables in the park. He did look a little odd to next to the pink. "I'm not sure the color suits you."

He laughed as though he was carefree, but she could see the exhaustion on his face.

"What do we need to do to make your nights better up there, Micah? Or do we need to take turns? I'm willing to sleep in the attic half the time."

He rubbed his hand over his face. "I can't let you do that. It's one thing for me to be tortured; it's another thing to let my wife be tortured."

Every time he said the word "wife," he made her want to grin like a fool. She felt like a wife in those moments.

"I'm sleeping on an old cot that we used when we were kids. I'd forgotten that we didn't just play up there. Sometimes we had campouts, so there was a stack of cots in the corner. I don't know if you've ever been camping, but if you really rough it and are sleeping on the ground, sometimes you wake up with a rock in the middle of your back that you didn't notice the night before. You wake up stiff and a little sore."

"It's almost as bad as that?"

"I would rather spend a week sleeping on that rock than one night on one of these cots. I'm trying my third one, and they're all terrible."

"Then let's fix it. Tonight after work, we are going to drive over to the superstore an hour away and get you an air mattress, which they must certainly have. Let's also check for an air conditioner, or at least fans to put at each end to pull air through. And what about if we had an ice chest with cold water in it or something like that? If you were warm in the night, you could have a drink of cold water."

As she spoke, his expression changed from one of despair to hope. "I like the idea that we can fix this. Let's do that. And I'll treat you to pizza."

"What about your grandmother?"

He frowned. "When she's here, I feel like I need to entertain her every minute of every day. Like she's a guest. But this is her house and her town."

"Micah, it's your house."

"Our house."

His words brought a smile to her face for about two seconds. Then she wanted to add what he hadn't: . . . *for what remains of the one-year agreement.*

"She has many friends who would happily invite her over for dinner."

"Could we encourage that? Maybe Mrs. Brantley would enjoy company for dinner tonight. She seems to love it when people stop by. I know Greg has been a lot busier now that he's engaged to Cassie."

"Then I will be guilt-free."

His tired eyes even looked happier. "What have you been working on case-wise?" She realized she should ask him about his work more often. Wasn't that what wives did?

"One was a simple property sale. That was easy. The other one hasn't helped my state of mind. It's a messy divorce case. I wish that people who can't get along wouldn't get married in the first place." His gaze came up and connected with hers. "Not that we don't get along."

No, they seemed to.

She stopped by Mrs. Brantley's right after lunch, a lovely lunch that had ended with them sharing their pie again, something that she now looked forward to since it was the only thing they did that made it feel like they were dating.

~

Micah was relieved to have a night off from having to be perfect in everything he said and did with Bella when his grandmother was nearby. Between his fake relationship and his awful nights, he felt like his life had been turned upside down.

They went to dinner first.

"I think this is our first time sharing pizza, isn't it?" Bella said as she took a slice of the loaded veggie pizza that had just been delivered to their table.

"It is. I must say that I've never had a veggie pizza before." He wasn't sure why he'd let Bella talk him into it. "Pizza should have meat."

"I'm sure you'll love it. If not, I'll buy you pepperoni."

"I can live with that." The look on his face as he ate his first bite of the pizza must have been what sent Bella over to order a pepperoni one for him. She ended up eating part of hers and part of his. She was tiny, but she could pack it in.

At their next stop, they found an air mattress.

"The box says it's like sleeping on a cloud."

"That always sounds a little damp to me," Bella said. "You know clouds make rain."

He chuckled. "That sounds preferable to what I have been sleeping on." He grabbed it and put it in their cart. They also found an air conditioner that needed to be vented through the window, and he thought he could set that up.

"My one concern as I look at that is that it has a motor, and it might make sounds. I have been very careful because Grandma is sleeping underneath the attic room. I'm not sure what she would think if she heard footsteps above her." He looked down for a moment. “I honestly don’t want my grandmother to know that I am not sleeping with my wife.”

Bella looked away. “I can understand that.”

He pushed the cart forward to the checkout. “I don’t think we have a choice. This is for however long she plans to stay. I’m in the middle of a web of deception.”

There hadn’t been any actual lies, but a web was nevertheless growing more and more tangled around them.

CHAPTER TWENTY-SIX

Bella reached to the nightstand beside her, patting the surface as she tried to find her phone so she could stop the incessant alarm. Finally grabbing it, she held it in front of her face and cracked open one eye. *4:00 a.m.* She turned it off and sank back into the pillow.

As she felt herself happily drifting off to sleep again, she opened both eyes and sat up. That dress would not be ready for a noon wedding if she didn't help with finishing details. She swung her feet over the side of the bed and sat up, rubbing her eyes. This was one morning she knew that Micah was not going to be up with her cup of tea ready.

She took a shower, put on shorts and a T-shirt, and went to work. She'd come back later to get dressed for the wedding. As she'd put on the mascara and lip gloss—because the world could only take so much of an unmade-up Bella—she'd realized one of the benefits she hadn't noticed before about doing weddings in a small town. She could walk from here to some of the venues. The church. The park. Even in heels, both were almost doable.

She was the first one to her shop, but April and Dora came

in right behind her, and they all trudged upstairs with the same heavy, tired footsteps.

"Today, we have one goal. That's it. Nothing else happens today until Honoré's dress is absolutely perfect."

"I was planning to get some work done on that dress that needs to be done next Friday," Dora said.

"No. You are excellent at the fine details. I'm going to have you work on the bodice while April and I add tiny beads to the skirt."

An hour into it, April leaned back and sighed. "When you said this was going to be a simple design, I was picturing plain white satin and we were done."

Bella chuckled. "No matter what, she is still a high-end bride. It is beautifully simple and elegant though."

Dora ran her hand over the fabric. "It's stunning. I hope someday I get to wear a dress like this down the aisle."

"I'm sure you will."

April patted her rounding stomach. "I'm looking forward to watching my little girl go down the aisle."

Bella and Dora squealed. "You know it's a girl! And you didn't tell us?"

April looked embarrassed at the attention. "We found out earlier this week, and there's been such a push to get this dress done that I didn't think I should say anything."

Bella got up and hugged her. Looking down into her face, she said, "There's always time to celebrate good news. And if there's anything you need help with"—she looked from April to Dora—"there's time for that too. I've come to think of you as family. I'm so glad that you followed me here."

April positively glowed. "Daniel and I are thrilled. We bought the cutest little house and were able to move right in. We were barely able to afford a two-bedroom condo in the not-so-great parts of the city. Here, we got a whole house. And the baby's room was already painted light yellow. That's the color I wanted."

The rest of the morning passed in a blur of tiny beads, thread, and the occasional sigh. An hour before the bride was due to arrive, Bella looked up from where she was working. "Did we finish this?"

Bella stood and shook out the dress so that it lay in front of them. The front looked perfect. She turned it to the side. Also perfect. She kept going until they'd seen the whole dress twice.

"It's done." Bella looked at it in astonishment.

"You sound surprised," April said. "I wondered if it would get done on time, but you assured us that there was no problem."

Bella laughed. "If I'd told you it couldn't be done, we would have believed that. I knew we were skirting the edge of impossible, but we did it. Well done, ladies. All of you get a bonus after Honoré has paid us."

"Thank you, Bella. There's a crib I've been wanting."

They carried the dress downstairs, being careful not to let it catch on anything. There wasn't time to fix problems. Bella had to hope that Honoré hadn't gone on some sort of fast this week and lost five pounds.

They hung the dress up where the bride would see it as soon as she walked in the door. Bella checked her phone. "We have a short time to spare. I'd like to go home and change. Both of you look great already. You must do better with early mornings than I do."

April said, "You go ahead. We've got this. And if she arrives earlier than expected, we will call you."

Bella headed for the door. "I expect her to be exactly on time. She has been for every other appointment." That gave her somewhere around a half hour to change and look professional. If only she could use that half hour for a nap.

~

They arrived at the wedding site, and Bella's jaw dropped. "Cassie, how did you do this? I mean, my wedding was absolutely gorgeous, but it was simple. This one looks anything but simple, no matter what the bride said."

Cassie said, "Simple is in the eye of the beholder. For some people, that would be jeans and barbecue. For Honoré Michelson, it's a full sit-down dinner with live music."

"That's the string quartet from the bridal fair, isn't it?"

"It is. That worked out beautifully. She liked how they sounded and hired them on the spot."

Bella noticed children playing on the swing set. "I hope you don't have kids squealing with glee in the middle of the best man's speech."

Cassie leaned closer. "Between the two of us, Mrs. Brantley makes my planning skills look amateurish. She has that under control and thought of it long before I did."

"And?"

"She arranged for Dinah to provide a free piece of pie to any boy who shows up with a little gift card she gives them. The price to them is that they don't play while there's a wedding."

"Seems kind of a shame that they don't get to play, though. I feel sort of cruel."

Cassie said, "Do you know how much those boys like Dinah's pies? I don't think there will be sadness on their part."

The bride arrived right after the groom. Bella knew she'd decided not to ride in a limo. Honoré stepped out of a car, and Cassie hurried over to her with Bella right beside her.

"Bella, that dress is stunning! You did that in one week?" Cassie greeted her client when they drew near. Then she dropped her voice and leaned closer to Bella. "Did you use pieces of the old one?"

"No. The best pieces of that went into my wedding dress. This was a hundred percent from scratch. And thank you. I'm rather proud of it myself."

The groom waited for his bride on the bandstand. A violin began playing softly, and the audience grew quiet. The other instruments joined in as the volume rose. It was nothing short of magical watching Honoré walk up the rose petal-strewn path to her groom with the birds singing and the stringed instruments playing the standard "Bridal Chorus." The couple said their vows, surprising Bella by using the traditional version instead of ones they'd written.

Honoré's mother and father were there, but not her Aunt Sandy, an absence that Bella did not regret. The newlyweds came back down the aisle to the reception tent and took their seats, with the other guests following. Quiet reigned in the park, so the children who had been playing on the swings must have accepted the offer of pie. The dinner that Micah's friend Nick served smelled wonderful and looked even better. Judging by the smiles on everyone's faces, it tasted as good as it looked.

Bella wandered over to talk to Nick as the dinner service ended. "Everyone seems quite happy with lunch."

"I always bring extra. Would you like the leftovers?"

"Are you kidding? I would be thrilled to have the leftovers. Then I don't have to make dinner. You'd better head out of here soon, though, because you have a long ride back."

He shrugged. "I've done that drive so many times that it doesn't bother me as much as it would someone like you, a Two Hearts newcomer. I would, of course, rather not be making a long drive." He looked up at the wedding party in front of him. "Maybe someday I'll be able to make that happen."

He packed up and left, but not before handing her a Styrofoam ice chest packed with the leftovers.

Micah stood off to the side of the tent.

"What are you doing here?" she asked him after walking over to what seemed to be his post.

"Greg is all about safety. He asked me to help as extra security for the wedding. Apparently, Cassie thought something ugly might happen between a family member and the bride. My guess is Aunt Sandy."

"That's smart. I don't think we need to be concerned, though. I'm going to run this home right now. It's leftovers from lunch that Nick gave us."

"Oh, good. I am hungry. We didn't get lunch out here."

"Neither did we. Do you want a piece of cake after it's been cut?"

He looked over at Cassie. "I don't know if that would hold up the elegant image of this wedding. A guy standing out here alone, eating a piece of wedding cake."

"You're probably right. Maybe we can get some of that to go later too."

She drove the food home so she could put it in the refrigerator, but hurried back to the event.

When she walked up to the house afterward, the only thing she wanted was a hot shower, some of the food she had brought home earlier, and to crawl under the covers to go to sleep. Would it be an early night? Yes. That sounded wonderful.

She pushed the door open and found . . . chaos. Large open boxes were scattered around the room, and Micah's grandmother was throwing stuff into them. Bella couldn't help the strangled sound that came out of her mouth at the sight of the mess when she needed peace.

"Bella, I'm glad you're here." The older woman stood. "Sometimes you have to make a mess in order to make things right."

While there may have been truth in that, did she have to do this right now? "Are you buying new things to replace these?" She took a step into the room to peer into a box that was half filled with accessories from the house. Bella set down her purse on the side table near the door.

His grandmother held up a pillow from the couch. "Do you like this?"

It had flowers all over it in a pattern that belonged in a country house. Then again, she was in a country house. "It isn't my personal taste. I like things a little simpler."

"Me too." Micah's grandmother threw it in one of the boxes. "I loved all these things. I collected them over a lifetime, so I certainly should have. But it's now time for you to turn this into your home. I'm clearing out everything that I don't think is your taste, so you can bring in those things that are. The wife in a home should have the power to do that."

Bella blinked furiously to hold back the flood of tears that threatened to burst free. His grandmother was nice. No wonder Micah had turned out the way he had. "That's kind of you." She could already picture the room more as she'd prefer.

His grandmother picked up a framed family photo. "What about the photos and pictures?"

"That's more a question for Micah. It's not my family."

Micah's grandmother stopped what she was doing and stared directly at Bella. In a measured voice, she said, "Bella, they are now your family. You haven't met them, but they're yours every bit as much as they're mine."

This time Bella couldn't fight the tears. One trailed down her cheek, and she swiped it away with her hand, hoping that nobody would notice.

"Oh, honey. Your family isn't very nice, is it?" The older woman winced. "Perhaps I should word that a different way."

Bella shook her head. "No. You said it correctly. My parents should have never had a child, because they didn't want to spend time with one. My grandmother was lovely, but unfortunately, I lost her when I was a teenager. I never knew one grandfather because he apparently ran off with someone. No one would really tell me what happened there."

"Well, you have family now. They love you. I know I'm growing fond of you, and I haven't known you very long. And Micah obviously adores the ground you walk on."

Bella gasped. Micah had put on a better show than he'd realized. "He is rather wonderful."

"See, you have family already." She picked up a crocheted afghan, looked at it for a few seconds, and threw it in another box. That was good. Bella had never liked the colors that were in it, and the big loopy pattern left a bunch of holes between the strands of yarn. What good was something to cover yourself with if it didn't actually cover you?

"What have you been up to today? I have been so busy with my friends that I haven't spent as much time with you as I should."

Bella stood in place, not sure if she should take a step forward to go to her room—well, Micah's room—or stay where she was. "I got up at four to finish a dress for a wedding that was at noon in the park."

"Our city park?" The incredulous tone in her voice told Bella that she had not been by there since she'd returned.

"It has been completely renovated. The bandstand is absolutely gorgeous. You should have seen it today. Wait!" She grabbed her phone out of her purse and scrolled through the photos to those of the wedding. "Look at this."

Bella held the phone up to show her one of the picnic tables she had painted.

"Pink?"

"I've taken a lot of grief over that. I just thought it was a pretty color. Why do picnic tables always need to be brown?"

Micah's grandmother chuckled. "You have an excellent point, my dear. I'm stunned to see what has happened in this town in a short time." She gestured around the room. "I'd better get back to work. What do you think, so far?"

"I love what you're doing. It's already starting to feel more me." She put her hand over her mouth. "Forget I said that."

Micah's grandmother laughed. "You've had every right to not feel this was yours." She surveyed the room. "What about the curtains?"

"I like the yellow. It's my favorite color. Well, that and pink. Those were the colors for our wedding."

"I'm going to continue cleaning if you just want to move along and pretend that I'm not here. I know you need to de-stress right now."

Truer words had never been spoken. Bella started for the kitchen. "I brought some leftovers home from the wedding. The chef is someone Micah knew. Nick."

"Oh, I've been to his restaurant in Nashville. It has delicious food. I don't want anything now, but I would love to have some later, if there's enough."

"There is." Bella fixed a plate and sat down at the tiny kitchen table to eat. Her goals were unchanged: get to bed, go to sleep, wake up refreshed.

Sounds woke her. Footsteps? Then she realized it was Micah upstairs, making his way across the room to his bed. She hoped his grandmother didn't hear him, because he seemed unusually loud tonight. The clock showed 2:00 a.m. She hadn't slept nearly long enough to function well today.

A thud followed by a howl came from upstairs. She sat up in bed. How could his grandmother not hear that? It looked like she'd have to wrap up a twenty-four-hour period with very little sleep by explaining why they weren't sharing a room.

The sound of tapping on her door got her out of bed. She figured it was Micah, but the door wasn't locked, and he'd probably just enter at this time of night. She opened it and found his grandmother standing there with a terrified expression.

"I don't want you to worry. You probably slept through it, and I've called Greg." She gulped and pointed to the ceiling. "Someone is upstairs."

She needed to call Micah and have him stop Greg. His best friend would not be happy about getting up in the middle of the night and driving across town for this. And the level of humiliation was too extreme to even fathom.

"Go back into your bedroom and lock the door. Let me put on a robe and get presentable." Bella closed the door before the other woman could respond and ran for her phone. As soon as Micah answered, she said, "Your grandmother called Greg because she thinks there's an intruder upstairs."

"The inflated bed burst. It's probably sitting on a rough spot or an old nail sticking out of the floor. I'm on my way down."

Bella watched and waited. Micah soundlessly opened and closed the door to the upstairs, tiptoed down the hall, and slipped into her room. "I called Greg and stopped him. I'm going to tell Grandma that we knew there'd been a creature in and out of the attic. I checked, and whatever it was is gone."

Bella thought over the words. There wasn't a lie in there. He had been living upstairs, and no living creature was up there now.

"She's scared, so you'd better do that now and let her know that Greg isn't on his way." Bella kept the door open a crack to listen. Everything went fine, and then she heard the conversation shift.

"I know, Grandma. Yes, I know I married her in a hurry."

Bella smiled. How many times would they have to explain that?

"No. I never wanted to marry her, and I couldn't love her. It's time to accept the situation and to stop suggesting that." After a pause, he added, "Regrets? I have many."

She closed the door. Okay, the man she had fallen in love with apparently regretted being married to her. That was easy to fix. She wouldn't stay where she wasn't wanted.

Bella pulled out her small suitcase and started throwing things in there, not caring what they were. As long as she stayed angry, she wouldn't cry. Another tap sounded on her door. She opened it.

Micah whispered, "Everything's okay. I'm going back upstairs for the night. I'll sleep on a cot again, but it won't be as bad as before because now I have air conditioning."

Bella nodded and pushed the door closed. Looking around the room, she wished so many things had turned out differently, and she regretted so much.

Now that she'd been paid for both the old and new dresses, she could find a place to live in Nashville. Her shop was here, so their paths would cross, but she wouldn't be married to him anymore.

When she opened the door the next time, the house was still. Bella tiptoed down the hall to the living room, pausing for a last look around. This could have become her own creation, a home for her and Micah. There was no point in mourning over more things that she'd lost. She hurried through to the door and outside.

Carefully closing the car door so she wouldn't wake anybody up, she started the engine and drove out of town. Unlike the last time she'd left and hoped it would be for good, this time the thought didn't bring happiness.

CHAPTER TWENTY-SEVEN

Why had she trusted Micah? And not just trusted him with her life. She had trusted him with her heart. How stupid did that make her? The man was a better actor than she'd realized. He'd been so caring with her. So gentle. Even when other people weren't around.

She'd bought the lie.

Her headlights cut through the dark countryside. As it neared four o'clock—a time when she should be sound asleep, again—more and more houselights were on as farmers arose to milk cows and tend to other chores.

Her car ate up the miles as she drove to . . . nowhere. She'd have to check into a hotel for a few days, maybe longer if she couldn't find an apartment to move right into. Something on this side of the city, so she wouldn't have to cut through rush-hour traffic, morning and night, when she went to and from her new shop in Two Hearts. That had to stay where it was. Too much was invested in it, and her employees had already moved.

Her eyelids grew heavier and heavier, and her head dropped. Jerking it upward, she opened her eyes wide, swerving on the road.

This was bad. She should have waited until morning and walked out of there with her head held high instead of running with her tail between her legs in the night. If Micah didn't want her, he didn't want her. That was that.

As her eyes started to droop again, she saw a lighted sign up ahead for a motel and pulled in, not caring what it was as long as she wasn't going to be eaten alive by insects. The partly burned-out pink neon letters read: *Be t M tel*. It must have been the "Best Motel" at some point, but any truth in that name no longer existed.

Inside, the man at the counter had a nasty leer as he leaned over toward her and said, "How long did you need the room for, baby?"

Bella took a step back. "Just until checkout today."

He laughed, and it made her skin crawl. "So you think you'll need that, what. . ." He glanced at the clock on the wall to his left. "About six hours?"

Bella considered. "That sounds right." This was one very strange motel.

He handed her a key, pressing it into her open hand and holding his there a moment too long. She slipped her hand away, knowing she would have to wash it several times to feel clean again.

"Out the door to the left, you'll see room twenty-two. There's a place to park right in front of it. If anyone else arrives." He gave her a long wink.

She had stumbled into a shady place, but she didn't have the energy to do anything about it. She stepped outside, more nervous than she had been when she'd arrived, but nothing moved in the parking lot. She made her way to her room, opened the door, and reached for the light to the left. With the space illuminated, it seemed clean, and the bed beckoned her. She locked the door and the sliding bolt.

Bella stretched out on the bed and closed her eyes. Even as

exhausted as she was, her thoughts wouldn't calm. She had fallen deeply in love with Micah Walker. Nothing was ever going to change that. He was the man for her, but he clearly didn't want her.

She put her hand over her aching chest. She'd survived heartache before. You couldn't get to thirty and not have somebody break your heart. As her eyes grew heavy, she pictured Micah's smiling face and sighed. Why him?

Bella must have drifted off because the next thing she knew, flashing lights through the slits in the window blinds shone in her eyes.

"No! Can't I get a good night's sleep anywhere?"

Red, blue, and white strobes lit the room as she went over to the window to peer between the blinds. Three police cars of some variety, probably from whatever county she was in, were parked at odd angles like they had pulled in and stopped in a hurry.

Beyond the cars, the sun lit the horizon, but it was still dark outside. Checking her watch, she saw that she'd slept an hour or two. Maybe.

Shouts outside caught her attention. A woman fought officers as she was dragged to one of the cars in handcuffs and stuffed into the backseat.

Had she stopped somewhere that wasn't safe? She stepped back as her muddled mind tried to come up with what to do.

Someone pounded at her door, and she jumped.

"Sheriff's Department. Open the door. We have a search warrant."

A check through the peephole in the door showed a man in uniform, so she did as asked. The man stood with his hand on his hip over his holster.

"Ma'am, I need to search the premises."

"You're welcome to, sir. I checked in not long ago. I think."

He stared at her for a moment. "You don't look like the usual clientele. May I ask what brought you to this place?"

"I was driving, and I got tired. You're always told to pull over when you're tired. I did that, and this is where I ended up."

He studied her for a moment before responding. "You ended up in the wrong place. I am going to have to search your room, though."

She stepped back. "Be my guest. Just know that if you find anything here, I didn't put it there." Should she call Micah so she had a lawyer ready to help?

He searched and, thankfully, came back to the door with nothing in his hands. "I suggest you get out of here as soon as possible. I would not normally recommend that someone drive tired, though."

Fifteen minutes later—she'd had to wait for the vehicles to leave so she could back out—Bella sat in her car, wondering where to go. Nashville would be alive with morning traffic by the time she reached the city limits. She could head that direction, stop at another motel or hotel, and take her chances. Or she could go where she knew she'd be safe.

Pulling out the exit, Bella made a left toward Two Hearts. She'd get an hour of sleep before her employees arrived, and that would have to do. She focused on the road, staying between the lines. As she passed the recently repaired *Welcome to Two Hearts* sign, a smile began and grew.

"Oh, my goodness! I like it here." She zigged on the road, but straightened out, pointing the car toward home.

Then she saw flashing lights for the second time tonight. This time, they were behind her car.

Bella pulled to the side of the road, got out her license, and rolled down her car window. When an officer got out of his car and trooped over to hers with heavy steps, she knew she was in trouble. "Officer—"

"Bella?" Greg looked through her open window. "You were weaving between the lines. Where's Micah?"

"Probably at his home in bed." She rubbed her eyes with the heels of her hands. "I'm sorry. I'm just so tired."

He glared at her in an official way much like the officer had earlier. "I'm not going to ticket you—this time. I'm concerned, though."

His unspoken words said she wasn't competent to drive on her own, and she had to agree.

"I'm going up Main Street to my shop."

After one more sheriff-worthy glare, he said, "Then I'll follow you there. That's only a few blocks."

It seemed he thought she could manage the short distance. She hoped he was right, because her eyes were getting watery and blurring. It couldn't be from tears.

A few moments later, Bella pulled into a parking space, grateful she didn't have to try to parallel park between cars. Greg idled on the street beside her car as she tried to get into her shop, somehow managing to fit the key in the lock after only four tries. He must have decided she was safe, because he pulled away as she closed the door behind her.

Wiping her eyes, she trudged up the stairs, glad they'd stabilized the railing, because she definitely needed it right now. A folded-up tulle wedding dress underskirt made a pillow, and a bolt of silk shantung unrolled over her became her blanket on the wooden floor she barely felt as she stretched out and closed her eyes.

Micah woke to his ringing phone. When his grandmother had calmed down, he'd crept back upstairs and managed to sleep on the deflated air mattress—until now. His good friend Greg's photo appeared on the screen, so he answered.

"What did you do to her?"

Micah sat up. "Who are you talking about?"

"Your wife. Who else would I be talking about?"

Micah thought his words through before he spoke. "Greg, *buddy*, my wife is sound asleep downstairs, so I'll ask again: what are you talking about?"

"She isn't."

Was this a nightmare? He knew he was in the same dusty attic he'd slept in the last few days. Daylight trickled in through the windows on either end of the room. Surely, it would be pitch dark in an actual nightmare.

Before he could speak again, Greg added, "She's in her shop."

"Well, she must have gotten up early to work. That's no problem."

Greg sighed deeply, and Micah heard the undertones that said he was an idiot and why couldn't he understand?

"She was crying. I stopped her as she was coming into town because she was weaving between the lines."

"Bella?" None of this made sense. Micah grabbed his pants and pulled them on as fast as he could and then yanked a T-shirt over his head. She'd left in the night?

"She was exhausted and upset."

"I'm on my way." Micah ended the call, then barreled down the stairs and, in his bedroom—one mysteriously without Bella in it—pulled on sneakers without socks.

When he ran out his door, his grandmother came out of hers. "What's going on?"

"Bella left me."

"She left you?"

He nodded. "I don't know why."

"Another fishy thing about this marriage."

"I don't have time for that right now, Grandma."

"Do you love her, Micah?"

"More than anything."

"Did you make sure she knows that? If she ran, it's because she doesn't know how much you love her. Do you understand?" She gave him a stern stare, the same one she'd used many times as he was growing up.

"Yes, ma'am."

"Bring your bride back here. I planned to tell you this morning that I'm moving in with Emmaline Brantley for as long as I'm in town. She's lonely, and a young married couple needs to be alone in this house. It hasn't helped you to have me here. Across the hall from what was basically your honeymoon bedroom?"

He could not believe his grandmother had mentioned his bedroom with that thought. Only one person had been sleeping there the whole time, though.

"Go! I'll be gone by the time you get back."

He leaned forward and kissed her on the cheek. "Thank you, Grandma. You're the best."

She pinched his cheek. "I know."

He laughed as he started down the hall, and then he remembered what his mission was in the first place and frowned. Bella had put herself in a dangerous situation by driving tired.

When Micah pulled onto Main Street, Bella's car sat alone at the curb.

Using his key, he went inside. She wasn't downstairs. "Bella?" he called softly as he climbed the stairs.

When he reached the top, he found her curled up next to a pile of fabric, breathing deeply. Not wanting to startle her too much, he said her name more loudly.

"Huh?" She opened what he could tell were red-rimmed eyes. She blinked a few times, and then her lips tightened as she recognized him. "What are you doing here?"

There was no mistaking the anger in her voice. "I'll ask the same question."

"You don't want me." She rolled away from him.

He knelt beside her. "Bella, honey. That's not true."

What had put such an impossible idea in her head? Memories from the past few weeks filled his mind, one by one. Her smile when he handed her a morning mug of tea, the two of them playfully arguing over who got the flavor of pie, climbing through wild brush to make her dream of the bandstand come true.

If she didn't know how much he wanted her in his life after all that . . .

Quietly, he asked, "Did you leave me?"

Tears now poured down her cheeks. "I heard you talking to your grandmother saying that you would never care for me and that she needed to stop even suggesting it."

He rubbed her back as she cried.

He stretched out next to her on the floor and pulled her into his arms. He had done so many things with her and for her. The one thing he hadn't done yet . . . was tell her how he felt. He took a deep breath. "Bella, are you listening to me?"

She nodded against his shoulder.

"I was talking about Michelle. My grandmother made a comment that I should have married Michelle."

"She doesn't like me." She sniffled.

"No. It's that she's having issues with letting go of her dream. She's wanted to match me with Michelle all my life. She's friends with her grandmother. We were probably toddlers when they decided our future."

"It wasn't about me?" She hiccuped. "Because, Micah, I think I love you."

His heart leaped, and he tightened his arms around her. "Aww, Bella. I love you."

She rolled over and snuggled closer. "You do? But you haven't wanted to be anywhere near me. You're sleeping upstairs and suffering instead of coming to share the bed with me, your wife."

"I thought that's what you wanted. I thought you wanted us to keep completely separate lives. Besides you only *think* you love me. I need you to love me for sure."

"I'm sure." She leaned forward and kissed him, putting her arms around him. He deepened the kiss.

A voice said, "Excuse me!"

Bella looked up to find April and Dora staring at them, openmouthed, from the top of the stairs.

Sitting up, he said, "Bella, grab anything you brought here and let's go home."

"That's a great idea." She stood. "I need a shower and some sleep." To her employees, she said, "Ladies, you're on your own today."

As he carried her bag out, he said, "And Grandma is going to move into Greg's mother's house. She said a young couple needed to have their time alone."

She leaned her shoulder against his arm and let out a sigh. "Everything you have said is wonderful. And when I actually get to sleep for a while, I think I'm going to be very happy."

He laughed. "So you're happy that you're staying in Two Hearts?"

As they drove off, she put her hand over his on the steering wheel. "Anywhere you are is home."

EPILOGUE

"You must be wondering why I've called you here," Mrs. Brantley said to Bella and Cassie as she opened the back door of her house, which led to her kitchen.

Bella had been curious, but this sounded more like a meeting of spies than the casual cup of tea she'd expected.

"I have a plan." Mrs. Brantley gestured toward the small table.

Cookie gave a small "woof" and wagged her tail. Bella knelt for a moment so she could scratch the dog's ears, then continued to the table.

After placing a cup of coffee in front of Cassie and tea by Bella, Mrs. Brantley added a plate of cinnamon-scented cookie bars that made Bella's mouth water. "Micah and I just repainted our living room. It's now a pretty shade of teal, but that came on the heels of working on my shop, so please tell me this idea doesn't involve more paint."

The older woman laughed. "Not a drop of it. Especially no *pink* paint." She grinned.

Comments about her picnic table color choice had been

abundant. She'd gotten to the point of wanting to repaint them. "About that, maybe I should —"

"Don't consider it. Our park has never had so much attention. Families are going just to see them. We're getting more and more weddings in town, and that color fits them perfectly."

"If you're sure."

"I am." Mrs. Brantley was sounding more like a mayor every day, even though they hadn't had time to have an election yet. Cradling her mug in both hands, probably because of the recent drop in temperatures, she put her elbows on the table. Lowering her voice in a conspiratorial manner, Mrs. Brantley said, "It's about CJ."

She didn't sound worried, so it must not be his health.

Cassie asked, "CJ?"

"He's single."

Bella glanced at Cassie. Her friend's grin must match her own. "The world has many single people. I was recently one of them." Bella didn't dare say that the woman mentioning it also fit that category.

Mrs. Brantley set her mug on the table and glared at them. "He has spent years moving from one place to another, never staying long enough to make true friends. Until he moved to Two Hearts."

Bella chose one of the bar cookies and took a bite. The warmth of cinnamon filled her mouth. Between bites, she said, "CJ likes it here. He told me that last week."

"Of course he does. What's not to like about Two Hearts?" Mrs. Brantley spoke with such affection about the struggling town that Bella had to hide a smile.

Cassie carried her mug to the coffee pot and refilled it. Walking back, she said, "When he built a bookcase for my office, he mentioned several times how much he liked the town and the people."

Concern filled Mrs. Brantley's eyes. "Then why does he want to leave?"

Bella asked, "Are you sure he plans to do that?"

"Yes. He said it was almost time to be moving on."

When Cassie ate a bite of the sweet treat, a swoony sigh left her. "Oh, my, these are good." Two bites later, she added, "CJ is the best finish carpenter I've ever seen. Every detail on my book case is perfect."

"We haven't had a good carpenter here since I was young. He's *needed* in Two Hearts."

Bella watched the exchange of words, wondering what Greg's mother had in mind. "If CJ's ready to leave, he must not feel any ties to the town. Maybe we should fix that."

"Exactly." Mrs. Brantley's evil grin might have surprised her law enforcement son.

A men's night out like pizza with the guys came to mind. Mrs. Brantley had other ideas.

"He needs a wife."

Bella shot to her feet. "No matchmaking. I won't be part of that. Not after what I have recently been through." Sure, she'd considered it herself when she'd first met him. Hearing it proposed out loud made her realize how wrong that would be.

Mrs. Brantley motioned to the chair, and Bella grudgingly took her seat again.

"Think about it, Bella. You're happy now, aren't you?"

Picturing her life since she and Micah had finally talked about love a couple of weeks ago, she knew she couldn't argue. "I've never been happier." The kiss Micah had given her this morning brought heat to her face.

And his grandfather had finally paid them a visit. Micah had turned down the offer of a check, because they had learned to do well on their own. Bella wondered if that had been the man's goal all along.

"Then we need to find someone for CJ."

"To get him to stay?" That sounded self-serving.

"So he will be as happy as you are."

Bella couldn't argue with that.

"One of the women in town will be perfect for him."

"I don't think he's dated anyone here." Bella hadn't noticed him in deep conversation with anyone in particular. "He seems to be friends with the single women."

"I've noticed that. Just like Greg and Micah, these women collect more male friends than dates." Her frustrated expression spoke volumes. "We need to have him fall for one of them."

Cassie shrugged. "It's possible that a new woman will drive into Two Hearts, and he'll be interested in her."

Mrs. Brantley smiled widely. "That's even better. I want the town to grow. Maybe this mystery woman will have skills you can use with your wedding businesses."

That didn't seem likely. They'd work on one thing at a time, and the current project seemed to be CJ.

"Are we all agreed?" Mrs. Brantley asked.

They should leave him alone. It wasn't nice to interfere with someone's life. "Well . . ."

When Cassie and Mrs. Brantley glared at her with the same expression, Bella knew she had no choice. "What should we do first?"

The unsuspecting man wouldn't know what hit him. His only hope was to find a woman on his own before they went to work.

Thank you for reading Bella and Micah's story!

1. If you enjoyed this fun book, *FINDING HER FOREVER* is the next book in the Wedding Town romance series. CJ and Grace have different plans in life. She wants to settle down. He's ready

to move on. When matchmakers decide who they should date, the two of them team up. It's friendship and a way to avoid the chosen matches. Their relationship could never become love.

2. Carly and Jake have their own story: *HOW TO MARRY A COUNTRY MUSIC STAR*. She's a down-on-her-luck country music star, and he's the wealthy man who hires her to be his housekeeper. Get it FREE at cathrynbrown.com/marry.

ABOUT CATHRYN

Writing books that are fun and touch your heart

Even though Cathryn Brown always loved to read, she didn't plan to be a writer. Cathryn felt pulled into a writing life, testing her wings with a novel and moving on to articles. She's now an award-winning journalist who has sold hundreds articles to local, national, and regional publications.

The Feather Chase, written as Shannon L. Brown, was her first published book and begins the Crime-Solving Cousins Mystery series. The eight-to-twelve-year-olds in your life will enjoy this contemporary twist on a Nancy Drew–type mystery.

Cathryn's from Alaska and has two series of clean Alaska romances. You can start reading those books with *Falling for Alaska,* or with *Accidentally Matched* in the spin-off series which includes *Merrily Matched.*

Cathryn enjoys hiking, sometimes while dictating a book. She also unwinds by baking and reading. Cathryn lives in Tennessee with her professor husband and adorable calico cat.

For more books and updates, visit cathrynbrown.com